I0577278

IF THE RING FITS

CAMILLA ISLEY

Boldwood

First published in Great Britain in 2025 by Boldwood Books Ltd.

Copyright © Camilla Isley, 2025

Cover Design by Alexandra Allden

Cover Images: Shutterstock

The moral right of Camilla Isley to be identified as the author of this work has been asserted in accordance with the Copyright, Designs and Patents Act 1988.

All rights reserved. No part of this book may be reproduced in any form or by any electronic or mechanical means, including information storage and retrieval systems, without written permission from the author, except for the use of brief quotations in a book review. This book is a work of fiction and, except in the case of historical fact, any resemblance to actual persons, living or dead, is purely coincidental.

Every effort has been made to obtain the necessary permissions with reference to copyright material, both illustrative and quoted. We apologise for any omissions in this respect and will be pleased to make the appropriate acknowledgements in any future edition.

A CIP catalogue record for this book is available from the British Library.

Paperback ISBN 978-1-83633-363-0

Large Print ISBN 978-1-83633-362-3

Hardback ISBN 978-1-83633-361-6

Ebook ISBN 978-1-83633-364-7

Kindle ISBN 978-1-83633-365-4

Audio CD ISBN 978-1-83633-356-2

MP3 CD ISBN 978-1-83633-357-9

Digital audio download ISBN 978-1-83633-358-6

This book is printed on certified sustainable paper. Boldwood Books is dedicated to putting sustainability at the heart of our business. For more information please visit https://www.boldwoodbooks.com/about-us/sustainability/

Boldwood Books Ltd, 23 Bowerdean Street, London, SW6 3TN

www.boldwoodbooks.com

To all of us who have realized our fathers won't ever marry us off to the morally-gray—rakishly hot—son of their mortal enemy, and we won't get to share one bed. Our marriage of convenience fantasies will have to remain confined to the pages of a book—I hope you'll enjoy this one.

1

ROWENA

I'm in love with my husband—and it's the single worst catastrophe of my life. The bitter thought churns in my head as I march through the sprawling corridors of Hartman & Associates, one of Manhattan's elite law firms. With each step, the dread builds in my chest, constricting my lungs, my heartbeat matching the hurried cadence of my heels striking the marble floors.

My instincts tell me to turn and flee, but I have to face the reality that I can't force Adrian to stay married to me if he doesn't want to. So, I continue forward until I reach the glass-walled conference room where our future will be decided.

The panoramic windows showcase a dazzling

bird's-eye view of New York City, all gleaming sky-scrapers and bustling streets far below. But the magnificent vista barely registers through the haze of my spiraling emotions. All I can focus on is the fast-approaching moment when the end of my marriage to Adrian will be inked in black on white, making our separation official and permanent.

I pause outside the door, collecting myself before I enter this lion's den of ruthless lawyers. Squaring my shoulders, I push my way in, my eyes immediately finding Adrian's. He rises from his seat, cutting an imposing figure in his impeccably tailored charcoal suit. His chiseled features are an inscrutable mask, but when our gazes collide, a powerful jolt ricochets through me, equal parts anguish and yearning.

"Rowena."

His deep baritone twists my insides. How can he sound so calm, so unaffected, when I'm splintering apart inside?

"Adrian," I reply, hating the vulnerable waver in my voice. I tear my gaze from him and nod stiffly to the suited vultures flanking him. "Counselors."

As I claim my seat across the expansive table, the distance between us is both too little and insurmountable. Adrian regards me intently, his dark brown eyes unfathomable.

I wonder wildly if he has an inkling of how much I don't want this. Then curse myself for the umpteenth time for falling in love with my husband. Feelings were never included in the arrangement. Our marriage was supposed to be strictly business.

But somewhere along the way, between the sleepless nights tangled in each other's arms and the quiet moments of vulnerability, I let my guard down. I let myself believe he harbored genuine feelings for me, too.

I blink back the threat of tears, pushing my nails into my palms to ground myself. But the fantasy still clamors for entry, and merciless memories invade my mind: Adrian's tender smiles, the gentle brush of his lips against my forehead, his body moving on top of mine, the adoring look on his face when he told me he was all in.

He was lying. They all lie. And I was wrong to believe him. So very wrong.

The truth cuts deep, a searing ache that radiates from my sternum outward. I was a fool, blinded by my desire for a connection. While Adrian's heart remained untouched, his focus solely on his ambitions.

A young secretary enters, oblivious to the charged undercurrents swirling in the room. "Can I offer you any refreshments, Mrs. West?" She calls me by his name and doesn't know how deep it cuts. "Tea, coffee, a latte perhaps?" Her polite eagerness is almost comical against the backdrop of my crumbling world.

"A latte would be lovely, thank you," I hear myself reply automatically, the words foreign on my tongue. As if a shot of caffeine could somehow fortify me against the looming heartbreak.

My gaze drifts back to Adrian, the magnetic pull I feel toward him torturous and unavoidable. Those dark, impenetrable eyes bore into me, betraying nothing, simultaneously igniting and chilling my blood. Under his unwavering scrutiny, I am stripped bare, every emotion laid out like an open book.

The same emotions I thought I could read on his face as we made love. But maybe for him it was always just sex—which also wasn't part of the plan. And it's been so long since he touched me, I can't even remember how it felt to have his hands on my body. That should've been a warning. One I chose to ignore.

As the secretary returns with my latte, I wrap my fingers around the warm ceramic of the mug, desperate for something solid to cling to amidst the emotional storm. The creamy liquid scalds my tongue as I take a sip, but I barely register the discomfort. My attention is entirely captured by the man across from me, the husband I've grown to love so deeply, and the despair of being alone in my feelings.

One of the lawyers on Adrian's side of the table starts explaining the terms of the divorce. Not that they come as a surprise. Everything was prearranged in our prenup. A peaceful dissolution of our fake union has always been the planned outcome of our marriage.

I've seen Adrian's determination, the way he can strip emotion out of any situation and look at the bare bones of it. So, I suppose it's fitting that our ending will be just as calculated and sterile as our beginning was.

The lawyer's monotonous voice drones on, each article of the prenup a dagger slicing in my gut. I nod mechanically, feigning understanding, but my mind is miles away, lost in a labyrinth of memories and what-ifs. I steal another glance at the unreadable enigma of Adrian's face and wonder if he feels even a fraction of the turmoil raging inside me.

As each new clause keeps being read aloud to

me, I fixate on the most trivial details—the way the sunlight glints off Adrian's silver cufflinks, the faint scent of his cologne that is a hook into my heart, the barely perceptible twitch of his jaw as he listens attentively to his attorney. I commit each detail to memory, a bittersweet catalog of all that I'm about to lose.

When the lawyer ends his speech, he hands a blue folder to the secretary, who brings it over to me, politely instructing me to sign on the dotted lines wherever they've placed a red plastic arrow. She gives me a pen.

The weight of it between my fingers feels like a stone tied to my feet, pulling me under. I stare at the crisp white pages before me, the red plastic arrows mockingly pointing to the spots where my signature will seal my fate. My mouth goes suddenly dry. A few strokes of ink, and I'll be erasing the last year of my life.

My gaze darts to Adrian's unmarked signature line, and a traitorous flicker of hope sparks in my belly. He hasn't signed yet. Why? Is he hesitating, too? Maybe, beneath that impenetrable exterior, there's a part of him that doesn't want to let go. But as quickly as the thought surfaces, I squash it down, refusing to indulge in any more delusions.

With trembling hands, I uncap the pen. My heart is drumming in protest against my ribcage as I poise the point next to the first red arrow. I've already scrawled the first letter of my name when the enormity of what I'm giving up sinks in.

I can't do this. Sign away my love, my hopes, my dreams, without at least trying to fight for them. I may be setting myself up for even more heartbreak, but I'll never forgive myself if I don't take a last stand.

In a moment of sheer desperation, I do the only thing I can think of to buy more time. With a calculated flick of my wrist, I send my latte toppling over, its contents spilling across the divorce papers in a creamy deluge. Shocked gasps erupt from the lawyers as they scramble to salvage the documents.

"Sorry!" I exclaim, feigning mortification. "I'm so clumsy. My hand slipped."

One attorney, a severe-looking woman with a tight bun, fixes me with a steely glare. "It's alright, Mrs. West. These things happen." She can hardly hide her irritation. "We'll print another copy."

As the lawyers bustle about, trying to restore order, I chance a glance at Adrian. His dark eyes are fixed on me, even more piercing, but a flicker of something deeper stirs in their depths. Curiosity? I can't quite put my finger on it.

Adrian lifts an arm, his tall frame commanding attention even while seated. "Counselors." His deep voice cuts through the chaos. "I'd like a moment alone with my wife. Please clear the room."

The lawyers exchange puzzled looks, but they don't dare argue with Adrian West. They gather their papers and file out of the conference room, leaving us with the tension of our unresolved future as our only companion.

My husband leans forward, resting his elbows on the table, his gaze locking with mine. The intensity in his eyes causes the hairs on my arms to rise in alarm as I wait for him to speak.

"Why did you spill your latte on the papers?"

The question is soft-spoken but cracks through the air like lightning. My heart is pounding so hard, I'm sure Adrian can hear it from across the table. Why is he asking? It doesn't matter. I wanted an opportunity to speak out and this is it. Okay, here goes nothing...

2

ADRIAN

Many months earlier

The city blurs past in a hazy mosaic of lights and shadows as I recline in the plush leather backseat of the town car, lost in thought. The first rays of sunlight glint off the gleaming skyscrapers, piercing the tinted windows and forcing me to avert my eyes. I check my watch—6.47 a.m. Right on schedule, as usual.

My driver glances up at me in the rearview mirror. "Everything alright back there, Mr. West?"

"Fine, thanks. Just getting ready for another day in the trenches," I reply with a wry smile. Sam chuckles and returns his eyes to the road.

I take a sip of steaming coffee from my Thermos, savoring the rich aroma and mentally preparing myself for the day ahead. The Calloway deal needs to be closed by the end of the week, and there are still a few sticking points to iron out. I also need to finalize the quarterly report for the board meeting and touch base with our legal team about the new compliance regulations.

As the car weaves through morning traffic, I pull out my phone and scan my inbox, firing off a few quick replies. The familiar motions center me, pulling my mind into work mode.

Ten minutes later, we slow to a smooth stop in the shadow of the imposing glass office tower where my office is. Another day, another battle. Time to enter the fray.

I tuck my phone away. "Thanks, Sam. See you tonight."

"Of course, Mr. West. Good luck today."

I flash him a confident grin as I step out onto the curb. "Won't need luck. But I appreciate the sentiment."

I stride past the spinning doors, my steps echoing through the luminous lobby as I cross the wide space, nodding at the security guard.

"Good morning, Mr. West," he greets me with a hint of deference.

"Morning, Reggie." I flash him a grin.

I check more emails as I ascend sixty-six floors to nearly the top of the building. With a chime, the doors open on my reign: the trading floor—the business core of any hedge fund. I emerge into the expansive space, floor-to-ceiling windows showcasing a magnificent view of the sun rising over the cityscape. Dozens of eyes flick up from glowing Bloomberg terminals as I enter the trading pit. The cacophony of loud chatter and clacking keyboards fades to a hush.

My traders, already hunched over their desks reviewing the latest market news and pre-bell indicators, shoot furtive glances my way before hastily dropping their gazes. I allow myself a small satisfied smile, basking in their respect and slightly intimidated dispositions.

"Good morning, team," my voice slices through the quiet. "Let's go make some money."

As if broken from a spell, the floor springs to life once more in a frenzy of activity and catcalls. I nod to the junior traders and enter the glass-walled office in the corner, where Sarah Lopez, my head of trading, is already waiting for me. Shutting the door, I turn to her.

"Alright, Sarah, what do we have on deck for open? I want to hit the ground running today." I loosen my tie as I slide into my chair.

"Futures are pointing to a higher open, but that employment report on GGY is going to be key." She swipes on her tablet. "If it beats expectations, we could see a rally..."

I nod along, ready to plunge into the deep waters of high finance where I'm the deadliest shark. There are millions to be made or lost in the blink of an eye. And I wouldn't have it any other way. I'm built for this game.

Bring it on.

The market bell rings and the trading floor erupts into its usual frenzy. Lights flash, phones ring off the hook, and a hundred conversations begin at once. I roll up my sleeves and dive right in.

As Chief Investment Officer, my day is a whirlwind of monitoring markets, adjusting positions, meeting with analysts, and strategizing. I'm glued to my Bloomberg terminal, watching the numbers dance across the screen. One minute the Dow is up, the next it's down. It's like trying to tame a wild beast.

"Adrian, Vanguard is on line two," my secretary, Wendy, calls out. "They have questions about that pharma stock."

I nod and pick up the phone, ready to explain our bull case and PE ratios. It's one call after another with high-profile clients. Between discussions of alpha, beta, short interest, and EBITDA, I barely have a moment to breathe. But I thrive on the rush, on the rapid-fire pace.

I stop only when my stomach starts growling like a caged lion. It's two thirty already and I forgot to eat lunch. I ask Wendy to put in my usual order at the sushi place downstairs.

I eat at my desk, eyes still glued to the terminal. The market waits for no one.

I'm just polishing off the last salmon skin roll when Wendy appears in my doorway, looking tense.

"Mr. Fulton wants to see you in his office. Right now," she says grimly.

My chopsticks freeze in midair as an uneasy feeling slithers up my neck. In all my years here, I can count on one hand the number of times I've been called to the CEO's office without notice. It's never been good news. And I don't like surprises.

3

ROWENA

I dart through the bustling New York sidewalks, my flats slapping against the concrete as I dodge businessmen engrossed in their cell phones. The late spring sun beats down on me, making me break a sweat despite my lightweight blouse. Normally, I'd relish the warm glow on my face, but today a sickening nausea swirls in my gut, casting a shadow over everything.

"Excuse me, sorry," I wheeze as I weave through the crowd, glancing at my watch. Damn, I'm going to be so late getting back to the office. I had to squeeze this doctor's appointment into my measly forty-five-minute lunch break, but the doctor was running fifteen minutes behind, so now I'm half an hour over. Ugh, it's already past two thirty; my boss, Brian, will get on my case again, the tyrant.

But that's the least of my problems. My mind reels, still processing the news that knocked the wind out of me ten minutes ago: I'm pregnant. Seven weeks along. The father is my dirtbag ex, Liam, who I mustered the courage to dump a month and a half ago—guess I should've been a week faster.

What. The. Actual. Fuck.

How did I not notice the signs? My bra has felt like a vise lately, but I chalked that up to PMS. The random puking I blamed on spoiled takeout. As for missing my period, well, that's not abnormal for me. My cycle is about as regular as the G train.

I press a hand to my still-flat stomach and feel a pang of... what? Regret? Panic? Irrational joy? Dizziness washes over me and I'm not sure if it's the pregnancy hormones or the enormity of the situation making me woozy. Single and knocked up was not in my thirty-before-thirty plan.

Gosh, I'll have to tell Liam. The manipulative jerk will probably see this as his chance to worm his way back into my life—or run for the hills never to be seen again, which, ironically, would be the preferred outcome. At the thought of facing him, a revulsion so visceral emanates through me, and I almost double over. I'm going to be sick right here on Broadway.

Angry horns blare as I duck out of the snarled traffic, cutting it close at a crosswalk. The acrid smell of exhaust hits my nostrils, and my stomach recoils. I suppress a gag against the bile rising in my throat, again dubious if it is morning sickness or just pure dread making me queasy.

I exhale slowly, trying to quell my spiraling thoughts as I hurry down the block to my office building. One crisis at a time, Rowena. First, grovel to Brian and pray he's in a merciful mood. Then survive the rest of the day at work. And after that? Collapse into bed with a pint of New York Super Fudge Chunk. Wrap my head around the news that there's a tiny person growing inside me. And make a plan.

As I step into the air-conditioned lobby of the office tower where I work as a junior software engineer, I beg my mind to shift into problem-solving mode. I'm a coder, after all—debugging is my specialty. But this glitch in my life's program feels impossible to untangle.

I join the throng of people waiting for the elevators. The up button is circled by a red light, signaling the call has already been made, but I poke it again and tap my foot as I follow the progress of numbers slowly descending on the overhead screen, willing the doors to open faster. *Come on, come on.*

The more I stand here, unmoving, the more questions pile in my head. How am I going to manage a baby on my own? My boss isn't exactly warm-hearted; he'll give me two weeks of paid maternity leave at best. And daycare costs more than my rent in this city. Maybe I could work from home for a while? That could ensure survival, but what about my career? I'm working my butt off to establish myself in a male-dominated field. How will having a kid impact my ability to keep pushing?

The elevator dings and I wedge in among briefcases and power ties, my bag clutched to my churning stomach. As we ascend, I take long, calming inhales, the effort futile when trapped in a metal box thick with conflicting colognes. I just need to make it to the seventeenth floor without puking.

Taking in my reflection in the mirrored walls— looking pale and shell-shocked—I'd say my chances of not retching on the suits are fifty-fifty.

Think of something else.

I close my eyes, trying to picture myself as a mom. All I can conjure is an image of me with spit-up on my shirt, dark circles under my eyes, and code scrolling endlessly on my laptop while a baby wails in the background.

Unstoppable tears carve paths down my face. I feel lost, like I'm stuck in a maze with no exit in sight. I wish I could call my mom for advice, but I'm not ready to confess to my parents the colossal mess I'm in, how spectacularly I've botched my life.

The elevator opens on my floor and I press through the throng of bodies to get out. I remove my black-rimmed glasses, wiping the tears from my cheeks and pasting on a neutral expression before I make my way to my desk. As I cross the open-space office, I avoid eye contact with my coworkers, eager to hide in my cubicle.

I slide into my chair and stare blankly at my screen, the lines of program I left unfinished before lunch blurring before my eyes. I drop my head in my hands, one thought drilling through my skull. I'm having a baby. On my own. With Liam as the father.

A light rap on my cubicle wall followed by Brian's signature throaty cough—the one he deploys before he bites your head off—alerts me to my boss's looming figure.

Oh no. I peer up, already cringing as I meet Brian's unforgiving scowl. "Rowena." He greets me with a thin smile. "How nice of you to finally join us."

I plaster on a forced grin, trying to disguise my queasiness. "Sorry, I had a doctor's appointment that ran late."

His eyebrow arches skeptically. "How convenient. Well, now that you've graced us with your presence, follow me." He turns on his heel, striding toward his office without waiting for my reply.

Crap. My stomach sinks further as I trail after him.

He sits at his desk, instructing me to close the door. I do as I'm told. The latch's click rings ominously in my ears.

I cross the room—small by any office standard, but endless compared to the size of my cubicle—and perch on the chair across from Brian's desk, hands clenched together to hide their trembling.

"I'll cut right to the chase," he begins, leaning back and leveling me with a cool stare. "The project you were assigned to has been discontinued. And with the budget cuts, your role is no longer... shall we say, essential."

Wait, what? My mouth falls open, but no words emerge. Is he saying what I think he's saying?

"To put it bluntly, Rowena, we're eliminating your position. Effective immediately."

It's the second cold shower in an hour. Only this one feels more like an ice shower where instead of ice chips, solid cubes are being thrown straight at my head. "What?"

"I'm sorry, Rowena, it's out of my hands."

His lips curl into a smug smirk. He's not sorry at all. If anything, he seems to relish delivering this devastating news.

The floor wobbles beneath my feet as the message sinks in—I'm being fired. Canned. Let go.

First, I'm having a baby, and now this? Jobless and pregnant, with no partner to lean on. I can't raise a kid alone in New York City with no income. Already, I was going to be grasping at straws with my salary. Now, it's going to be impossible.

A sour taste rises at the back of my throat and saliva floods my mouth. Oh, fuck. It's happening. I'm going to hurl. Right here, right now, all over my boss's pristine designer suit. He'd deserve it, the insufferable prick.

I clamp a hand over my mouth, fighting the urge to projectile vomit my disgust and despair on Brian and see if he can keep his smug expression. Maybe I should do it, a last act of defiance.

But my stomach refuses to cooperate. Better this way; I need a good reference, not a criminal record for assault with a biological weapon.

"What about severance? Do I at least get a payout to tide me over while I look for a new job?" I hate how small and weak my voice sounds. Like I've already been defeated.

Brian slides a manila folder across his mahogany desk. "It's all outlined here. Three months' salary. That's the best we can do."

Three months. I quickly do the mental math. It'll cover my portion of the rent in the apartment I share with Nina and Hunter, my best friends, for a while. But not all the upcoming doctor visits and baby supplies I'll need. Without medical insurance, I'm royally screwed.

I want to argue, to stand up for myself and demand more. I've poured my blood, sweat, and tears into this company for three years. But the fight has drained out of me, replaced by an exhaustion that seeps deep into my bones. What's the point? He wants me gone.

"Fine."

"Great. You have to go see HR, sign a few things, then security will escort you out once you've gathered your belongings. Company policy."

And there it is. The final nail in the coffin of my career. I nod numbly, then turn and exit his office on shaking legs, the taste of failure bitter on my tongue.

When I get back to my desk after signing a million release of claims papers, my laptop is already gone. Good thing I made it a policy never to store anything private on it, not even a single picture to use as a screensaver. As I gather my few personal items from my cubicle into a cardboard box someone has conveniently dropped off, the enormity of my situation crashes over me in waves. Jobless. Pregnant. Alone. The three words swirl in my mind, a taunting mantra of despair.

I can't afford to live in New York without a steady income. But I don't know if I can muster the energy I'd need to interview for new jobs. Even making it to the office today felt like a Herculean effort with the constant nausea and fatigue. And what's even the point? As my pregnancy progresses, my baby bump will become a flashing neon sign: "Don't hire me! Maternity leave imminent!"

I'll have no choice but to crawl back to Omaha with my tail between my legs and move in with my parents. The thought makes me cringe. I love Mom and Dad, but returning to my hometown as a knocked-up, unemployed failure is the stuff of nightmares.

Balancing the box precariously against my hip and flanked by a burly security guard, I keep my gaze on the floor as I walk toward the exit. Even if I don't see them, I can feel the shocked stares of my colleagues on me. I can't get out of here fast enough. At the elevator bank, I jab the down button with more force than necessary.

As the bell chimes with an annoyingly cheerful ding, I ask my escort if he's coming all the way down with me. Showing more empathy than Brian did, he shakes his head. But he still asks for my access badge back.

I snap the cord off my neck with a yank and hand it to him. We share a small nod of perhaps commiseration for him and gratitude on my part for a basic display of humanity, and then I push the lobby button. The elevator doors close swiftly on life as I knew it.

As the floors tick down, the meager breakfast bagel I ate on the way to the doctor threatens to make a reappearance. By the time I reach the lobby, I'm gulping for air, praying I can hold it together until I'm outside.

No such luck. My stomach clamps painfully, and

a cold sweat breaks out over my forehead. I make a mad dash across the lobby for the restrooms, barging inside and abandoning my box of belongings outside a stall.

I don't even have time to close the door before I'm hunched over the toilet, splattering the contents of my stomach into the bowl.

As I heave and gasp, tears streaming down my face, a hysterical laugh shakes me. Could this day get any worse? Then again, maybe puking my guts out in my former office building is the perfect metaphor for my life right now—a complete and undignified mess.

I flush to purge the awful smell, then sink back, dropping my butt on my heels. I'm not sure I'm done throwing up and I'm not ready for a packed subway ride home. Eventually, I'll have to face the world. But for now, I allow myself a break. This one moment to fall apart.

Because starting tomorrow, I'll have to be strong. For myself, and for this unexpected life growing inside me. I'll have to make this work.

Even if I have no idea how. Fuck. I'm going to be sick again.

Still bent over the toilet, I hear the restroom door slam open, followed by hurried footsteps and the heavy thud of someone crashing into the stall next to mine.

Retching sounds erupt from the newcomer, and my stomach churns in sympathy, prompting another violent wave of nausea. I clutch the cool porcelain as my body convulses, wondering who the stranger in the stall next door is and what happened to them.

4

ADRIAN

"Should I tell Mr. Fulton you're on your way?" Wendy asks.

I give a curt nod. "Yes."

I'm not about to make the CEO wait. I drop my chopsticks and stand, brushing off my Armani suit. "Alert Sarah I'll be unavailable. She has the floor until I return."

Wendy scurries behind me as I head to the elevator bank. "Anything else, Mr. West?"

"No, thank you, Wendy." I push the up button, my mind spinning. What could Dominic want? Our fund is up 28 per cent YTD, we just landed the Calloway account—but he might not know about that yet... I rack my brain but come up empty.

The doors slide open with a muted ding and I step inside, only to find myself face to face with a familiar head of perfectly coiffed blond hair. Preston Harris, the company's CFO, looks up from his phone with a tight smile.

"Adrian," he greets me smoothly. "Ah, you've been summoned, too?"

My brows furrow as the doors close and the elevator begins its ascent. "Dominic?"

Preston nods, pocketing his phone. "His assistant was very insistent. Wouldn't say what it's about, though."

Curiosity piqued, I lean against the handrail, studying my colleague's profile. After the CEO himself, we're the top two executives at the firm. Why does he need to see both of us? Is he selling out? I hope the fuck not. I didn't spend the last ten years building this company from the ground up to get tossed aside like yesterday's news. I sacrificed too much for this job. Relationships. Time with family and friends. Vacations. *Sleep.*

The doors open onto the hushed expanse of the executive floor, which Dominic keeps all to himself —not because he needs an entire floor, but because he can. His assistant waves us in with a practiced smile. "He's expecting you."

I allow Preston to exit first, bringing up the rear with a confidence I don't entirely feel.

In the corner office, Dominic rises from behind his massive desk, silver hair glinting under the recessed lighting. "Adrian, Preston, please get comfortable." He gestures for us to take a seat.

I sink into one of the chairs, legs crossed, projecting an air of nonchalance I'm far from feeling. Preston perches ramrod straight beside me.

Dominic's craggy features are unreadable. "I'll cut to the chase, gentlemen. I've decided to retire at the end of the year. And one of you will be taking over."

Every muscle in my body goes taut, my earlier fears evaporating. He's not selling out; he's announcing his successor. This is it. The opportunity of a lifetime. I keep my expression neutral, but inside, I'm already envisioning myself in this corner office—bigger than mine and a few floors up. Preston may be good, but I'm better. I've got this in the bag.

"Over the next few months," Dominic continues, prompting me to focus on the present and not on a distant fantasy, "I'll be evaluating you both personally and professionally. We'll be spending some time together outside the office, too. Starting with a weekend at my Hamptons estate two weeks from now. I expect you both to attend. Families are welcome."

Preston shifts beside me. "Of course, sir. My wife and kids will be delighted."

I suppress a smirk. Preston's picture-perfect family-man image won't help him here. "Count me in," I announce. "Though I'll be coming solo." No time for attachments in my world.

Dominic nods, already reaching for his phone. "Excellent. My assistant will send over the details." He waves a hand in clear dismissal.

Considering how monumental the announcement was, it took a record short time to deliver. But Dominic, like me, is all about efficiency.

Mind still reeling, I follow Preston out, making calculations. A weekend in the Hamptons, schmoozing with the boss. I can do that in my sleep. Really, Preston has no chance.

I walk beside him toward the elevators, his mop shining under the fluorescent lights, my mind already narrowing on all the steps I need to take to impress Dominic and lock the promotion in. I should start by telling him we closed Calloway this morning.

I stop halfway down the hall. "Hey Preston, you

go on ahead. I have to clarify something with Dominic."

The CFO nods. "Sure thing. See you downstairs, Adrian." He steps into the open elevator.

I stalk back toward Dominic's office. His door is slightly ajar. I'm about to knock when his secretary's voice drifts out.

"I don't understand, sir. Why put on this contest if you've already decided who to name as your successor?"

My hand freezes inches from the door as my heartbeat thunders in my ears. Could it be that Dominic isn't just choosing a replacement, but an heir? He has no children and isn't romantically attached to anyone that I know of. Could the company—Dominic's entire legacy—be up for grabs?

Dominic chuckles. "Well, between you and me, Adrian is the obvious choice for driving profits. The man's a machine."

A grin spreads across my face. I knew it! My relentless work ethic, the grueling hours I've put in to bringing this firm to greatness—it's all paying off. I'm about to burst into Dominic's office and shake his hand when his next words stop me cold.

"...But Adrian, he's too much like me. Ruthless. No family, no life outside this place. I don't want to pass down my life's work to someone who will repeat my mistakes and leave no legacy behind besides a pile of cash."

My mouth goes dry as Dominic's voice drops to a heavy sigh. "No, it'll have to be Preston in the end. The company needs someone with roots. Someone with children who wants to make the world a better place for them. Unless Adrian proves I've misjudged him, that's how things will go."

Children? Make the world a better place? Who is this man talking? Not the cutthroat founder of our multi-billion-dollar fund. The Dominic I know is a cold-blooded killer. This Dominic, will he start to sing "Kumbaya" next?

My head spins as I back away from the door in a daze. I bled for this company, lost pieces of myself along the way... and now I'm being told it's not enough? Anger simmers under the shock as I turn on my heel and make a run for it. I burst past the stairs' emergency entrance, too agitated to wait for a fucking elevator.

On my floor, I crash into my office and slam the door behind me, heart pounding. A few quick flicks of my fingers and I've loosened the knot of my tie as I pace back and forth. This can't be happening—I'm the better man for the job, no question. I worked my way up from nothing to get here. And now Dominic is going to pass me over for the promotion because what, I don't have kids? Where's the justice in that?

I collapse into my chair, my hands clawing through my hair as I glance at the neatly stacked folders on my desk, the product of endless late nights. With an angry shove, I swipe the entire pile to the floor. Papers fly everywhere. I should hand in my resignation right away.

I wheel closer to my computer and I'm already opening a blank document to write my notice, when I hesitate, fingers poised on the keyboard. The cursor blinks, waiting for me to type the words that will set me free. But the thought of stepping away—of walking into the unknown—before I have another job lined up keeps me frozen. I started working after-school jobs when I was fourteen, and I haven't gone a day since then being unemployed. I know too well what it feels like to have nothing—to struggle in ways I swore I'd never let myself face again.

Not having a job is not an option. But the idea of having to start fresh at a new place, to have to prove myself all over again feels like too much. Next year, I'll turn forty, I'm at a time in my life when I should be collecting the fruits of my hard work, not having to start from scratch.

Should I just flip the bird to everyone, retire early on an island somewhere in the Caribbean, and just manage my investments? I've made millions in my years at Fulton. How much more do I need?

But it's not really the need for more money that keeps me here—a cog churning in the wheel—is it? It's more the fear of losing it all. Which could happen overnight. The stock market could crash at any moment. Volatility has never been higher; 2008 has proven not even real estate is safe. The pandemic has done the same for oil and natural gas. And with the global turmoil of the last few years, even safe-haven assets have been on a roller coaster of ups and downs.

Despite the uncertain economy, I probably won't lose *all* my money in the blink of an eye, but the idea of being jobless—like my father—even for a single day, rips through me like a live wire, electrifying every muscle, leaving me paralyzed, my breath locking in my lungs as blood roars in my ears.

I'm still blocked, when a new email pops up in my inbox. It's the invitation to the company retreat in the Hamptons. Without thinking, I click "RSVP" and select "plus one." What am I doing? I don't have anyone to bring. But some irrational part of my brain tells me this is my chance to prove myself, kids or no kids.

I hit send, and lean back in my chair closing my eyes. I reopen them a heartbeat later only to stare at the ceiling. Around me, the wide windows of my office, once a symbol of my success, feel like they're mocking me. Like the entire city out there is poking fun at me.

A minute or an hour later, I couldn't tell, my landline rings. It's Dominic's direct line. I swallow my apprehension and answer.

"Adrian! I just saw your RSVP. I thought you said earlier you were coming alone?"

My palm goes clammy against the receiver, and I blurt out the first thing that pops into my head. If Dominic wants a legacy, I'll give him one. "Oh, right. The thing is..." I pull in a wobbly breath. "I'm bringing my fiancée."

"Your fiancée?"

"Yeah. I—we—are getting married... to... err... put down roots, be a family, you know, that kind of stuff?"

I pass a hand over my face. What the fuck am I blabbering?

"Yes, Adrian, I know." Dominic chuckles. "That's

usually the reason why people get engaged. Why didn't you say so right away? I'd love to meet the woman who's managed to lock you down."

Why? Why? *Why*? "Umm, the thing is... she... she's pregnant. We're having an heir—I mean a baby. But it's still early days, and she's been feeling sick a lot. I wasn't sure if she'd be up for the trip to the Hamptons. But I called her and she said she wants to come and support me."

There's a long pause. "Wow Adrian, a baby? I had no idea! Congratulations, you must be thrilled to become a father," Dominic replies, sounding genuinely happy for me.

"Thanks, we haven't told many people yet since it's still early on..." I trail off, my stomach churning with the enormity of the lie.

"Of course, I understand. Well, I look forward to meeting her!"

"Great, she's excited to meet you too." I hang up, feeling lightheaded. What the hell did I just do? I don't have a fiancée to bring to the Hamptons, let alone a pregnant one. This lie is going to catch up to me so fast.

I can't breathe. Glass or no, the walls of my office are closing in on me. I need to get out of here. I stumble out the door, unsteady on my feet. Wendy asks me something but I don't hear her over the ringing in my ears. I have an objective, getting out of this building. I need fresh air. Now.

The elevator ride down takes forever, but I'm finally in the lobby. I eye the front doors but before I can reach them, a wave of nausea hits me. That sushi platter I had at lunch churns violently in my stomach. Oh, for fuck's sake. Not here.

In a panic, my eyes snag on the public restroom in the corner.

I charge through the door, barely registering a cardboard box lying on the otherwise pristine tile floor. Ducking into the closest stall, I bend over the toilet just as my stomach heaves.

I cough and sputter, gripping the sides of the bowl.

As the first wave passes, I notice a strange sound. Glancing to my left, I realize with horror that someone is throwing up in the next stall, too.

5

ROWENA

Seven weeks pregnant

Flushing the remnants of my misery away, I slump back, my forehead beaded with sweat. In the momentary quiet, a deep, velvety voice drifts over the thin metal barrier, smooth and oddly calming despite the circumstances.

"Are you okay?"

The rich timbre sends a shudder down my spine, landing somewhere low in my belly. I try to keep my voice steady as I reply, "Not really. You?"

A scoff echoes off the walls. "Not even a little."

I wince, feeling a strange camaraderie with this unseen stranger. Misery loves company, right?

"What happened to you?" I ask, my curiosity piqued.

There's a heavy sigh, followed by a bitter chuckle. "I lied to my boss. Big time."

A strangled sound escapes my throat, somewhere between a laugh and a sob. "Well, at least you still have a boss." My voice cracks as I confess, "I just got fired. I don't know what I'm going to do next."

The weight of my words settles heavy in the air, mingling with the lingering scent of sickness as a dizzying spiral of worst-case scenarios flash before my eyes.

I squeeze my lids shut, willing the images away. I can't break down, not here, not now. Not in front of this stranger with the sexy voice and his own set of problems.

"Shit, I'm sorry." Genuine empathy laces his words. "That's rough."

"Yeah, it is." I nod miserably, forgetting for a moment that he can't see me. "I guess we're both having a pretty crappy day, huh?"

"Yep."

I hear him pulling on the roll of toilet paper, probably to clean his mouth or something. I'm almost afraid he's going to leave. Having him in here with me is weirdly consoling.

But then his voice filters through again. "So, what do you do for a living?"

"I used to be a senior technology developer engineer at the fintech company on the seventeenth floor."

He lets out a low whistle. "Damn, impressive. You must be smart, then."

"Not so smart, apparently." I trace my fingers in idle patterns on the cool metal wall. "Got axed today along with the project I've been busting my ass off for the past six months. Budget cuts they said, but I suspect my boss couldn't wait to get rid of me."

"I'm sorry. Bet he's a walking midlife crisis."

I crack a wry smile despite myself. "That's strangely accurate." I sigh. "I never thought I'd regret not having him lord himself over me."

"Hey, I wouldn't sweat it too much," he assures me. "This city is crawling with hedge funds, banks, brokerages... They're always hungry for talented software engineers. I could even put in a good word at my firm, see if we have any openings."

His words give me pause. That's... incredibly kind of him to offer. "Where do you work?" I ask.

"Fulton Capital. The hedge fund on the top floors."

My eyes widen. Fulton Capital is among the elite

wealth management funds in the city. I vaguely re-call the sleek logo emblazoned on the building's di-rectory—they're one of those innovative investment firms always splashed across the financial news.

This guy must be the real deal.

A single tear rolls down my cheek. After the traumatic emotional blows of the day, ironically, it's his compassion that has me breaking down. Hot, salty water streams down my face against my will. I've lost control of everything, even my body. I choke down the sobs, but a muffled one claws his way out of my throat.

"Hey," he says gently, no doubt hearing my snif-fles. "What's wrong? Talk to me."

"I'm sorry, I didn't mean to cry, I just... That's such a thoughtful offer, and I appreciate it, but..." I swipe at my wet cheeks, snorting pathetically. "I... I can't take you up on it right now." I blow my nose, wiping it on a wad of toilet paper. "I'm not hiding in here just because of the job loss," I admit, my words echoing in the confined space. "Actually, me getting fired is the least of it."

There's a pause. "Oh?" His voice sounds sur-prised, but still kind. "Do you want to talk about it? I mean, only if you're comfortable. No pressure."

I grip the toilet paper harder as the truth bubbles up inside me, wanting to spill over. And why not? This guy is a total stranger; it's not like I'm ever going to see him again—not that I've seen him now.

"I found out this morning that I'm—I'm pregnant. With my ex-boyfriend's baby." Saying the words out loud makes it real. Tears well up again and I choke back another sob. "We only just broke up and he... he's not a good person. At all. And now I'm stuck with this... this situation." Once the floodgates open, I can't seem to stop. "I'm exhausted. And scared. The thought of interviewing, trying to find a new job in my condition..." I let out a humorless laugh. "No one will hire me when I'll need to go on maternity leave in less than a year." I bury my face in my hands, shoulders shaking with silent sobs. "But I don't know what to do without insurance. Without money. Without a job... I'll have to move back to Nebraska. Live with my parents." A whimper slips from my lips. "Leave my friends behind. My life here is over. Everything is ruined."

My stomach roils again and I fight down another wave of nausea. I must be trapped in a bad dream. I had a plan—focus on my programming career, find someone to share my life with, and start a family when we were ready. Not like this. Not alone and powerless, hiding in a bathroom.

"I'm so sorry." His voice is full of sympathy. "That's... a lot. I can't imagine how overwhelming it must feel."

"Yeah. It's a disaster. My life is imploding as we speak." I stare at the gray metal stall door, wondering how things spiraled so far out of my control. "I bet your lie doesn't sound so bad now."

A mirthless laugh sails over to my side. "No, still does. But look, our company has great policies for working parents," he encourages me. "Generous leave, flexible hours. I'm positive we could work something out if there's an open position that fits your skills."

His optimism is sweet, but misplaced. I shake my head before realizing the futility of the gesture. "That's kind of you, but I don't think—"

My stomach suddenly bloats and an uncontrollable, loud burp forces its way out, reverberating off the bathroom walls. Mortification burns through me. "Oh gosh. I'm so sorry." I want to disappear into the floor. "See? Even if I landed an interview, I doubt I could make it through without puking on the hiring manager. Not a stellar first impression. So, unless you can find me a job that requires no interviewing skills, has great health insurance, unlimited sick days, and doubles my salary..." Between hurls, I re-did the math and realized I couldn't afford New York as a single parent on my old wage anyway. "I'm screwed."

Despair settles over me like a gravity blanket, wrapping me into the opposite of comfort.

Seconds tick by in heavy silence. I wonder if I've scared off my surprisingly supportive bathroom confidante. Then...

"How badly do you want to stay in the city?"

His question takes me by surprise. I frown at the stall divider. "Um, a lot? I never wanted to live any-where else. But what does that have to—"

"Because I might have an offer for you," he inter-jects. "I've been thinking, and... well, just hear me out before you say no, okay?"

I blink, taken aback by his sudden intensity. "Okay..." I reply slowly, bafflement and curiosity whirling inside me. "I'm listening."

6

ADRIAN

I stare at the sleek, paneled ceiling, brain whizzing with a crazy idea taking shape and figuring out the best way to expose it to her. To this mystery woman in the next stall, whose face I haven't even seen—but who could solve all my problems. I must be out of my mind. Or maybe not—because things like this don't just happen. It's almost too good to be true, like the universe is handing me exactly what I need at the precise moment I need it. The timing, the situation—it's all lining up in a way that's hard to ignore, like it's meant to be. And maybe that's why I should go through with it. It's not just luck; it's a door opening, and I'd be a fool not to walk through it.

I only need to convince her.

Okay, I can sell anything to anyone. Just think of this as another pitch.

"I've poured my entire life into my career," I begin. "Sacrificed so much to get to where I am."

"Tell me about it." Her melodic voice floats over the divider, tinged with a shared exhaustion. "I learned the hard way today just how fickle a job can be. How meaningless all that effort feels in the end." Her words are like a silky caress, and I marvel again at how enticing she sounds.

"I agree 100 per cent," I reply, shifting on the floor. "But I'm not ready to throw in the towel just yet. My boss called me and the other senior VP into his office earlier. Said he's planning to choose one of us as his replacement."

"I sense a great injustice is about to take place." Her tone is laced with mock seriousness.

Despite the gravity of the situation, she pulls a genuine laugh out of me. "You bet. I was already uncorking the champagne, but then I overheard him saying he wouldn't pick me, even though I'm the best man for the job. All because I don't have kids and I won't leave a legacy behind."

"What? That's ridiculous!" she exclaims, her

tone indignant. "It's discrimination, you should sue him."

"I'm not positive suing my boss would help me get the top job." I shrug, the absurdity of the conversation mirroring the insanity of what I'm about to propose.

"No, you're right," she concedes. "But it's still totally unfair."

"Exactly. Which is why..." I lean my head back against the icy metal wall, the next words feeling heavier than they should. "I may have invented a pregnant fiancée."

Silence hangs heavy between the stalls. Shit, I've really stepped into it now. She probably thinks I'm a lunatic.

"Wow," she finally says. "That's—wow. I take it your fiancée... err... isn't pregnant?"

Is it my impression or is there a veiled interest in the question?

"I'm not engaged," I confess, tugging at my sleeve anxiously. "I don't even have a girlfriend."

"Ah. Oh, well, what's your boss going to do?" she muses. "Come to your house and check your closet to see if you live alone? Demand copies of the ultrasounds?"

"No." I chuckle despite myself. "But I might've

told him she'll be accompanying me to a weekend at his Hamptons mansion in two weeks."

"Okay, then you're screwed," she declares in a matter-of-fact tone that cracks me up.

"Unless..." I offer, trailing off, teasing the scheme I'm about to outline.

"Unless?" she prompts.

I drum my fingers on my knee, working up the courage to give voice to what I'm thinking. The idea that's been swirling in my mind since she told me she's pregnant and out of options. "Listen, this is going to sound absolutely insane but... what if we teamed up? You need a break; I need a pregnant wife-to-be. We could help each other out."

My body is rigid with anticipation as I await her response. Have I just made the craziest proposition of my life to a total stranger in a public restroom?

Yes. Yes, I have.

"Are you asking me to be your fake girlfriend?" Her voice is tinged with incredulity. I don't think she grasped how serious I am, however bizarre my suggestion must sound.

"Um, yeah. But the thing is, for it to work, the arrangement would need to be a bit more... err, solid."

"Solid? What do you mean by *solid*?" Her tone is a mix of curiosity and worry.

The words tumble out before I can think better of it. "Marry me?" I cringe at how dubious I sound, even to myself.

I'm being impulsive, reckless even, but I can't ignore the serendipity of it all. How right it feels. It's like when I hit the green button on a risky trade, spotting patterns no one else can see, feeling the certainty I'm right in my bones. Besides, it's not like I'm asking her to spend the rest of her life with me. It's a temporary fix, a means to an end. Once I've secured the promotion and built my so-called legacy in Dominic's eyes, what happens after won't matter.

Maybe the fake engagement alone will do the trick, and we won't need to actually get married. But if that's not the case, I'm ready to walk all the way down the aisle to convince Dominic. And we're not in the Middle Ages when a marriage was forever. Reversing everything afterward won't be hard. A divorce would be clean, simple, with no strings attached. She gets her stability; I get my title—everyone wins. If I have to play family man for a little while, so be it. I've done crazier things to get ahead.

And once it's done, Dominic won't be able to take the job back even if I don't get married or get divorced. Investors wouldn't have it. A change in CEO requires a good explanation to be justified. Having me installed and then removed for no apparent reason a few months later would only project uncertainty. The last thing any hedge fund wants.

Her laughs fills the air, bringing me back to the present. "Haha, you're funny!"

I stay silent, letting the gravity of my impromptu proposal fill the void.

After a long pause, her voice takes on a more somber edge. "Wait... are you being serious right now?"

I exhale. "I know it sounds bonkers. But I'm totally serious. That's how desperate I am."

"Yes, but a fake engagement?"

"Look, my boss is no fool. It'll take time to convince Dominic. I'll need to fully commit to playing the part of the family man—engaged with a kid on the way." I fidget with my cufflinks, hoping she'll see the logic in my admittedly mad plan. "And you'd be taken care of. I'd put you on my medical insurance. It would give you space to get back on your feet financially with no pressure while you figure out your next career move and have the baby."

The seconds stretch endlessly as I wait for her reply. I can't believe those words came out of my mouth.

I wait and wait, my mind racing as I strive to imagine what her face might look like and try to guess what she's thinking. Will she laugh in my face? Call me insane and storm out? Or could she see the twisted brilliance of this plan? My palms are slick with sweat as I wait some more, giving her time to absorb the enormity of what I've said.

Finally, she speaks again. "I might be old-fashioned, but shouldn't you at least ask my name before you propose?"

I grin at her witty comeback. "You're right, I'm sorry. I'm Adrian West, and you are?"

"Rowena Taylor."

"Rowena," I repeat, letting the lovely name roll off my tongue. "That's such a beautiful name."

She chuckles, the sound light and silvery. "Definitely makes me fake wife material?"

"Absolutely." I grin like an idiot. Her sense of humor is refreshing.

"You've never even seen me," Rowena points out, amusement lacing her tone. "What if I'm hideous?"

"This would be a platonic arrangement." Trying

to be tactful, I let out a soft, hesitant hum, adding, "So it wouldn't matter how you look."

"But aren't investment bankers supposed to have wildly beautiful wives?"

"An ugly wife-to-be could make me appear less shallow," I quip back without missing a beat.

Her infectious laugh echoes through the bathroom, and a foreign warmth twists deep in my stomach, knowing I'm the one who made her laugh even on her lowest day.

"Well, that sure takes the pressure off," Rowena says, still chuckling. There's a pause and then, "So, how would this arrangement work?" Rowena asks hesitantly.

"Since you said you can't make rent, and we'd have to pretend anyway, you should move in with me. You'd have your own bedroom and private bathroom, of course." I picture my spacious penthouse apartment, imagining a faceless woman inhabiting one of the airy guest rooms. "It's a big place with plenty of space. We wouldn't step on each other's toes, and I'm at the office most of the time. We'd just need to put on a bit of a show on public appearances."

"How many public appearances?"

"Who's the one worried about me being repulsive now?"

"If we only have to be roommates, I care more about you being kind and... *clean*. Also, hopefully not into heavy metal."

I laugh again. "Definitely not into heavy metal. And I have cleaning ladies."

"But what if we're not compatible?" she presses me.

"If you're pregnant, we mustn't be too far apart in age," I reason. "And you sound nice."

"Yeah, you sound nice as well."

"But, Rowena, we'd still lead completely separate lives." I hope this sounds as reassuring as I intend it to be.

"Ah," she jokes dryly, her tone lightly mocking. "That sounds like all my Cinderella dreams coming true."

A smile tugs at my lips. Her wry humor is contagious, despite the circumstances. "I understand I'm asking a lot. You might not want to do this at all."

She sighs. "I've no idea what I want."

"You don't have to answer right away. But if you're open to considering the proposal, we can iron out the details later."

A beat of silence stretches between us, broken

only by the muffled sounds of the busy lobby beyond the door. When Rowena speaks again, her
voice quivers. "Shouldn't we, um, come out of these
stalls first? Meet face to face? This is starting to
sound like an episode of *Love Is Blind* on steroids."
She gasps. "Not that I was implying love is involved;
you know what I mean, right?"

My lips pull into a grin. "I do. And you're right,
we should meet." My pulse quickens at the suggestion, an inexplicable excitement buzzing through
my veins.

I rise to my feet, smoothing down my suit and
adjusting my sleeves. I push open the stall door, anticipation coiling in my gut as I step out to stand before the woman I've just asked to marry.

7

ROWENA

I slowly rise from the tiled bathroom floor, my legs wobbly beneath me like a newborn foal taking its first steps. The nausea seems to have subsided for now, but I gingerly place a hand on my stomach just in case. I want to make sure I'm 100 per cent in control before I get out. Puking again in front of Adrian is not on the list of humiliations I strive to add to this day.

A swarm of bees buzzes in my belly at the thought of meeting him face to face. I don't know why I'm so nervous, excited even. He's just some random—albeit kind and sexy-voiced—stranger I happened to vomit next to. And who asked me to marry him. Nothing to get worked up over. Right?

I glance down, scanning my black trousers and top for any rogue flecks of upchuck. The last thing I need is to walk out there with puke on my clothes. Thankfully everything appears clean, just a bit rumpled. I tug at the hem of my blouse to smooth out the wrinkles.

Clothes set, I clasp and unclasp my hands at my sides, wiping my palms on my pants before I reach for the stall door and open it.

My vision narrows on Adrian standing just a few feet away from me but taking up a lot of space.

Holy hot damn.

I'm unprepared for how devastatingly handsome he is. Easily over six-foot tall with a lean, muscular build that his impeccably tailored charcoal suit does nothing to hide. Thick, raven-black hair with a hint of a curl at the nape. Chiseled jaw dusted with just the right amount of scruff. Full, sensual lips quirked in a slight smile.

But it's his eyes that draw me in more than anything else and make my knees go weak—two pools of fall twilight, both mysterious and inviting, fringed by obscenely long lashes. Those bedroom eyes meet mine and it's as if an electric current zings through my body, making every nerve ending tingle.

He emanates this raw, primal sort of sex appeal

that pulses down to my very core. It's not just that he's classically handsome, there's an allure to him, an edge of danger and dominance cloaked in a crisp, polished veneer. I have the sudden urge to muss up his perfect hair and tear off that expensive tie with my teeth.

I'm staring slack-jawed, probably with drool gathering at the corner of my mouth. Fantastic. Way to play it cool. I snap my gaping pie-hole shut and pray my cheeks aren't as flaming red as they feel.

Aside from being panties-dropping handsome, Adrian looks pallid, no doubt from being sick, but he's still a hundred times more attractive than any man I've ever dated. Not that he wants to date me. Adrian is promising only minimal interactions and completely separate lives.

If looking a little ashen is what a single hurl did to him, I'm afraid to so much as glance in the mirror, certain I'll find a hot mess of tangled hair, smudged mascara, and green-tinged complexion staring back at me.

But then his lips curve into a full-blown smile and I swear I hear a chorus of angels singing.

"Hello, Rowena," he says in that honey-rich baritone, smooth and sweet, yet with a rasp of sandpaper grit. Hearing him say my name in that sinful voice makes the skin of my upper back prickle. Like a thousand tiny pins are being stabbed across my shoulder blades.

"H-hi," I stammer, hating how breathy and shy I sound.

I step forward, arm extended for a handshake, but then snatch it back hastily as it occurs to me where that hand has recently been. "I should um, wash up first," I say with a queasy grimace.

"Good thinking. I'd better do the same." He flashes me another knee-buckling grin.

We head over to the sparkling chrome sinks side by side. Hyperaware of Adrian's towering figure next to me, I fumble with the dispenser, pumping foamy soap into my palm. As I lather up, I can't resist peeking at him in the full-wall mirror, trying to be surreptitious. But then his deep-set eyes snag mine in the glass and hold. Busted. Heat floods my cheeks.

Quickly ducking my gaze, I rinse the suds away, the water feeling icy against my flushed skin. When I'm done, I tear off a length of rough brown paper towel, the sound as loud as a thunderclap in the quiet of the public restroom. My fingers tremble as I pat my damp hands dry.

We turn to face each other again, a weird tension pulling between us. Mustering my courage, I thrust out my arm. "Nice to officially meet you."

"It's a pleasure, Rowena." Adrian envelops my hand in his much larger one. His skin is cool from the water, yet it ignites a flash fire in my veins. I feel the scrape of a callus on his palm—maybe from lifting weights at the gym—and the firm, assured pressure of his grip. Solid. Strong. Capable.

When Adrian releases my hand, I immediately mourn the loss of contact. "I'm glad we ran into each other." His eyes sparkle with interest as he talks. "Unconventional as the circumstances may be."

I twist a lock of hair around my finger, my gaze flicking up to meet Adrian's as I keep blabbering nonsense. "So how would I do as an investment banker's wife?" I ask, aiming for playful but wincing inwardly at the note of self-doubt that creeps into my voice.

Adrian's gorgeous brown eyes sweep over me appraisingly. The unhurried scrutiny ignites a flicker of heat low in my spine. He tilts his head, shoving his hands casually into his pockets in a way that somehow makes him even more attractive. A tiny smirk tugs at his lips.

"I think," he drawls, "you're going to make me look *very* shallow."

My cheeks flush hotly at the veiled compliment.

I bite my lip to hold back the ridiculously giddy smile threatening to break free. Adrian finds me beautiful. Or he's just telling me what I want to hear to get me to agree to his proposal.

"How about me?" He theatrically sniffs the air. "Any body odor that disturbs you?"

"The jury is still out on that." I clear my throat, trying to regain my mental balance. "Our stomachs' recent rebellion sort of covers everything else."

Adrian barks out a surprised laugh, his eyes crinkling at the corners. "Ouch! That's cold."

"But accurate," I counter swiftly, the words sharp but my smile softening the blow.

Adrian nods solemnly, although the twinkle in his eyes is still playful.

Gosh, he makes me so nervous.

"How old are you?" I blurt out, trying to fill the silence.

Adrian arches an eyebrow. "Should I be offended by that question?" Amusement laces his words.

"No! I mean—that's not what I—sorry." Mortified, I stammer an apology and wish not for the first time today that the floor would swallow me whole.

"I'm thirty-nine," he cuts in smoothly, mercifully halting my verbal floundering.

I blink. Thirty-nine. A solid eleven years my senior. Suddenly, all the men I've previously dated—Liam included—seem woefully juvenile in comparison. Boys playing at adulthood. But Adrian? He exudes maturity, capability and raw masculinity from every pore.

Every inch a man.

"I'm twenty-eight," I offer even if he hasn't asked me.

An awkward silence descends on the room. I fidget, fingers twisting together. What now? Should I say something else? Crack a joke?

Luckily, Adrian talks before I further embarrass myself with a knock-knock pun. "I know this is... *unorthodox*. But I hope you'll seriously consider my proposal for..." His gaze holds mine, dark and intent. "... a mutually beneficial arrangement. No pressure, of course."

Mutely, I nod. My head's still spinning, thoughts tripping over themselves. Engaged. To a veritable stranger. It's crazy. Absolutely bananas. And yet...

"Could I get your number?" Adrian produces his phone, sleek and gleaming. "To discuss details whenever you're ready."

"Um, sure." I recite the digits and watch as his fingers fly across the screen. A second later, my cell buzzes in my bag.

"There. Now you have mine, too." A hint of a smile plays at the edges of his mouth.

I bob my head again, feeling like one of those bouncy-headed dashboard dogs. "Thanks. I'll... I'll think it over and get back to you soon."

"Wonderful." His eyes crinkle at the corners. "Where are you going from here? Home, I suppose?"

"Yeah, I feel better."

"How are you getting there?"

"I'll just take the subway. It's only a few stops to my place. I'll be fine now that the naus—"

"Nonsense. My driver will take you." His tone brooks no argument.

"Your driver?" I quirk a smirk. "How loaded are you, exactly?"

If his polished leather shoes and expensive-looking watch are an indication, he must be rolling in it.

Adrian gives an insouciant half-shrug. "I do alright for myself."

He steps forward and for a deluded moment I think he's going to hug me or something, but he merely brushes past me—still close enough for me to detect the smell of his aftershave, a rich and earthy scent that momentarily scrambles my brain cells. Yeah, BO won't be a problem.

Bending down, he scoops up the cardboard box containing the riffraff I kept in my cubicle. "Shall we?"

I trail after him, marveling at the strangeness of it all as we exit the restroom. Adrian West, my investment banker in shining armor, escorts me to his luxury motorized stallion. The sleek black town car is already waiting parallel parked at the curb when we step outside, gleaming under the late afternoon sun.

So this is how the other half lives, I think to myself.

Adrian pulls open the rear door and sets my box on the leather seat before turning back to me. "Tell Sam your address. He'll take you wherever you need to go."

"Thank you. I appreciate it." I hesitate with one hand on the door frame. "For all of this. The ride, and well, you know..."

"The impromptu marriage proposal?" he offers.

"That too." I duck my head to get into the car.

Adrian's expression sobers. "I'll be in touch soon.

Take it easy in the meantime, you've had a long day."

"That's an understatement," I mutter. With a parting nod, I slide into the buttery soft rear seat. "Thanks again. Bye, I guess."

He gives me a small smile and shuts the door with a solid thump, rapping twice on the roof.

As the car pulls away from the curb and merges into traffic, I twist around to peer out the back window. Adrian stands on the sidewalk, an imposing figure in his dark suit, watching us drive off. My stomach does a little flip that doesn't seem vomit-related for once. He disappears as we turn a corner, and I face forward again, slumping against the seat with a shuddery exhale.

Wow. I'm sitting in a car that must cost more than my yearly salary. With a box of my pitiful desk whatnots. Because I just got fired. And then proposed to by a stranger. A millionaire from the looks of it. To be his wife. His fake, contractual wife precisely, but still.

I glance out the window at the blur of signs and shop windows whizzing by. It feels like a metaphor for how quickly my life has spun off in a new direction. In a few hours, everything familiar is shrinking behind me as I careen into the unknown.

Resting my forehead against the cool glass of the window, I close my eyes and try to slow my racing thoughts. The only certainty: life as I knew it is already just a memory. I'm hurtling down an unbeaten path, destination unclear.

Goodbye, old life. Let's see what the future holds.

8

ROWENA

We get stuck in a bit of traffic, and by the time Adrian's sleek black car pulls up to the curb in front of my building, it's already past five. At once, Sam exits from his side and comes to open my door. I thank him and I'm about to pull out the box with my office stuff when I glimpse Hunter rounding the corner, her dark wavy hair bouncing with each step as she walks home from work. My heart leaps into my throat. I shove the cardboard box back onto the seat, desperate to hide the evidence of my disastrous day.

Giving Sam one last, weary nod, I slide out and force a smile as I greet my roommate. "Hey."

Hunter's eyes widen as she takes in the luxury vehicle and personal chauffeur idling behind me. She lets out a low whistle. "Well, well. Look at you, Miss Fancy Pants. What's with the limo service?"

"It's not a limo, just a... nice car." I glance at Sam, mortified. But Adrian's driver smiles warmly and wishes me a good evening before returning to his post at the wheel.

Hunter and I watch him as he speeds away into traffic.

"So?" my roommate prompts.

"It's a long story."

"Ooh, I can't wait to hear all about it." Hunter loops her arm through mine as we head inside. I might not be ready to rehash the day's events, but her nearness is comforting.

We take the elevator up to our apartment, the ache in my chest growing with each floor we pass. Where will I even begin to tell her everything that happened today?

As we step inside—my dilemma worsens as it's not just my roommate in the house. A chorus of greetings rises. Nina, radiant as always, bounds over to pull me into a tight hug. Her brother, Dylan, of-fers a wave from the couch where he sits beside

Nina's boyfriend, Tristan. It's weird for everyone to be already home from work. We all have high-demand careers—or I used to. None of our jobs are nine-to-five. What's everyone doing here?

Nina pulls back, her brow creasing as she studies my face. "Are you feeling okay, Winnie? You look a little pale."

"Must be the lack of sunshine from being chauffeured home in a luxury car," Hunter quips with a smirk.

Nina arches an eyebrow at me, but I whiffle her off. "I'm fine, just tired. It's been a day."

They're all watching me, waiting for an explanation. But I'm not ready. I paste on a weak smile, hoping it's enough to hold them off... for now.

"Well, I hope you're not too tired, because we've got pizzas on the way."

My stomach churns at the mention of food, the mere thought of eating making me queasy again.

As Nina drifts back to Tristan, I pull Hunter aside. "Why is everyone here so early?"

She frowns. "Didn't you get the text from Nina?"

I haven't checked my phone since before lunch. "No, what is it?"

"I don't know." Hunter shrugs. "She just told us

to be home early." Then she studies me, perplexed. "What's up with you today?"

Thankfully, Nina chooses that moment to clap her hands, her eyes sparkling with excitement. "Come on guys, we have something to share before the pizzas arrive."

I'm grateful for the distraction. Anything to postpone the moment when I have to confess my bombshell.

We all settle into the living room, finding our usual spots. I sink into the oversized armchair, pulling my legs up and hugging them to my chest. It feels like I'm trying to physically hold myself together.

Hunter perches on the armrest of the couch, her eyes trained on Nina. "Okay, spill!" she tells her. "What's this big announcement?"

Nina's smile widens. "Well..." She pauses for dramatic effect, and I lean forward despite myself, momentarily swept up in her excitement. She laces her fingers with Tristan's, her eyes shining as she looks around at all of us. "We're moving in together!"

Nina's words hang in the air as Hunter and I stare at her—Dylan doesn't seem surprised; he must've known already.

My first thought is that even if I had the strength to find a new job that came with a larger salary by some miracle, I'd still have to move to a cheaper neighborhood. I can't cover my rent here with a kid, and I sure as hell can't pick up half of hers on top of that.

But Nina hastens to add, "I know you guys must be worried about covering my portion of the rent. But don't stress." *Don't stress?* I'm basically *made* of stress. "Dylan said he'd be happy to take over my room if you two are cool with it. Since Tristan and I want to move in together as soon as possible, and Dylan needs a place STAT, it works out perfectly! Right, Dylan?"

She looks expectantly at her brother, who gives an affable shrug. "If they're okay with it, I'm game. No worries either way, though."

I press my lips together, trying to mask my rising panic. Oh gosh. An unpleasant roiling grips my abdomen again. They probably expect us to say something, but I'm not eager to rain on their roommate swap parade.

I glance at Hunter to gauge her reaction, but she seems lost in thought, sneaking furtive peeks at Dylan. She's not speaking either.

The other three must've expected a different response because Nina's face falls, Tristan looks uncertain, and Dylan is smiling awkwardly.

But then Nina's brother flashes a charming grin. "I promise I don't smell. I shower at least once a week." He winks at Hunter and me conspiratorially. "I figure we can all see how this cohabitation goes until your lease on this place is up. What do you say?"

"Yes." Hunter, out of her trance, almost falls on her butt in the exuberance of her reply. She always has had a huge crush on Nina's brother, and Dylan moving in is probably a dream come true for her. One that I'm about to shatter.

All eyes turn to me expectantly and I have no other choice than to burst their bubble. Suppressing a sob or a burp—I can't even tell at this point—I confess everything. That this morning I found out I'm pregnant with Liam's baby and lost my job half an hour later. I tell them about Adrian and our meet-puke in the bathroom, and that I'm seriously considering marrying a total stranger, but that either way, I'll have to move out.

To say that my roommates look at me shell-shocked would be the understatement of the century. Once they recover, they ask me a million questions: how far along am I? Does Liam know? What about Adrian? Who is this guy? And have I lost my mind?

They volley questions at me like one of those tennis-ball shooting machines. Hunter, to her credit, seems only concerned about me and not her smashed dream of moving in with her crush.

Next, they ask whether my parents know, and that finally breaks me. I sob uncontrollably while I shake my head.

Without another word, both my best friends stand up and envelop me in a bear hug, nearly squeezing the air out of me.

"You can stay here rent free for however long you want." Hunter pats my shoulder.

I blink, rejecting the idea of becoming a charity case. "You can't afford to pay double."

"I won't move out," Nina jumps in. "Between the two of us we can pick up the difference."

"Guys, I appreciate your offer to let me stay here without paying rent. But I can't accept. It wouldn't be right."

Nina opens her mouth to protest but I hold up a hand. "And what about when the baby comes? I'm going to need a plan, security, and stability. I can't just rely on your generosity forever."

Hunter snorts sarcastically. "And you think

you'll find stability by moving in with some random dude you met in a bathroom? By becoming a kept woman?"

Her words sting, and I flinch. Nina shoots Hunter a sharp look. "Hunt! Don't be like that. This is her choice to make."

I nod gratefully at Nina before turning back to Hunter, forcing more confidence into my voice than I feel. "I know it seems crazy. Trust me, I'm aware. But please don't judge me for considering it." I twist my hands together anxiously. "I haven't decided anything for sure yet. But if I do this, it will be my choice. Can you respect that, even if you don't agree with it?"

Hunter's skeptical expression softens. "Of course. I'm sorry, I didn't mean to come off so harsh. I just worry about you, Winnie." She rubs my arm. "First Liam and now this."

I manage a small smile, blinking back the fresh tears that threaten to spill over. "I know." The idea of moving in with Adrian, of tying myself to a virtual stranger, terrifies me. But the fear of facing this pregnancy alone, with no support, looms even larger. I turn to Hunter. "And I'm sorry you're going to have to move out, too, because I can't keep a stupid job."

She hugs me fiercely. "Don't be silly, that is the least of our problems."

"But what if the landlord doesn't let us out of our lease early?" I sob into her shoulder.

Behind us, Dylan clears his throat. "Err... actually if you're moving out, I could take up your room as well and turn it into a home office." He stares at Hunter. "If that's cool with you." She nods, and he adds, "But you don't have to go, seriously. If you want to stay, we'll all chip in to cover your rent until you get back on your feet."

"Yeah," Tristan agrees. He scratches his chin thoughtfully. "Pretending to be engaged to this rando isn't your only option."

"Thank you, but it's not just the rent, it's medical expenses, too. I don't have insurance anymore and I'll need to go to a lot of appointments, plus buy a million things for the baby... I... I..." I trail off, overwhelmed.

Dylan rakes a hand through his golden fringe. "I'd tell you I could check if we have any openings, but the head of the informatic division at our firm is a total douche. I wouldn't want you to work for him."

"But I can hire you," Tristan jumps in eagerly. "We could always use a talented software engineer."

"Please, Tristan, you told me two weeks ago that you phased out your entire legacy Java stack in favor of microservices and cloud-native architecture. Your IT department is already over-staffed."

"You're too smart for your own good," he scoffs. "But how is me offering you a job worse than a stranger paying your expenses while you pretend to be engaged to him?"

I wring my fingers. "I know this may sound weird, but you're doing it for me. He's doing it for himself. It's an equal exchange. And having you as a boss would be too weird, anyway."

"Fair enough." Tristan nods. "You said this dude works in your building?"

"Why?" I pause, frowning. "Are you going to google him?"

Hunter nods, pulling out her phone. "That's a great idea. Name."

"Adrian West," I reply, feeling a knot in my stomach.

Tristan and Dylan both low whistle.

"Why?" My voice rises. "You know him?"

"We know *of* him. Dude's a legend on Wall Street," Dylan says with admiration. "Everyone calls him the next Warren Buffett."

"But he's also known as a bit of a shark," Tristan adds, his eyebrows knitting together.

"Like he's dishonest?" I ask, alarmed.

"No, just ruthless, at least in a business context," Tristan clarifies. "I don't know him personally."

Hunter gasps loudly as she stares at her phone. "Is this him?" She turns the screen to face me.

Brown eyes, dark as aged leather, bore into me, making my insides squirm even from within a picture. "Yep."

"Oh, wow," Hunter exclaims, her nose almost glued to the screen. "And did you just forget to mention your future husband was going to be this hot?"

"Let me see." Nina scrambles next to Hunter. "Holy shit! That man could make a nun reconsider with just one look!"

"Excuse you?" Tristan broods from his corner.

"Well, just look at him. Bet he could seduce even you."

Tristan barely glances at the screen before grinning. "Nah, I'm more into blondes."

Dylan bats his lashes at his best friend, making his voice shrill. "Oh, good to know."

"Sorry, man." He pulls Nina into his lap. "Talking about another Thompson." He kisses Nina, and Dylan rolls his eyes, averting his gaze.

They really get into the kiss, and Dylan shoves his best friend on the shoulder. "Come on, man."

Tristan reluctantly breaks the kiss and elbows Dylan good-naturedly. "Alright, alright, so what are we doing here? Are you still moving in with me?"

"Not until she's okay." Nina scowls.

"I am okay," I lie. "If Dylan can pay two-thirds of the rent here and use my room as an office, I just have to move my stuff out and decide where to go."

"There's no hurry," Dylan offers once again.

I give him a thankful smile. "I can't make the next lease payment without going broke, so I'll have to make up my mind before the end of the month."

They all look at me and nod supportively, except for Nina.

"Honey, today has been a lot." She meets my eyes with a steady, encouraging gaze. "You don't have to decide anything right at this moment even if rent is due soon. I agree it's not a forever solution, but we can cover you for a month if you need more time. We're all here for you. Just let us, okay?"

I nod.

Hunter squeezes me into another hug. "Take all the time you need; we'll support you whatever you decide. But don't make any rash decisions because you're in a panic."

It means the world to know they have my back, but this is a decision I have to make alone as it will impact the rest of my life. I just hope that whatever path I choose, it'll be the right one for me and my baby.

9

ADRIAN

Bass vibrates through my bones as I nurse a whiskey on the rocks, the clink of the ice cubes punctuating each beat dropped by the DJ. Limbs sway around me on the rooftop lounge, traders grinding the night away over another multi-million-dollar close. Their elation swirls like the technicolor lights reflecting off the glass and steel skyscrapers surrounding us, a buzzing energy I'm disconnected from.

I fish my phone from my pocket and check the Asian markets for the dozenth time, but the numbers on the screen blur. I don't have the focus for this right now. Feeling the weight of the day, I down my drink and push through the sweaty throng of bodies to the exit.

"Calling it a night already, boss?" Tyler, one of the junior traders, shouts over the music with a dopey grin.

I force a tight smile. "Early start tomorrow. Don't stay out too late, yeah?"

He throws me a sloppy salute before melting back into the crowd. I push forward, envying his carefree abandon. When was the last time I enjoyed myself at one of these outings?

The elevator ride down to the lobby is blessedly quiet, a reprieve from the relentless noise above. I scroll through my apps and tap a request for a generic black car. Sam's day ended a while ago.

Ten minutes later, a Mercedes-Maybach purrs to a stop at the curb. The unknown driver hops out and opens the passenger door with a tip of his cap. "Good evening, Mr. West."

I nod back and slide into the seat, welcoming the calm hum of the engine as we merge into traffic. I should pop champagne right now, riding the high of another insanely profitable quarter. But I'm just... tired—worried. Terrified that all that I've achieved will be for nothing. This job, these wins—they're all I've ever wanted and fought tooth and nail for since I first set foot on Wall Street.

And now, I stand to lose it all because I don't

have a wife and kids. And I lied to Dominic about it. If Rowena doesn't accept my proposal, I can kiss my future goodbye. My hands shake and I have to grip my knees to make them stop.

What have I done?

I can't even wrap my head around it. I lied. Flat-out lied to Dominic, to the one person whose trust I've spent years building. And not just a harmless little white lie. No, I conjured a relationship—*an entire fake life with a pregnant fiancée*—out of thin air. Who does that? I'm not the guy who spirals into impulsive decisions, not the type who lets fear dictate his actions. But today, I did.

The pressure is about to crack my skull open. This is reckless, even for me. I've always been calculated, methodical, driven by logic, not emotion. But today? Today, I let the visceral dread of my teen years coil together with the fresh fear of losing everything. That same fear I thought I'd left behind —the one that haunted me when I was young, when nothing felt secure—mixed with the terrifying possibility that everything I've worked for could disappear. My career, my reputation—it all felt so fragile, slipping from my grasp. And instead of controlling it like I should've, I let it control me. I panicked. And in that panic, I made a decision that could ruin not only me but this stranger I've dragged into my mess. A woman who's pregnant, no less, and with a life that's already in chaos.

And for what? To keep my position? To prove to Dominic that I can build a life beyond this office? Gosh, what if Rowena says no? What if she thinks I'm insane and bails? What if I have to face Dominic and admit it was all a lie? The fallout would be catastrophic. He'd fire me on the spot, and then good luck finding another job once I become a running joke on Wall Street.

And what about her? She's got her own problems to deal with—what kind of person am I to put this on her?

Before I can spiral further, the driver pulls into the underground garage of my building. I mutter a goodnight and take the private elevator up to the penthouse.

Outside my door, I find a familiar cardboard box. Rowena's stuff from her desk that she left in my car and that Sam dropped off with my doorman. I pick it up and fumble with my keys. The soft click of the lock is amplified in the night's quiet. I toss the keys on the large console table in the entry hall and drop Rowena's box next to them.

I peek inside at the scant remains of her professional life as I wonder for the millionth time since this afternoon how I could be so reckless as to ask a woman I barely know to upend her entire world. To bind herself to me, share my home, potentially my name, and pretend her child is mine. It's insanity.

I scrub a hand over my face and look out the floor-to-ceiling windows at the glittering city below. For years, this view was enough. The pinnacle I clawed my way up to from nothing. But now, the sprawling space just feels... hollow.

"Jeez, I'm losing it," I mutter. I need to sleep. And to figure out how the hell I'm going to convince Rowena to agree to this crazy plan before Dominic figures me out.

I head down the hall, flicking on lights as I go, shadows nipping at my heels. I'll figure it out tomorrow.

I pause, undecided where to go. Before turning in, I should check on the Hang Seng and Nikkei indexes. Both had unusual volatility today, and I need to ensure we're not overexposed in the Asian markets. It's the responsible thing to do as CIO. But as I make my way to the office, my mind refuses to shift into work mode.

All I can think about is Rowena. Will she accept

my outrageous proposal? Move in with a stranger over a decade her senior? Uproot her entire life to play house?

I chuckle humorlessly. When I frame it like that, it sounds mentally ill. No sane woman would agree to it. But I have to try. My job, my whole fucking future, hangs in the balance.

On impulse, I deviate from my office door and go back to the foyer. Without giving myself time to rethink, I pick up the box of Rowena's stuff and bring it to the large living room table. Maybe her things will give me more of a pulse on what kind of person she is. I find sticky notes in a rainbow of colors. An army of markers and highlighters. But one pen stands out from the rest.

I pluck the novelty pen from the box, eyeing it curiously. It's a Disney princess. Belle, from *Beauty and the Beast*. The doll has long chestnut hair and big eyes, the skirt of her golden ball gown composed by a feathery pompom. The figurine kind of looks like Rowena—except her irises are not a solid brown, but spark into green on the outer rim.

Is this some kind of sign? Am I the beast in our twisted fairy tale? A monster trying to trap a beauty in his castle of glass?

I set the pen down with a huff of laughter. I'm losing my damn mind. Reading way too much into a silly trinket. But it makes me wonder... If Rowena is the princess in this scenario, then my cold, clinical business proposal won't fly. No woman—especially not one who wants a fable—dreams of an arrangement born out of necessity and nothing more.

Fuck. I'll have to find another way to persuade her. Appeal to her practical side... how?

I keep rummaging through the box, curiosity getting the better of me. A framed photograph catches my eye, and I pick it up for a closer look.

Rowena is with two other young women, all of them dressed in bright, half-soaked pink dresses and blonde wigs. Well, two of them have wigs on— the third seems to be a natural blonde. They're grinning at the camera, arms slung around each other. They look... happy. Carefree.

I study Rowena's face, taking in her brilliant smile, the way her eyes crinkle at the corners. She's stunning, even in a garish getup. But I decide that I prefer her as a brunette. There's something about the warm tones of her natural hair that just suits her.

Are these the friends she mentioned earlier? The ones she'd hate to leave behind? I can see why.

Will they be enough for her to choose New York? To pick me?

As I set the picture aside, a pang of something uncomfortable twists in my chest. Rowena has a whole life I know nothing about. People she cares about and who care about her. And here I am, eager to use it to my advantage... I really am the monster.

But offering her a way out that benefits me too is all I can do. I have a hunch she wouldn't go for charity. She didn't even want me to look into a job for her—which I did, anyway, only to find out the only open position we have is entry level and couldn't sustain a single mom in this city.

Shaking off the thought, I keep poking through her things. A mouse pad printed with the words "I survived another meeting that should've been an email" makes me chuckle.

There's more—a succulent plant that I handle with care, wary of the small but wicked-looking thorns. File folders. More pens. A stub ticket to Taylor Swift's Eras Tour concert.

At the bottom, I find something unexpected. A wad of tiny strips of paper held together with a binder clip—fortune cookies messages. I pluck one free and read it. "The one you love is closer than you think."

I scoff and move on to the next. And the next. Each message is more saccharine than the last.

"In dreams and in love there are no impossibilities." Debatable.

"Love isn't something you find. Love is something that finds you." Gag me.

But there are also some funny ones.

"Borrow money from a pessimist. They won't expect it back." Ha!

Or weird ones.

"He who throws dirt is losing ground." What does that even mean?

"Love is like wildflowers... it is often found in the most unlikely places." Okay, kind of pretty. I guess.

"True love is not something that comes every day. Follow your heart, it knows the right answer." This one's so cheesy it makes me shudder.

I flip another one. "For rectal use only."

A surprised bark of laughter escapes me. Then a chuckle. Soon, I'm cracking up, shoulders shaking with mirth. Tears blur my vision as I give in to the hilarity.

Gosh, what a roller coaster. This last message was so unexpected, so irreverent. This glimpse into her personality... it's enthralling. Appealing.

I want to know more about her. But not just because I need her to say yes to me more than I've ever needed anything.

I read the last fortune cookie message. "If you eat something and no one sees you, it has no calories." I chuckle, shaking my head.

I replace everything into the box except for the plant, my fingers lingering on the cardboard. It feels wrong that I snooped, but I'm also sort of glad I did. With a sigh, I glance at the succulent. Does it need water? I have no idea. I've never been much of a green thumb.

But it seems important to her, so I decide to err on the side of caution. I'll leave it be for now. It's a succulent, right? They don't require frequent watering. Instead, I carry it over to the windowsill, where it'll catch the morning light. There. That should do it.

Suddenly exhausted, I head to my bedroom. I strip off my suit, leaving a trail of expensive fabrics on the floor, eager to collapse into bed.

The mattress welcomes me like an old friend. For a long moment, I stare at the ceiling. My phone is a lead weight in my hand. I want to text her. Ask if she has thought about what she's going to do. But it could come across as me pressuring her or appearing too eager, too desperate. Even if I am.

My thumb hovers over her contact. Rowena Taylor. I can't tell if the flutter in my chest is nerves or excitement. Both, maybe.

Before I can second guess myself, I open a new message. The cursor blinks at me, mocking. Taunting. I flex and unflex my fingers... and start to type.

10

ADRIAN

I decide to keep it simple.

ADRIAN

Hey, this is Adrian

I send the text and stretch an arm behind my head, my back sinking comfortably into the propped-up pillows.

ROWENA

Hey?

The quick response pops up. It's nothing exceptional, but it gives me a thrill, anyway. I wonder what she's doing still up. Hopefully the nausea isn't keeping her awake.

ADRIAN

> How are you feeling? Was the ride home okay?

I wait, tapping my fingers against the back of the phone, wondering if I'm sounding too keen.

ROWENA

> More than okay, you know how to travel in style

I chuckle, relieved she's taking things light-heartedly.

ADRIAN

> *Cool emoji*

> You left your box in my car

> On purpose, Sam said?

There's a pause, and I flip the phone in my hand, anxious.

ROWENA

I bumped into my roommate
outside my building and panicked

My screen lights up again before I can respond.

ROWENA

I needed a minute before having
the whole "I'm pregnant I got
fired" chit chat

Did you look into my box?

Guilt ripples down my spine.

ADRIAN

I did

ROWENA

What's your take from snooping
around in my stuff?

I could play it cool and pretend I have paid little attention. But instead, I type a genuine answer.

ADRIAN

> You're a secret romantic who believes in fairy tales, you love books—but not self-help ones. You have a great sense of humor, and your best friends mean the world to you. You're a Swiftie. You can keep a plant alive.

My fingers hover over the little blue arrow, uncertainly. But then I hit send with a bit of a "fuck it" attitude. No point in holding back.

ROWENA

> *Shocked emoji*

> You got all that from my box of office crap?

ADRIAN

> Yep

ROWENA

> I can see why you're good at your job

A few seconds pass, but her typing bubbles keep moving until another message flies in.

ROWENA

But how did you guess the bit
about self-help books? (Spot
on, BTW)

ADRIAN

Fortune cookies are chock-full of
motivational quotes, but you
didn't keep a single one

ROWENA

I'm impressed

ADRIAN

Are the women in the photo your
roommates?

ROWENA

Yep, on the night we met

ADRIAN

Did you tell them… everything?

A nervous tension simmers in my gut. The input
of her friends will be important in what she does.

ROWENA

Yes, they were very supportive. A
little shocked

ADRIAN

Did you also talk about me?

I'm curious, maybe too keen for her answer. I toss an extra pillow behind my head.

ROWENA

Extensively

We also googled you—great job on the SEO

My heart gives an intrigued kick. I press for more details, unable to stop myself.

ADRIAN

Oh? Verdict?

ROWENA

Great bone structure—possibly ruthless?

I grin amused by her teasing about my looks, but I'm not sure if I should worry about the ruthless part.

ADRIAN

Where did the ruthless part come
from? I don't believe it's in my bio

ROWENA

My best friend's brother and
boyfriend both work in finance.
Apparently, you have a reputation

My smile fades a bit. The finance world is small, after all. And I do have a reputation—not to mess with me—that I've spent years building. I'm respected and, yeah, also feared by some.

ADRIAN

Taylor Swift has a Big Reputation,
too

ROWENA

Don't try to distract me with—
admittedly good—Taylor
Swift puns

So, are you? Ruthless?

ADRIAN

I go after what I want. I have no
problem admitting that

I send the message with a firm nod, owning up to my nature.

ROWENA

> And now you want a pregnant fiancée

I rub the back of my neck, unsure how to reply. Pretend I'm not after something? No, because I am. My future is in her hands. I decide total transparency is the best way ahead.

ADRIAN

> I honestly didn't write to pressure you

> I just wanted to check on you

> But, yeah, I want you to be my fiancée for all the wrong reasons

> It's not romantic, and probably not what you might've dreamed for yourself

> But if you're going to say no, I'd rather know

> The sooner I come clean with my boss the better

I send the flurry of texts, each one making my chest tighten, then wait.

ROWENA

I don't know what to do

ADRIAN

Is there anything I can do to make the decision easier?

I want to help, to smooth things out for her.

ROWENA

Actually, yes

Can we meet on Saturday, talk some more?

Relief washes over me. She didn't say no.

ADRIAN

Yeah, sure. I can show you my apartment

I grimace at how that might come across, immediately regretting the phrasing.

ADRIAN

I'm sorry that totally sounded
serial killer of me

And now I've made it worse.

ADRIAN

I promise I'm not a serial killer

I add quickly, hoping to inject some humor back
into the conversation.

ROWENA

That's exactly what a serial killer
would say

I chuckle, relieved she's still joking.

ADRIAN

We can meet in a public space if
that's more comfortable

I just thought you might want to
see where I live

Also, where you'd live

Your plant misses you

ROWENA

Talk to her every morning and
she'll be fine

Coffee sounds great

fingers-crossed emoji I'll be able
to keep it down

ADRIAN

Is the nausea still bad?

ROWENA

Better than this afternoon

My roommates made me
ginger tea

ADRIAN

Glad to hear

I'll have Sam pick you up at ten

Does the time work for you?

ROWENA

Ten is perfect

See you Saturday

ADRIAN

Goodnight

I want to say more, but I wouldn't know what to add, so I leave it at that.

It's a while before another message from her comes in. Was she thinking, too, of something else to add?

ROWENA

Night

ADRIAN

PS. If you have questions before Saturday, text me whenever

I set the phone down and I've just switched off the night lamp when another string of texts arrives.

ROWENA

Off the top of my head, in no particular order

How do you feel about pineapple on pizza?

Do you believe in ghosts?

Is double dipping at a party ever acceptable?

What's your take on socks with sandals?

How many times is it okay to hit
the snooze button?

If I steal a fry from your plate, will
it start a war?

Related, do you share dessert?

How competitive are you at board
games?

What's your weirdest habit that I
should prepare for?

Are you a dog person, cat person,
or the kind who watches animal
videos and wishes?

I'm the latter in case it wasn't
clear

I stare at the barrage of questions and a rush of
adrenaline cures my exhaustion as I begin to type
back.

11

ROWENA

I stare at my phone, my face glowing in its pale light —the only illumination in my dark bedroom. What was I thinking, bombarding Adrian with that crazy volley of questions? He's going to think I'm a total nutcase.

Liam always used to tell me how annoying and silly my sense of humor is. How *extra* I am. Now Adrian is probably thinking the same.

I flop back onto my pillow with a sigh, ready to toss my phone aside and attempt to sleep, when I notice the three little dots appear. He's responding. My heart kicks into double-time and I bolt upright, clutching my phone tightly.

"Please don't let it say 'Lose my number, you lunatic'," I mutter, gnawing on my bottom lip. The seconds stretch like cotton candy as I wait. And wait. The dots disappear. Reappear. Disappear again. Jeez, is he writing me a novel? The suspense is killing me.

"Just rip off the Band-Aid already," I groan, shaking my phone as if that will make his response materialize faster.

While I wait, I imagine his strong hands typing out a reply, his dark eyes narrowed at the screen. Maybe a smile tugging at the corner of his mouth? Or a disturbed grimace? Ugh, I can't tell. Is he going to play nice just because he's desperate and he needs me?

I squeeze my eyes shut for a second. Please let him get my oddball sense of humor. Please don't let him be scared off by my quirky late-night ramblings. I've been told I'm an acquired taste. Liam loved to remind me constantly how lucky I was he could endure all my eccentricities.

My phone vibrates in my hand and my eyes fly open.

ADRIAN

I see you're going straight for the important stuff

I laugh.

ADRIAN

Also in no particular order:

Double dipping at a party is
NEVER acceptable

Now I'm full-on grinning.

ROWENA

But what if the nachos are huge
and the salsa really, really good?

ADRIAN

Still a no go

thumbs-up emoji to pineapple
on pizza

I'd even go as far as endorse hot
honey pizza dips

My eyes widen.

ROWENA

Ew, gross

You're disgusting

ADRIAN

skeptical emoji have you at least
ever tried it?

ROWENA

I also haven't tried Oreos dipped
in orange juice

But I still know they'd be horrible

ADRIAN

laughing emoji point taken, but
don't knock it til you try it

My phone buzzes again before I can craft a witty
rebuttal.

ADRIAN

I don't snooze

Oh, I don't have a problem believing that.

ADRIAN

Don't own a single pair of sandals,
but if I did, I'd never wear them
with socks. Even if, weirdly
enough, I don't mind socks with
sliders

I read the text and snort a laugh, shaking my head in disbelief. Who is this guy?

ROWENA

> Agreed. Sandals and sliders are two distinct categories when it comes to footwear and sock-wearing

ADRIAN

> I'm neither a cat nor a dog person, but if you move in with me, you can get two of each

ROWENA

> Are you trying to bribe me?

ADRIAN

> Shamelessly

> You can also take all my fries, and I share dessert

> But you don't want to play a board game with me, that might *actually* start a war

I'm aware I'm swooning a little as I type a reply.

ROWENA

I had a feeling you were the competitive type

ADRIAN

My weirdest habit... I never make a trade if it's 11:11

ROWENA

Isn't that supposed to be a lucky hour?

ADRIAN

I don't believe in luck

ROWENA

I hope my fortune cookie messages are in a separate room where they can't be subjected to your misbeliefs

ADRIAN

laughing emoji

I promise never to express my skepticism in front of them

But I hope I've answered all your questions for now

ROWENA

You didn't tell me about ghosts

This time he doesn't shoot back as fast as before. The answer takes longer to come in.

ADRIAN

I shouldn't believe in ghosts. But tonight, I feel like mine are circling me in the darkness

Wow, he went from playful to deep fast. I'm having a bit of whiplash when the next text pops in.

ADRIAN

Sorry, that sort of put a damper on the mood

But I'm stressed. I hate not being in control and I'm spiraling

ROWENA

I'm not the most collected person but I get it. Today was hard. For both of us

ADRIAN

I'm going to let you go to sleep now, you and the baby need to rest

Goodnight to both

My eyes go as big as Puss in Boots'. Is it just me, or is he really sweet?

ROWENA

Keep your lights on and wear a sleep mask instead

Ghosts don't like light

He sends me a picture back of his night lamp lit up. I glimpse a stylish bedroom in the background.

Something in my chest pulls. If I'd sent a message like that to Liam, he would've ridiculed me—if not worse.

Instead, now, even after what has been the most horrible day of my life, I close my eyes, dropping my phone on my chest, enveloped in a vague, unjustified sense of hope.

* * *

Two days later, the mid-June heat slams into me as I step out of my apartment building, the stifling air clinging to my skin. I squint against the bright sunlight, my eyes still adjusting after spending the past forty-eight hours mostly in bed with the curtains drawn. Queasiness churns in my stomach, an unpleasant reminder of how much I've been throwing up since getting fired. But I'm determined to push through the morning sickness. I need to get out of the house, get some fresh air. And if I'm being honest with myself, I'm really looking forward to seeing Adrian again, despite my roommates' warnings.

Nina's voice echoes in my head as I walk down the curb. "Winnie, are you sure about this? Going to meet some rich guy alone at his place?"

"It's just coffee first," I assured her. "I'll text you every hour to let you know I'm alive."

Hunter chimed in, "And if he tries anything, knee him where it counts and run like hell!"

I waved a hand. "I'll be fine. Adrian's not an ax murderer."

At least, I'm pretty sure he's not... 99 per cent sure.

"Alright, but keep your guard up," Nina said. "And your pepper spray handy."

"Yes, Mom," I said, rolling my eyes good-naturedly as I exited the apartment.

I chuckle to myself, grateful for their concern even if they're being a tad overprotective. Apprehension flaps in my stomach as I spot Adrian's car waiting. Sam, his driver, steps out and opens the rear passenger door for me.

"Good morning, Miss Taylor," he greets me politely.

"Morning, Sam. And please, just call me Rowena." I slide into the backseat, the cool leather a welcome relief from the oppressive heat outside. The AC hits my skin, further cooling me just as the door shuts with a light thud.

Moments later, Sam merges onto an empty lane, and I pull out my phone. Nina and Hunter will be expecting that first text. I switch to the camera app, angling it to capture my face against the backdrop of the car's posh interior. Flashing a grin and a thumbs up, I snap a selfie.

Tapping out a message, I attach the photo and hit send, officially starting the clock on my promised hourly check-ins.

My stomach flips again as the reality of what I'm doing hits me. Gosh, I'm so nervous to see Adrian. After our text exchange a couple of days ago, he's only messaged me once to confirm today's appointment. What will he say? What will *I* say?

I smother my plain T-shirt down. I wanted to look cute, wear a sundress, but practicality won out

—I'm in jeans and an easily washable top in case I need to kneel on a questionable restroom floor and spill my guts out. Definitely not a dress day.

As the car weaves through the quiet weekend streets, my mind spins with thoughts of tall, intimidating, darkly handsome Adrian. I have to keep reminding myself this meeting is just business. A contract. Nothing more.

So why do I feel like I'm heading to a first date instead of a business negotiation? I fiddle anxiously with my hair, twisting a lock around my finger. I need to stay detached, be clinical about this. Even if his deep brown eyes make me want to melt...

The temptation to stare at the picture of him I saved on my phone is strong. Instead, I plonk the device back into my bag and focus on the scenery flashing by the tinted windows, hoping to calm the butterflies rioting in my stomach.

Soon the car slows and I glance up as Sam speaks. "We've arrived, Miss Taylor—Rowena."

My stomach swoops and I swallow hard against a surge of nausea. Morning sickness or just nerves about facing Adrian. Maybe both.

"Thank you, Sam," I manage, trying to inject some confidence into my voice. I can do this. I *need* to do this.

Before I can gather myself further, the door is opening, releasing a flood of bright sunlight into the back of the car. I blink against the sudden glare, my eyes watering. Sam's hand appears, palm up in invitation.

Drawing one last fortifying breath, I place my hand in his and allow him to assist me out. The heat hits me again like a wall after the cool air conditioning, making me almost recoil back into the shade of the car.

Instead, I stand tall and step fully out onto the sidewalk. The door shuts with a muted thump behind me and I'm suddenly aware I'm still clinging to Sam's hand. Blushing, I release him and raise my hand to shield my eyes as I take stock of our destination. We're somewhere in Tribeca, just a splash from the river but not in view of the Hudson.

Nerves jangle through me and my stomach twists into a tighter knot as I say goodbye to Sam. This is it. No more stalling. Time to face the ruthlessly handsome millionaire who wants to marry me.

I lower my shading hand, blinking as my eyes adjust. I'm standing in front of a quaint coffee shop decked out with stylish blue wooden paneling punctuated by a flower arch just above the entrance door.

To the side, there's a cart with plants for sale—spider plants, succulents, and some potted herbs. A mini garden market. The vases are recycled cans that look stylish despite being essentially garbage. On a normal day, I would've stopped to look, maybe bought something. But today I don't have either the money to spare nor the certainty of a home in which to put the plant. So, I push past and enter the coffee shop.

Inside, the rustic charm of wooden shelves meets the elegance of neatly arranged bouquets, and the smell of dark roast gives a rich undertone to the delicate floral notes while the enticing scents of vanilla and butter waft from the display of pastries.

Indie music is playing just loud enough to vibe to. I barely take this all in, my eyes searching the room for Adrian. I almost pass him over and then do a double take. Out of a suit, I almost didn't recognize him. He's seated at a corner table, casually relaxed as he scrolls on his phone in fitted jeans and a white polo shirt that highlights his toned arms.

This weekend version of him seems less intimidating. Still devastatingly handsome, though.

Adrian glances up from his phone and notices me, a warm smile spreading across his face. My insides do a cha-cha-cha across my digestive tract and this time, I'm sure the dance has *nothing* to do with morning sickness.

Raising my hand in an awkward little wave, I make my way over to where he's sitting. As I approach the table, I notice a steaming mug already waiting at my place. Did he order for me? A jolt of unease shoots through me. Liam used to do that—decide what I wanted without bothering to ask, as if my opinion didn't matter.

"Hey," Adrian says.

My tongue feels like sandpaper. "Hey."

I avoid eye contact, still fixated on that mug.

But then Adrian trails my gaze and speaks in his deep, soothing voice. "I got you a honey ginger tea, it might help with the nausea. But please, if there's anything else you'd like—food, another drink—just say the word and I'll get it for you."

Relief floods through me, dissolving the knot of tension. He was trying to be thoughtful, not controlling. This is Adrian, not Liam. I need to remember that.

I give him another tentative smile. Despite being

a cutthroat professional in the high-stake game of Wall Street—at least if Dylan and Tristan are to be believed—Adrian seems to be more nervous than me as he keeps talking.

"They have a high-protein granola yogurt that's also supposed to be good for expectant mothers," he continues, his brow furrowing. "But I wasn't sure if you felt up to eating anything; I didn't want to presume."

The considerate gesture warms me from the inside out, chasing away the last of my unease. "Thank you, that's sweet of you. The yogurt sounds perfect right about now. And maybe some water too, if you don't mind?"

Adrian's face lights up. "You got it. One granola yogurt and a water, coming right up." He stands, and I can't resist sneaking a glance at how his jeans hug the muscular curve of his backside as he heads to the counter. Hot damn.

The man fills out a pair of Levi's like it's nobody's business.

Tearing my gaze away, I wrap my hands around the warm mug and breathe in the soothing scent of ginger and honey.

I take a tentative sip of the tea, savoring the way

it soothes my throat. I'm surprised by how different this casual breakfast is from any interaction I ever had with Liam. My ex never would've gone out of his way to find something to ease my discomfort. With him, it was always about what he wanted, what worked for him, what I could do for him. But Adrian... he seems to care. Or at least he's good at making me feel like he does.

I'm just taking another careful swallow of tea when Adrian returns, setting a glass of water and a bowl of creamy white yogurt sprinkled with granola in front of me. "Your order, milady," he announces with a playful little half-bow before settling back into his seat.

"My hero," I quip, surprised at how easily the banter comes. Usually, I clam up around guys I'm attracted to, my wit drying up like the Sahara. But something about Adrian puts me at ease, despite the unconventional circumstances. "Seriously though, thank you."

"It's nothing." Adrian's smile softens as his gaze meets mine, warm and sincere. "I know this whole situation isn't easy. But I want to make this as un-complicated as possible and for you to be comfort-able with everything that we discuss today."

Right, because we're only here to discuss a business arrangement. I must drill that concept into my head.

Just.

Business.

12

ADRIAN

The second I mention what we're here to discuss, Rowena becomes shifty again. She looks like a scared lamb standing in front of a big, bad wolf, ready to hop away at the first sign of distraction from the predator.

I need to tread lightly. Already, I almost fucked up by ordering her that drink without asking first. She came in smiling, knocking the breath out of me in her simple clothes: jeans, a plain T-shirt, no makeup, black glasses perched on her button nose, and her chestnut hair cascading freely. Then, one look at the mug on her side of the table, and that beautiful smile dropped. I mentally kicked myself for getting her the ginger tea; she must've assumed I'm a prick who orders for his partners.

Hopefully, I turned that around with the yogurt.

I wait for her to have a few spoonfuls of granola before I say, "So…"

Rowena smiles tensely. She's still a tad pale, but in better shape than the other day. It's a relief to see. "You want an answer from me."

I nod, no point in denying it. "Sorry for insisting, but if I have to admit the truth to my boss, I should do it right away."

She turns the mug in her hands, avoiding eye contact. "How would the agreement work?"

Out of my backpack, I fish out a manila folder. "I've had my lawyers look into what would be the safest way for us to frame this agreement, for you specifically…" I pause because the next part might put her off.

Rowena raises an eyebrow at me. "That bad, huh?"

I hesitate, forcing a tentative, encouraging smile that I'm sure comes off as more of a grimace. "Well, the short of it is that it'd be way easier to manage everything if we actually got married."

Ginger tea goes down the wrong pipe, and she sputters, coughing. When she's recovered her breath, she stares at me appalled. "I shouldn't be surprised. You proposed to me after half an hour, it makes sense we'd move from a fake engagement to a real marriage in less than two days."

"Well, getting legally married gives you more rights and more protection. Like alimony and such. I had my lawyers draft a prenup with all the details." I slide the documents over the table to her. "I've asked them to keep all the legalese out of it and write it as straightforward as possible so you don't need a lawyer to check it."

Rowena eyes the documents as if they make her more uncomfortable than at ease. "Give me a rundown."

"In simple terms, you agree to be married to me for at least six months. All your expenses medical or otherwise will be taken care of, for the baby, too. And once we divorce, you'll get an alimony to put your annual income at $150,000 a year regardless of what you make or until you marry again."

"What if I don't have a salary?"

"Then, you'll get the full 150K from me."

Her mouth gapes. "Are you joking?"

"If I get the top chair at Fulton, 150K will be a drop in the ocean for me."

"Okay, Scrooge McDuck." She narrows her eyes

playfully, crossing her arms. "Glad to hear you have a pool of gold to dive into."

I sit back in my chair and give her a breather. "Sorry if I'm coming on too strong. But I want you to see that once I get my side of the deal and we divorce, I won't leave you hung out to dry."

Her eyes shift again and finally she looks at me. "No, it's okay. I asked. And you'd just be okay getting married?"

"Look, the prenup protects my assets, too. I won't lie about it. This way, we're both safeguarded. And saying I do will prove to my boss I'm serious beyond the shade of a doubt."

"Wow. You make it sound so straightforward. I just never imagined... you know..." I raise an eyebrow because *I don't know*. She adjusts her glasses. "I never imagined this is how I'd get married."

I give her time to elaborate. But when she still doesn't speak, I prompt, "Did you have questions?"

She takes a sip of tea. "I guess just, what would be your relationship with the baby?"

My jaw tenses. I could sugar-coat it for her, but she needs to come into this agreement with a clear idea of how things are going to go. "I wouldn't have one. It'd be better that way, less messy for everyone once we split up." She gives me big eyes so I explain further, "We'd be married in name only and for my work functions, the rest of the time, we'd be leading separate lives."

"Yeah, you've said," Rowena replies in a small voice. "What about you, do you have any questions for me?"

I stare at my coffee before I tell her the heaviest doubt on my mind because it's another delicate subject. "I guess, only... how will the father take the news that you're living with me? You mentioned he's not a good guy."

She winces. "He doesn't know I'm pregnant."

"Are you going to keep it that way?"

She looks out the window, lost. "I don't know..."

If she decides to bring this dude into the picture, it sounds like a problem future-me will have to deal with. But for now, the most important thing is to get her on board, so I don't press the subject. "I'm sorry this isn't how you'd imagined your life going..."

"Yep, me, too," she scoffs. "But I thought about it, and I don't want to go back to living with my parents or rely on my roommates' charity." Rowena stares directly at me now. "So, yes, Adrian, I will marry you."

The words sink into my chest harder and hotter than any deal I've closed before.

13

ROWENA

Eight weeks pregnant

After I say yes to Adrian, things move at light speed. And just the next day, I'm standing in the middle of his sprawling penthouse, my new home, feeling completely out of place. He's out on a business lunch that apparently is lasting well into the afternoon even if it's Sunday—he wasn't kidding when he said he is a workaholic. The doorman let me and the movers in.

I study the space. Floor-to-ceiling windows, sleek modern furniture, an intimidatingly vast kitchen. Adrian's apartment is like a spread right off of *Luxury Home Magazine*.

"So, this is home now," I mutter under my breath, getting out of the way of one of the movers.

I glance at the tower of moving boxes stacked in the entrance hall, feeling almost dizzy with how fast everything is happening. After I accepted his proposal, Adrian asked how soon I could move in and I blurted out, "Right away." My next rent payment was looming and well, better to rip off the Band-Aid.

The rest of the weekend has been a whirlwind of frantic packing. I started boxing up my stuff with the help of Nina and Hunter, but then Adrian's people showed up and like little Tasmanian devils, they packed up my entire world in a blink—did most of Nina's things, too, for her move to Tristan's place. And now they're here, reversing the process, unpacking everything for me.

Once the movers are finished, I poke around, exploring my room. The walk-in closet is bigger than my entire bedroom at my old place. In the en suite, the shower has more nozzles and knobs than a spaceship. I bet even the toilet is top of the line.

I wrap my arms around myself, suddenly homesick for my tiny apartment with its leaky faucets and squeaky floorboards. Even if I was renting, it felt like mine. And I shared it with people who loved me.

Still, I wouldn't want to be there either. My

besties kept shooting me dubious looks as they helped me box up all my worldly possessions. Nina and Hunter are being as supportive as they can—more understanding than I probably would've been if the roles had been reversed—but I'm almost relieved to get some space from them. Their constant worried side stares and raised brows were making me rethink my life choices every five seconds. Not that I can backtrack now. Dylan has officially taken over my and Nina's leases, and I'm here.

But as I sit alone in this ridiculously luxe apartment, doubts creep in again. What have I gotten myself into? Playing house with a man who makes my palms sweat and my brain short-circuit with a single glance, but who clearly stated he isn't interested in anything romantic.

But I've made my fancy bed—actually one of Adrian's cleaning ladies (he has several, apparently) did as she helped me unpack—now I have to lie in it.

I go back into the bedroom and search the million drawers for a pair of leggings and an oversized T-shirt. It takes four tries, and another one to find a hoodie. I still shiver after pulling it on. Outside it's easily eighty degrees, but the air conditioning inside is polar-bear friendly. Does Adrian run hot? Is that why he keeps it at subzero temperatures in here? My teeth clatter as I hunt for the thermostat.

After fiddling with the buttons for a while, I set the temperature to a more humane habitat. I don't hear or notice any changes, the air conditioning is so quiet, but after a few minutes, I stop shivering.

Since the movers already unpacked everything and I've got nothing to do, I settle on the creamy suede couch, feeling small and almost like an intruder amidst the sleek, modern décor. This house feels more like a showroom than a home—all steel and sharp angles, too tidy, and not loved enough. Grabbing a throw pillow, I tuck it behind my back, trying to get comfortable.

Three remotes sit on the glass coffee table. I stare at them blankly. "You'd think a gazillionaire could spring for a universal remote," I mutter. But no, that would be too easy.

I pick one up and aim it at the massive flatscreen mounted on the wall. Click. Nothing happens. I try another. The stereo system comes alive with a blast of music, techno beats pulsing through the surround-sound speakers and making me jump. I push buttons madly until the music stops, and, finally, the third remote brings the TV screen to life. I cycle through the channels mindlessly, too drained to focus. Instead of watching TV, I should prepare for the future, make a plan on how to turn my career around and become self-sufficient as a single mother. But I've barely eaten anything today, kept down even less and, frankly, I'm exhausted.

I watch a romantic movie, crying more than I should for a comedy and get hungry by the end. The nausea seems to have let up for the day, and since my light lunch ended up down the toilet, I could use a snack.

Pushing up from the couch, I pad to the kitchen. I yank open the double-door fridge, not sure what I'm expecting to find. Bottles of champagne? Caviar? The tears of Adrian's enemies?

Instead, the shelves are lined with stacks of pre-made meals in microwave friendly glass containers. They look like something out of a cooking show, with pretty garnishes and perfect grill marks. Definitely not frozen dinners.

I pull out a few, reading the labels. "Broccoli chicken." My stomach turns at the thought. Meat of any kind is my enemy lately. "Veggie lasagna. Slightly more promising. Lentil soup..." I wrinkle my nose. "Hard pass."

I settle on one container labeled pesto pasta and

stick it in the microwave, punching the buttons and praying Adrian won't mind me raiding his fridge.

As the microwave hums, I lean against the marble countertop and rub my temples, still wondering how I ended up pilfering pasta in some millionaire's McMansion kitchen.

The microwave dings, and the scent of basil and garlic fills the air. My mouth doesn't exactly water, but at least my stomach isn't roiling in protest. Baby steps.

I go back to the couch, picking at the healthy dinner I re-heated. The TV drones on but I'm only half paying attention, senses alert as I wait for my new "roommate" to arrive. It'll have to be soon. How long can a lunch last?

I finish my pasta and drop the empty bowl on the coffee table. Just as the clock ticks to 7 p.m., I hear the jingle of keys and the lock clicking open. I fumble for the remote to mute the TV.

Adrian strides through the door looking like he stepped out of the pages of *GQ* in another expensive tailored suit. He tosses his keys on the entryway table and reaches up to loosen his tie with a sigh. That simple, unconscious gesture oozes masculine sex appeal and makes me feel as if gravity has suddenly doubled.

"Hi," I squeak.

"Oh, hi, Rowena." He glances my way with a flicker of surprise, as if he forgot I'd be here. "Did the move go alright?"

I hop up from the couch, smoothing my T-shirt self-consciously—with a mild climate reinstated, I was able to remove the hoodie about an hour ago. "Yeah, great, thanks." As I walk toward him, I still feel like the G-force is working extra hard to make my knees buckle. "Your people took care of everything, I barely had to lift a finger."

He kicks off his shoes and leaves them scattered on the floor, reassuring me I haven't moved in with a total neat freak. "Glad to hear."

I gesture lamely to the kitchen. "I hope it's okay that I ate one of the pre-made meals..."

His face softens into a smile, making him look less intimidating. "Of course, that's what they're there for. Mrs. Doherty—Rosa—is an excellent cook. Let her know if you have any favorite dishes you'd like her to make."

We have a chef! I'd figured seeing all the gourmet meals in the fridge, but hearing it is still so out there.

"Err, thanks." I hover awkwardly, unsure what else to say.

Adrian studies me, his dark eyes unreadable. Silence blankets us, fraught with uncertainty.

I'm suddenly very aware that we're alone in a house with no less than five beds. Not that we will use them, I remind myself. At least not together. I'll sleep in my room, he'll sleep in his. And we'll live platonically ever after.

Oblivious to my inner meltdown, Adrian shrugs out of his suit jacket, revealing a crisp white shirt that stretches across his broad shoulders. He drapes the jacket over a chair and moves toward the couch, loosening his tie further until it hangs slack around his neck.

I try not to stare at the triangle of tanned skin exposed by his open collar as he settles on the opposite end of the sofa from where I was sitting. Even slouched against the cushions, his tall frame is commanding. He rakes a hand through his dark hair and rolls his neck from side to side, clearly trying to unwind from a long day.

I perch back down, unsure whether I should stay and attempt to chat or give him space.

I clear my throat softly, hoping to break the silence without startling him. "Did your meeting go well?" I venture, keeping my tone light and conversational.

Adrian's eyes flutter open, and he turns his head to look at me, a wry smile unzipping lazily from the corner of his mouth. "Yeah."

Concise, to the point, he probably doesn't want to make conversation with me—another piece of business he's been forced to bring home.

I'm about to excuse myself to my room when he stretches his long legs out in front of him, crossing them at the ankles. "Is it okay if we discuss a few things now or are you tired?"

Nope. Apparently, Adrian West never rests. He is business, business, business. I mentally snap my finger three times.

I settle down on the cushions. "Sure."

"This week we need to go shop for a ring." He whips out his phone from his pocket. "I can make time Tuesday afternoon."

Oh, so we're scheduling life-changing decisions like they're dentist appointments?

I duck my head to hide my disappointment. "My calendar is wide open, so Tuesday works for me."

Adrian seems to sense my discomfort and speaks more carefully as he says, "Sam will pick you up and bring you to me."

Despite his softer tone, I feel like one of those virgins in auction romances being brought to their captor for deflowering. Except, I'm no virgin—as the baby in my uterus testifies—and I'm here of my free will.

"Anything else?" I ask, trying to keep it together.

"Yes."

Of course there's more.

"Friday we leave for the Hamptons to spend the weekend at my boss's house," Adrian continues. "We should talk before that and define a few details. Like how we met, how I proposed, and so on." I nod. A bathroom meet-puke probably wouldn't fly in his circles. "I can do dinner on..." He scrolls his calendar again. "Thursday night."

"Sure." I nod.

I discreetly spy his screen as he types "dinner with Rowena" into his phone and allots an hour for the event.

We're mapping out our future in thirty-minute slots. I wonder what will happen if the conversation runs late; will he ask me to reschedule?

Adrian puts away his phone and looks up at me. And nothing in his gaze fixed over me feels businesslike. "Sam drives me to work and back every day, and if I have meetings in the city, but other than that, he's at your disposal. If you need to go anywhere just buzz the doorman, and Sam will be waiting for you downstairs."

I have a doorman, a personal driver, a chef, two cleaning ladies... what else?

"I've ordered a credit card for you; it should arrive tomorrow."

Ah, money. Of course he's also giving me an allowance.

I'm getting more uncomfortable with this conversation by the second. "A credit card?"

"Yeah, to buy clothes, groceries, stuff for the baby... whatever you need."

I feel utterly shitty asking the next part, like I'm a mix between a kept woman and a teenager negotiating with her parents for pocket money. "Okay... err... how much can I spend?"

Adrian raises an eyebrow at that. "The card limit is twenty K a month."

"Twenty thousand dollars?" I gape. "Per month?"

He smirks now. "You didn't take me for a full, stingy Scrooge McDuck, did you?"

Oh, so he's not a total cyborg. Good to know. I relax a bit and crack a smile at the joke. "I won't be spending twenty grand a month."

His expression is more open now. "Don't worry. I said I'd be taking care of you and I will.

To which effect." He takes his wallet out of his pocket and fishes out a business card. "I've asked around, and this is the best neonatal doctor in town."

He hands me the card, where over a polished logo that reads Clinlada, the name and qualifications of a specialist are printed out:

Dr. John Raikes
Double board-certified OB/GYN, sub-specializing in maternal-fetal medicine and fetal and neonatal surgery.

"I've added you to my insurance and asked my secretary to book you an appointment first thing tomorrow morning."

I blink. When did he have the time to do all this? He truly is a machine. A Terminator. Pity, he's not getting involved with the baby or I could've given him all the night feeds. I bet he doesn't even need sleep.

"You should go see him about your morning sickness. I know it's normal, but just to be sure."

Despite his businesslike attitude, I'm moved by Adrian's mindfulness, maybe too transported. In my previous relationship, I wasn't used to my boyfriend being considerate about my personal struggles. My standards are low.

"Thank you."

He shrugs. "It's nothing."

Adrian is looking at me with half a smile and those smoky brown eyes, and I can't stand it. I bounce up. "I'm going to head to bed now."

Before I go, I notice how Adrian's gaze flicks to my empty bowl. Heat rushes to my cheeks. Way to be a slob, Rowena. I pick up the dirty dish from the coffee table and carry it to the kitchen, chastising myself for leaving a mess behind.

I've just dropped it in the dishwasher when a deep voice jolts through me. "Rowena."

Spinning around, I find Adrian leaning against the threshold, looking unfairly sexy with his tousled dark hair and sleeves rolled up over toned forearms.

"This is your home, too, now." His dark eyes glint with amusement. "You can leave stuff around. I'm not the nit-pick police."

A surprised laugh escapes me. He's so different from Liam, who used to bite my head off over the smallest things; my ex would make a monumental case of even minor accidents—like if I dropped something or booked the "wrong" restaurant.

"I'll keep that in mind," I reply. "Though this place seems way too pristine for not being policed."

Adrian grins, and the effect is devastating. "It's all Mrs. Doherty, not me."

"Oh, okay." I roll my eyes, hoping his housekeeper is not a Mrs. Rottenmeier. "Good to know I can clutter."

His lips twitch. "Night, Rowena." He touches two fingers to his forehead and then flicks them away with a swift, carefree motion. "Sleep well."

"Yeah, you, too," I say, slightly breathless.

I wait for him to clear the door before I move out of the kitchen. With the way his deep voice sunk straight into my core, I don't need to accidentally brush against his chest. It's great he'll be out of the house most of the time, otherwise I'd be in danger of forgetting all the reasons it's a good idea to keep my distance.

14

ROWENA

Sam pulls up in front of Tiffany's flagship store on Fifth Avenue, and I can't say I'm surprised Adrian would choose the iconic jewelers to buy me an engagement ring.

As the driver opens the car door for me, the famed Tiffany & Co writing gleams in the late afternoon sunlight. I mutter a quick thanks and step onto the sidewalk, smoothing my dress. Today I made an effort. Even if the occasion is fake, I still thought it'd be nice to look pretty in case we have to make a post on Instagram or something.

I'm also feeling incredibly well. I went for my first consult at Clinlada yesterday, and Dr. Raikes—a hottie with blue eyes and a mop of black hair—prescribed me a miraculous drug that's safe to take during pregnancy and that made the morning sickness almost completely disappear. I feel much more energetic now.

My phone buzzes in my bag with a new text.

ADRIAN

I'm already inside.

My stomach coils with nerves and anticipation. After two days of living under the same roof, I'm going to come face to face with the enigmatic Mr. West again.

So far, he's been a ghost in his own penthouse, leaving before I wake and returning long after I'm asleep. Apart from the day I moved in, we haven't had any contact.

Except maybe last night. I had dozed off on the couch, but when I startled awake at 3 a.m., a soft cashmere blanket was draped over me, cocooning me in warmth. Did Adrian put it there? At the thought of him tucking me in, a warm current corkscrews up my spine.

I shake my head, not wanting to read too much into the gesture. So, he caught me drooling on his couch and covered me with a blanket. It's basic

human decency. Doesn't mean anything. Our relationship is strictly business. Adrian needs a pregnant wife, and I need to be able to afford to live in
New York as a single parent. Simple as that.

I give my dress one last tug and march toward
the gleaming glass doors, my footsteps lost in the
bustle of Fifth Avenue. A gloved doorman ushers
me inside with a polite nod. "Good afternoon, miss."

"Afternoon," I respond brightly, despite my jan-
gling nerves.

I step into Tiffany's, taking in the gleaming expanse of the jewelry shop. Light hardwood floors
stretch out before me, the marble and glass display
cases sparkling under the carefully positioned spot-
lights. Diamonds and precious gems wink at me
from every direction, but despite the eye-catching
baubles, my gaze snags on Adrian. A different kind
of black diamond.

He's standing by a display case, deep in conversation with a shop assistant. Jaw-droppingly handsome as always in a dark tailored suit, he looks at
home amidst the glittering luxury of Tiffany's.

I sit at the opposite end of the spectrum. The
one where I feel like an underdressed fraud in my
simple cotton frock. Too late to go back home to
change, so I'll just have to fake it till I make it.

I approach them, forcing a shy smile. "Hi."

Adrian turns at the sound of my voice and does a double take, dark eyes widening almost imperceptibly as they swipe over me. "Rowena. You look... lovely."

A flush rises to my cheeks at the compliment. Adrian has never seen me in a dress and with a touch of makeup highlighting my eyes—and not turning me into a raccoon like the day we met. Does he really think I'm lovely or is it just a polite remark he'd offer to anyone?

"Thanks," I mumble, tucking a strand of hair behind my ear self-consciously.

"Hello, welcome to Tiffany's!" The perfectly coiffed blonde saleswoman Adrian was talking to glides over to me to introduce herself. "I'm Danielle. And you must be the lucky bride-to-be?"

More *for hire* than lucky, but... *details*. "Rowena, nice to meet you."

"Your fiancé was just telling me you're shopping for an engagement ring; may I show you a few options?"

Adrian flashes her a dazzling smile. "We would love you to."

"Of course! Right this way, please." Danielle

turns and starts across the wide foyer, her heels clicking on the hardwood floor.

Adrian extends an arm and, after a moment's hesitation, I slip my hand into the crook of his elbow, allowing him to escort me further into the glittering wonderland of Tiffany's.

The shop assistant guides us over to a plush velvet seating area. "Let me first explain some of our most popular styles." From a locked drawer she takes out a black case whose interior is divided into tiny squares, each occupied by a loose gemstone.

As I sink into the seat, I try to project self-confidence as if I regularly get shown to private booths to buy diamond rings.

Danielle launches into her pitch, rattling off a dizzying array of diamond cuts. "The Round Brilliant is our most classic style, with its fifty-seven facets to optimize sparkle. Then we have our patented Tiffany True cut, as well as cushion, princess, emerald, pear shape..."

My eyes glaze over as she points to each glittering stone. They're all so huge. How much would Adrian have to shell out for one of these rocks?

"...of course, clarity and color are important factors as well," Danielle continues eagerly. "We only sell diamonds graded VS1 or higher, and D through

G on the color scale for that icy white appearance that Tiffany's is known for."

Icy is exactly what these stones feel to me. Beautiful but cold. Like Adrian's penthouse.

Danielle turns to me expectantly. "So, do you have any particular preferences in terms of style? Would you prefer a solitaire or halo or trilogy?"

"Err..." My mind goes blank. I have no freaking clue. I glance helplessly at Adrian, silently begging him to take the lead on this.

He gives me a reassuring smile before addressing Danielle. "Why don't you show us a range, in your most popular cuts?"

"Of course!" Danielle gushes. "And in terms of size, are you thinking..." She trails off delicately, her gaze flicking to Adrian.

"Go big or go home, right?" He looks at me.

I force a smile, my cheeks aching with the effort.

Danielle seems much more heartened by the declaration and scurries off to pull out some rings, leaving Adrian and me alone in the boudoir.

He stares at me concerned. "You okay? You seem tense."

I furrow my brows and look away. "I'm fine! Just a bit... overwhelmed, I guess. This is all so..." I wave a hand vaguely at the opulent surroundings.

"Hey, we got this," he whispers, his deep brown eyes earnest and reassuring. "It's only a little bling, okay?"

I nod. It's just a ring. A stupidly expensive, blindingly sparkly ring...

Danielle returns bearing a black velvet tray lined with rings that would probably pay off my student loans. Twice over. She handpicks a monstrosity with an emerald-cut center gem flanked by triangle side baguettes, the band encrusted with more diamonds.

"This is one of our most popular styles this season," she enthuses, holding it out to me. "Three and a half carats, VVS1 clarity, E color. Quite spectacular, isn't it?"

I pluck the ring from the tray gingerly, afraid I'll drop it. It's ice cold and heavier than I expect. I slide it onto my finger and hold my hand out, blinking as the center stone catches the light and fractures it into a thousand rainbow shards.

It's positively gorgeous... and completely wrong for me. The ring wears me, not the other way around.

I glance up to catch Adrian watching me intently, trying to gauge my reaction. He wants me to make a quick decision, check a box and move on.

He probably has to return to work or something. But I can't pretend to love a ring that makes me feel like even more of an impostor in my own life.

I slide the ring off my finger and place it carefully back on the tray. "It's beautiful," I say diplomatically. "But a bit too much for everyday wear?"

Danielle's smile falters, but she quickly replaces it with another colossus, a huge round solitaire. "Perhaps something more classic, then?"

I dutifully try on ring after blinding ring, each one more soulless and ostentatious than the last. None of them feel right for me. I'm getting a tension headache from the stress of playacting this role.

After what feels like hours, Adrian leans forward. "Do any of these look good?"

They all look great; I don't know how to tell him I wouldn't want to wear any of them.

Abruptly, I slip out of the booth. "I... we need to reschedule," I stammer, backing away from the diamond-encrusted madness.

Adrian frowns, looking both confused and irritated. "Reschedule? Rowena, we have to go to my boss's house on Friday. There's no time."

I wave off the protest, already moving toward the door. "I'm sorry, I just... can't do this right now."

"Rowena, wait!" Adrian calls after me, but I keep

pushing through the glass doors, desperate for air that doesn't smell like wealth and expectations.

Outside on the sidewalk, I gulp down breaths, trying to calm my racing heart. What am I doing? I can't just leave Adrian hanging out to dry. He needs this, and he's been nothing but kind and understanding with me. But the thought of going back inside, of staring at more ridiculous diamonds and pretending to be enthusiastic about it—

"Hey!" Adrian's voice behind me makes me startle. He sounds more concerned than angry, and that gives me pause. If I'd pulled a scene like that with Liam, he'd already be all red-faced, yelling up my nose.

"What's wrong?" Adrian asks instead.

I turn to him, steeling myself. "I'm sorry, Adrian. But those rings are not me, and you don't want me to let you buy one. Trust me."

He tilts his head with an amused grin. "I'm pretty sure I *need* to buy you one. My boss has to understand we're serious, and nothing says long-term more than a big rock on your finger."

I roll my eyes. "You know what those rings say?"

He crosses his arms over his chest. "Enlighten me."

"Dude with no clue who just went to the

brand-name store to buy the biggest, most expensive rock he could find." His nostrils flare, so I attempt to sound less of a know-it-all. "You want to impress your boss, right? Make him think we're genuine?"

He drops his arms. "Yes."

"Then the ring needs to have a soul, a story." I point at my chest. "Look at me and think of a color."

"Yellow," he says without hesitation.

"Why yellow?"

"Like the Belle figurine on your pen." My jaw drops slightly. That's how he sees me? I almost want to laugh; I'm not exactly princess material. But before I can break into my usual self-deprecating routine, Adrian continues, his voice lowering, "You're the color of sunshine and of the flakes of gold in your eyes."

Okay.

I stare at him, even more stunned. My gaping must make *him* self-conscious because he scratches behind his neck. "At least that's how I'd describe you as a color."

I'd describe him as black. Like the depth of the night when it wraps around you, warm and protective. Not the cold, distant black of space, but something rich and enveloping. A beautiful nocturnal sky—vast, mysterious, impossible to ignore. With sparks of stars scattered across.

Sunshine and nightfall. Where there's one, the other can't be. Just another reminder that we're pretty much opposites.

But I don't say any of this. Instead, I smile. "Yellow is a beautiful color, and I know where we need to go to find a ring."

"Where?" Adrian asks puzzled.

"To shop vintage."

I grab his hand and drag him down the curb.

Ten minutes later we reach the corner of 47th Street and 6th Avenue—the edge of the Diamond District.

The street is lined with discreet, high-end shops, each boasting thick glass windows that house elegantly displayed jewelry. The air is heavy with the aroma of street food and the sound of chatter mixed with the occasional honk of taxis.

We weave through the rush-hour crowd, a tangle of professionals and tourists, inspecting every window we pass until we both stop dead in our tracks.

Sitting slightly apart under a spotlight is the perfect ring: a stunning cushion-cut yellow diamond that catches the light just right. The vibrant colored stone is securely clasped by four sleek, elegantly arching prongs and nestled between two tapered baguette colorless diamonds. The gemstones are set in platinum or white gold, the metal's gleam almost as captivating as the stones themselves.

I turn to Adrian. "It's perfect."

He smiles. "Sunshine in a stone." He stares down at the price tag next and frowns.

I follow his gaze to the hefty label, sitting just shy of fifteen thousand dollars.

"If it's too expensive, we can find a different one."

"Too expensive? It should have an extra zero. My boss is going to think I'm cheap."

I pat his chest. "Your boss will think you have a heart."

15

ADRIAN

I glance at my watch—7.00 p.m. sharp. The low hum of chatter filling our open-plan office fades as my traders shut down their computers and grab their bags, eager to escape for the evening. Someone taps my shoulder.

"Hey Adrian, a bunch of us are grabbing drinks at Sullivan's." Sarah flashes me an expectant grin. "You in?"

I hesitate for a split second before shaking my head. "Thanks, but I've got dinner plans with my girlfriend tonight." The word still feels foreign on my tongue.

Sarah's eyebrows shoot up in surprise. "Girlfriend? I didn't know you were seeing anyone!"

Her tone is light, but I detect an undercurrent of shock.

I force a casual shrug. "It's relatively new." And 100 per cent fake.

Sarah chuckles. "Oh, well, have a good one, then." She gives me a wave before heading out with the others.

As their voices fade down the hall, my muscles unwind with relief that Sarah believed I could have a girlfriend. My personal life has been practically nonexistent for years now, consumed by ninety-hour work weeks and an unrelenting drive to succeed. If it wasn't for this charade with Rowena, my evening plans would comprise a re-heated meal and spreadsheets, as usual.

I shoot Sam a text that I'm ready to head out and make my way down to the lobby, my mind already jumping ahead to tomorrow's meetings. But as I slide into the backseat of the car, my thoughts drift unexpectedly to Rowena.

When we first agreed to this ruse of an engagement, I saw it as just another obligation to juggle, one more complication in an already demanding life. But the other day, when we went to pick a ring, something shifted.

A strange warmth took residence in my gut as I

watched Rowena bypass the flashiest diamonds in favor of a vintage ring, one with a soul as she put it. One that reminds me of Rowena herself—quietly luminous, with hidden depths. And when she slipped it on to try, the way her eyes lit up, crinkling at the corners... I smile at the memory.

"Good day, sir?" Sam meets my eyes in the rearview mirror.

I settle back against the leather headrest. "Not bad, Sam. Not bad at all."

As the city blurs past the car windows, it hits me that for the first time in longer than I can remember, I'm looking forward to getting home. To seeing her.

Sunshine indeed.

A short while later, I stride into the foyer of my penthouse, loosening my tie and shrugging out of my suit jacket. The usual stillness of my apartment is punctuated by the unexpected clinking of dishes and the indistinct murmur of music. Curious, I follow the sound to the kitchen.

And there she is. Rowena is standing behind the island in leggings and an oversized T-shirt, transferring something from a skillet onto two waiting plates, her hair piled into a haphazard bun. She's singing along absent-mindedly to the pop song on her phone, her hips swaying almost imperceptibly to the beat.

And there it is again, this warmth ballooning in my chest, threatening to take up all the space.

"Hey."

Rowena startles as I come up behind her, then turns with a smile. "Oh good, you're home! I hope you're hungry."

I glance past her to the kitchen table, noting the place settings. I can't remember the last time I sat down to have dinner with someone else at home.

"You didn't have to go to all this trouble," I say, trying to navigate this foreign terrain of domesticity.

Rowena just laughs. "It was no bother. I hope you don't mind that I set up in the kitchen. That dining room table is so long, we'd have to text each other to pass the salt."

Under her glasses, her eyes dance cheerfully, making my lips twitch in response. "Fair point. So, what's on the menu?"

"A pregnancy-friendly feast, courtesy of the fabulous Mrs. Rosa Doherty. We've got frittata with chard and a quinoa salad. Your housekeeper was keen to cook for your pregnant future wife."

I raise an eyebrow.

Rowena shrugs, looking suddenly self-conscious. "I didn't know what else to tell the staff. I thought it was best to just go along with the whole fake marriage thing?"

I nod pensively. It's a good call. The fewer people who know the truth, the better.

We sit to eat and, after we've gotten a few bites down, Rowena picks at the food on her plate with her fork, asking, "So what is it you wanted to discuss tonight?"

I grab my phone and pull up the file I typed earlier with a list.

She mock-frowns at me. "Please tell me we're not mapping out our fake relationship on a spreadsheet."

I flash her a sheepish grin. "Are bullet points better?"

Her eyes go to the ceiling, but I catch a flicker of amusement there. "You're hopeless."

I set the phone on the table, sliding it to her side. "Not a spreadsheet, just some notes."

"Okay, Mr. Bullet Points." She slides the phone right back at me without looking at it. "What's the first item on the list?"

"Learning basic stuff about each other. Siblings, where we're from, foods we hate, allergies... things people in a relationship would know about each other."

She grins at me. "Let me guess, you made me a spreadsheet?"

I have, in fact, typed her a list. "Shouldn't computer programmers love spreadsheets?"

"We do." Rowena nods, chewing enthusiastically on her frittata. She looks more healthy, livelier. "Just not about our romantic lives, perhaps, fake or otherwise. But I'll make you a list and then I can quiz you on it."

"Great. We should also decide what the official story for how we met is."

She finishes chewing before saying, "We should stick to reality as much as possible. We used to work in the same building, bumped into each other in the elevator every morning or something until you asked me out. I mean..." She falters, a soft blush creeping up her cheeks. "If you asking me out"—she points at herself self-consciously—"might be believable."

I stop cutting into the frittata and lower my fork and knife over the plate, pinning her down with a stare. "I don't date. But if I did, I'd ask you out."

Rowena dips her chin as she asks, "You don't date, like ever?"

"I stopped a while ago. Anytime I tried to see someone on the regular, soon the complaints about me being married to my job started, and I just got fed up." I shrug. "Didn't see the point of trying for a relationship anymore."

"What do you do for sex?" she blurts, then her eyes widen as if she regrets the impulsive question. "Sorry, I didn't mean to pry—"

"I have people for that."

"Oh, okay." Her gaze shifts to her plate.

"You sound the opposite of *okay*."

"No, no." She's looking everywhere but at me. "I've got nothing against sex workers."

I rub the bridge of my nose. "I didn't mean *prostitutes*."

Rowena meets my eyes again. "You said you had *people*, like the ones you sent to help me move. I thought you meant for hire."

"No, just women like me, with high-stress careers and no time for relationships."

She smirks now. "Is there a special app where you high-flying executives meet?"

I lean back in my chair, folding my arms. "Manhattan is a small island. It's not that hard to meet people."

"Right."

I tilt my head. "Are you imagining me in some sort of perverse sex club?"

She snorts on her water. "Yes, sorry. It all sounds a bit ritualistic."

"Not really... Stress-relief sex can be very hot."

Now her face turns positively purple. I shouldn't have said that.

Rowena takes a long sip of water and nods. "I bet. So, were you seeing someone when you— when we—"

"Yes, but I won't be seeing her anymore." I wipe my mouth with a fabric napkin I didn't even know I owned. "And this is another thing I wanted to ask you. Even if this marriage is fake, I need it to be monogamous. Will that be okay for you?"

"You mean...?"

"I would prefer you not to have sex with other men while you're married to me."

"Oh, yeah. Sex isn't in my future." She chuckles. "In a few months, I'll turn into a small whale, and I doubt anyone would want to have sex with me." She plays with her napkin, not having any idea how wrong she is. "Then my vagina will be destroyed and I won't be able to have sex even if I wanted to, so... What about you? Won't that be a problem for you?"

"No, my work is my priority."

She looks at me dubiously, her eyes scanning my face with a hint of amusement. "Not even a little tempted to go to your secret clubs? I bet you all wear masks and no one would even recognize you."

I can't help the laugh that escapes me—a genuine one, not the strained chuckles I've perfected for boardroom diplomacy. "Rowena, I promise you, there's no secret society or masked orgies in my schedule."

Her lips quirk up, and she seems to mull over my response.

"Okay, then." Rowena polishes the last bite of her frittata. "Monogamy it is." She glances at the now-dark phone screen. "What else did you plan for our relationship itinerary?"

I swipe to unlock the device, scrolling through my meticulously organized list. "Ah, public appearances. We need a few of those to make this all seem authentic."

She nods thoughtfully. "Like what? Charity galas? Movie premieres?"

I smirk at the mention of movie premieres. "Do I strike you as the red-carpet type?"

"Not really, but hey, I'd prefer a movie than

being presented as your sex slave to your masked orgy buddies."

I downright guffaw at that. "I'm never getting that image out of your head, am I?"

"No, sorry."

"Charity events are more my speed," I say. "I have a few coming up."

Rowena nods, her hazel eyes glittering with that humor I'm beginning to appreciate more with each passing moment. "Got it. And what about... couple things? You know, grocery shopping together, arguing over where to go on vacation, Netflix binges... that sort of thing?"

I lean back in my chair, imagining the domestic scenario she's painting. The thought is oddly disarming, a stark contrast to the sterile, calculated life I lead. "Rosa does all the shopping and I haven't been on vacation in years, but I'm sure we can find other mundane activities to publicly bicker about."

Her grin is infectious. "No rest for the wicked," she deadpans.

I tap my fingers on the table, surveying her—the woman who's going to become my wife, in a manner of speaking. It strikes me how comfortable I feel around her, even during our peculiar discussion. "And as for Netflix, I can't remember the last time I watched something that wasn't news or market analysis."

She rolls her eyes. "Your life sounds riveting."

"Wait, it gets better," I tease. "Sometimes, I even read financial reports before bed. It's like a bedtime story, but instead of sending you to sleep, it just gives you anxiety about the Asian markets."

Her laughter fills the room, warm and infectious. It's been so long since my home has echoed with anything other than the click of a laptop or the distant hum of New York City.

"So, are we going to schedule in 'Netflix and chill' on that phone of yours?" Rowena asks with raised eyebrows.

She's not meaning *that* kind of chill, is she? And why don't I find the idea unappealing?

I tap on the screen thoughtfully. "I don't..."

"I'm just messing with you." Rowena smiles then shifts on her seat and stretches sideways as if the chair is uncomfortable. Time to move the conversation to the living room.

I scoop up our plates and walk them over to the sink. "I'll leave these here for Rosa in the morning. Want to move to the couch?"

Rowena nods. "I'll just make a cup of ginger tea first." She busies herself with the water boiler. A minute later, she pours the water into a dark-blue mug that must be hers as white writing on its side recites: *I am currently unsupervised.* The boiling water engulfs the small packet of tea already inside the mug, steam rising in fragrant wisps. With the heat from the water, a second part of the writing appears in bright pink. *I know, it scares me too.* The full slogan on the mug makes me chuckle silently; it's quirky and cute, just like her.

"How's the nausea?" I ask.

"So much better; that doctor you sent me to is a miracle worker."

"Glad to hear."

With the mug in her hands, Rowena pads out of the kitchen and over to the couch and settles in, tucking her legs underneath her. I join her, keeping a respectful distance.

She takes a sip and sets the mug on the end table, her brows furrowing. "So, I was thinking... when we see your colleagues and they ask why I'm no longer working in the building, should I tell them the truth? That I got fired?"

I shake my head emphatically, my voice coming out harsher than I intend. "You can't say that."

Her eyes widen in surprise. "Why? Isn't it best to stick to the truth as much as—"

"Rowena," I cut her off, intensity burning through my words. "If some asshole middle manager at a fintech start-up fired my girlfriend for *any* reason, I would buy the whole damn company and clean house. Every last one of their management team would be out on the street faster than they could blink."

She stares at me, her mouth hanging open. I soften my expression, clenching and unclenching my hands to come off less aggressive.

"Unless... that's what you want me to do?" I raise an eyebrow. "Say the word and I'll have my assistant making calls tonight."

Rowena lets out a laugh, shaking her head. "No, no, that won't be necessary. Your world domination plans can wait." She chews her bottom lip, contemplating. "Maybe we could just say I quit, then? Because of the pregnancy being too much to handle with work?"

I mull it over. It's not the full truth, but it's close enough without revealing the ugly reality of what those pricks did to her.

"Alright, it's settled then," I declare. "If anyone asks, you decided to focus on your health and our family. No mention of those ungrateful bastards who didn't deserve you." I drop my hands on my thighs. "We're good then... that was all for tonight."

Rowena shakes her head and leans in just a fraction. "Not so fast, tiger, we have to come up with a great proposal story first..."

She's right.

"Any ideas?"

"Nope." She cracks her knuckles. "Time to get your romantic mojo on."

I'm fucked.

16

ROWENA

Friday afternoon my phone buzzes with a new text.

ADRIAN

Waiting for you downstairs. Ready
to hit the road?

The simple message makes me almost light-headed. I'm about to spend the weekend with Adrian's boss and colleagues at some swanky estate in the Hamptons while growing a human inside of me and with a million lies to remember. I hope I won't make a total fool of myself.

I dry my sweaty palms on the skirt of my dress before typing a quick, coming down, reply. Adrian told me to just be myself and pack whatever I'm comfortable in—no fancy clothes required. I've settled on a breezy yellow sundress and flat strappy sandals—casual but cute. The skirt swishes around my knees as I grab my weekender bag and head out of Adrian's lavish penthouse to the elevator.

Downstairs, as I step out into the bright afternoon sun, I scan the busy Manhattan street. I expect to find Sam leaning against a sleek black town car, ready to whisk us away to high society for the weekend. But the sight before me stops me dead in my tracks.

There's no sign of Sam. Instead, Adrian leans casually against the hood of a low-slung, midnight black Ferrari, his dark eyes burning into me over the rims of his sunglasses. He's still in one of his power suits from the office, all sharp lines and confident authority.

Combined with the dangerously exotic car, he looks like a black panther poised to pounce.

Predatory. Primal.

Breathtaking.

He lowers the sunglasses completely and his piercing gaze rakes over me, leaving tingles in its wake.

But the little jolts of electricity surging through me are nothing compared to the impact of Adrian's smile when it breaks free. It's a rare sight, like the sun bursting through storm clouds and creating a rainbow, the brilliance exploding in my belly like confetti. He pushes off from the car with feline grace and strolls over to me, his stride as self-assured as ever. "You look great."

Hearing his gruff voice redoubles the confetti explosions.

I blush but manage a shaky laugh. "Thanks. You look... like you're about to steal an art masterpiece and then go play a high-stakes game of poker in a casino in Venice." I wave vaguely at the car and him.

Adrian chuckles, pushing the sunglasses on top of his head and becoming instantly ten times hotter. "Spot on—just don't blow my cover, okay?" He takes my bag with a casual familiarity that makes my pulse stutter.

"No Sam today?" I ask as he stows my luggage in the petite trunk.

Adrian smirks. "Nope, I'm driving. Disappointed?"

"In this discreet little number?" I joke, trailing my fingertips along the gleaming fender.

"In my field, a flashy ride is required. Keeps up appearances with the big-money clients."

I snort. "Your commitment to the job is admirable. I can only imagine the level of sacrifice driving a Ferrari requires."

He laughs, shaking his head. "Smartass." But the word is tinged with, if not exactly affection, at least a little fondness—familiarity at the bare minimum. Adrian's gaze lingers on me after the comment. A soft heat in his eyes that sends flutters rioting through my stomach again. "That dress is perfect on you."

"Thanks." I lower my gaze to hide how much the compliment thrills me. "Glad I didn't screw up the dress code."

"You mean for our heist? Nah, you're textbook. You'll distract all the guards. Actually..." Adrian's brow furrows mock-thoughtfully. "There is just one detail missing."

My heart sinks and my eyes dart down to assess myself. What did I overlook?

But then Adrian reaches into the inner pocket of his suit jacket and pulls out a small black velvet box. The same box from the jewelers the other day.

My pulse kicks up for no reason at all. It's not

like this is a surprise. But then, in a smooth motion, Adrian drops to one knee before me. I suck in a sharp breath, my heart ricocheting wildly behind my ribcage.

He flips open the box, revealing the stunning yellow diamond ring nestled inside. The sunlight hits it, scattering into a thousand dazzling beams.

Adrian gazes up at me, a playful grin tugging at the corners of his mouth. But there's a seriousness in his eyes, too. An intimacy that leaves me feeling exposed.

He reaches for my trembling left hand. "Rowena Taylor, will you do me the honor of being my fake wife?"

Electricity zings through my veins at his touch. I know this is all for show, but seeing this beautiful, powerful man kneeling before me, offering me a ring... It feels like a whirlpool churning in the pit of my stomach—I miss the confetti.

A few passersby have gathered, their murmurs of excitement adding to the surreal atmosphere. Some hold up their phones, capturing the moment.

All I can manage is a squeaky, "Yes."

Cheers erupt from the onlookers.

Adrian's grin widens triumphantly as he slips the ring onto my finger. It fits like it was made just for me. Which I suppose it was since we had it resized.

He rises fluidly to his feet, still clasping my hand. "Shall we then, future Mrs. West?"

Mrs. West. The name sends a thrill through me I don't dare examine too closely.

"We shall." I wave at the crowd and let him tuck me into the sleek sports car.

As Adrian shifts the Ferrari into gear and we zoom off, I can't stop stealing glances at the ring. The yellow diamond glitters in the sunlight, impossibly bright. As glitzy and unreal as this whole situation.

I twist it around my finger, marveling at the perfect fit, the solid weight of it. How right it feels despite being just for show. I wonder... If the engagement were real, how would it feel?

Stop it, I chide myself. This isn't some fairy tale. It's a contract. Less than a year from now, I'll take this ring off and go back to my normal life.

A life that has no Adrian in it.

I sneak a peek at him from the corner of my eye. His chiseled profile is limned in golden light, like some modern warrior god.

His eyes cut to me and linger.

"Shouldn't you be looking at the road while driving a space rocket on wheels?" I tease.

He refocuses his gaze on the bridge we're crossing. "Relax, Sunshine." *Sunshine? Since when am I Sunshine?* "I've never gotten so much as a parking ticket."

"Sunshine?"

He shoots me a cocky smirk. "I thought it'd be the perfect pet name for you. Make us look more couple-y."

"Ah. And what should I call you? It wasn't in your brief."

"Use your imagination."

I studiously tap my fingers on my chin. "I'll go with Bunny."

Adrian's laughter fills the car, a rich sound that sneaks its way right under my skin. "Can't I get something more virile?"

"No, you already have the Ferrari for that. We need to fluff you up."

His eyes flick to me again. "Fluff me up, huh?" He's clearly amused, the dark brown of his irises glinting with a dare. "Bunny and *Sunshine*, we're ready for a life of crime."

I turn to him mock-shocked. "Did you try to make it sound like Bonnie and Clyde?"

"No, I didn't." He presses his lips hard together not to smile.

"You *so* did."

As our laughter settles, a thought crosses my mind. "We've got the names down, Bunny, but we forgot to invent a story for our first date. What tale are we telling people?" I nudge him playfully.

"Do we have to say anything?"

"If Preston is bringing his wife, she might ask."

"Why would she ask something so personal?"

"Because she's a romantic?"

"A *nosy* romantic. We should keep it casual. I'm not big on... gestures."

"Yeah, seeing how you meet all your sexual partners at clandestine gatherings where everyone wears a mask, I got that romance isn't high on your list of priorities."

"Please don't joke about sex clubs in front of my boss." He sounds mildly terrified.

"Oh, that wasn't supposed to be a topic?" I feign innocence. "I'll put a note in my mental calendar... So, casual first date." I tap my chin, thinking hard. "How about lunch at that taco truck near the river?" I suggest. "The one with the amazing carnitas."

"A woman after my heart." Adrian theatrically

brings a hand over his chest. "I love tacos, then what? A long walk on the riverside?"

"Do I look like a long walk on the riverside kind of girl to you?" I give him some side-eye.

Adrian chuckles softly, accepting the dare in my eyes. "Yeah?"

"No, after tacos, we went back to the office, *obviously*, because I don't think you've ever missed an afternoon of work in your life. I'm pretty sure most times you eat lunch at your desk eyes glued to the monitors. Tacos are already a stretch."

His eyes flick to me, then back to the road.

I adjust my sunglasses. "You're not refuting the bleak picture I've painted of your lunch habits."

"Am not. So, that's it, tacos?"

"No. Mmm... that same night you invited me out for drinks and..."

"Dinner?" Adrian suggests.

"No, too tame, we went... uh, I got it... ax throwing."

"Ax throwing?" Adrian snorts. "No one would ever believe I did that."

"Exactly, we need to spice up your character."

"I thought we were fluffing me up?"

My grin widens, unfazed by his dubious expression. "We are, with a twist of danger to keep things interesting."

"Is there even an ax throwing place in Manhattan?"

"Sure, on Lafayette Street, just a fifteen-minute walk from the office."

"Should the fact that you know that scare me?"

"Tremendously." I smile innocently.

"And how did we do at ax throwing?"

"You sucked, but I was awesome!" I scoff playfully. "Nailed a bullseye on my first try and won us free nachos."

"Yup, nothing spells romance like flying axes and free nachos." Adrian nods enthusiastically. "And that's the moment I fell in love?"

Love. He says it so easily, so truthfully. I wish my poor fluttering heart could tell the difference.

"That's the moment," I agree.

"And what about you? When did you know you loved me?"

I bite my lip, stalling for time.

The car slows to a crawl as Adrian stops at a red light. He turns to face me, his dark brown eyes playful yet expectant.

"I knew when you made me laugh during my worst day—" I cut myself short because maybe there's too much truth in what I'm saying. He made me smile on the day I got fired and found out I was pregnant—more than once.

Adrian's eyes bore into me. The light turns green, but he doesn't drive forward. He keeps looking at me until the car behind us honks, and he finally presses on the accelerator, gaze back ahead.

"So, I can make a bad day good." His Adam's apple bobs while he keeps his eyes fixed on the road —tone of voice level, but also quietly thunderous. "And you love me for it."

The words hang over our heads like a sword ready to fall, the teasing note fading into something quieter. More charged.

Love. It might be harder to fake than I thought.

I look away from him, fixating on the posh beach mansions flashing by. When did we even make it to the Hamptons?

"Looks like we're almost there," I say. "Anything else we need to get straight?"

"We've got the basics sorted." Adrian turns the Ferrari smoothly onto a long, hedgerow-lined drive. "The rest we can improvise. Just... stay close to me in there, okay?"

I smile softly, touched by the protectiveness in his tone. "Don't worry, Bunny." I test out the endearment and appreciate the way it rolls off my tongue. "I'll be sticking to you like glue. You'll get sick of me."

"Wouldn't dream of it, Sunshine." His hand finds mine, fingers interlacing and squeezing.

As we pull up at the sprawling beach mansion, a new, anxious frisson skitters across the back of my scalp. Let the fake-dating games begin...

17

ADRIAN

I pull the Ferrari into the circular driveway of Dominic's sprawling Hamptons estate. The white mansion rises before us, all columns and balconies and sparkling windows. Rowena's eyes are wide as she takes it all in.

"Wow, your boss knows how to summer."

I smirk. "Just wait until you see the inside." A nervous tension settles on my shoulders as I come around to help Rowena out. This weekend has to go perfectly.

The front door swings open and Dominic strides out dressed in swimming trunks and a light-blue linen shirt, silver hair shining in the afternoon sun. His sharp gaze lands on Rowena as she steps out of the car. I watch his expression closely, trying to gauge his reaction.

Surprise flickers briefly in his eyes, quickly masked. Rowena is not strictly my type—she's a fresh-faced natural beauty, not the plastic Barbie doll or fellow Wall Street shark he probably expected. Her clothes are pretty but not expensive. Today was probably the first time she ever drove in a Ferrari.

Dominic takes this all in, and his mouth curves into a warm smile. "Adrian, welcome! And this must be the lovely Rowena." My boss steps forward to shake her hand. "A pleasure to finally meet you, my dear."

"Likewise, Mr. Fulton. Adrian has told me so much about you." Rowena unleashes a dazzling smile. I loop my arm around her waist, pulling her close.

Dominic's gaze drops to the diamond glinting on her finger. His eyebrows lift almost imperceptibly. Good, he's noticed I'm committed to this whole family thing.

"Please, call me Dominic," he insists. "And make yourself at home. How was the drive? Not too taxing, I hope, especially in your condition?"

"Oh no, it was very pleasant," Rowena assures

him. "Adrian found me this amazing doctor in the city who put me on a new medication. It's made the morning sickness a million times better."

She leans into me affectionately as she speaks. My chest expands with pride and warmth. Barely a minute in, and she's already making me look great, propping me up as the doting fiancé. So far, she's nailing this fake relationship act.

Dominic nods, looking impressed. "Excellent, I'm so glad to hear that. Well, please come in, both of you!" He waves over a sharply dressed valet who hurries to collect our bags from the Ferrari's trunk.

As Rowena and I follow Dominic into the house, I can't help thinking that this crazy scheme could work.

In the foyer, Dominic gestures expansively at the lavish interior. "Welcome to my humble abode," he chuckles. Humble, right. The place practically screams billionaire, from the gleaming hardwood floors to the original artwork gracing the walls.

I keep Rowena close, my hand resting lightly at the base of her spine. The casual intimacy feels surprisingly natural, and I catch her glancing up at me with a small, private smile. An unfamiliar warmth stirs within me.

Through barely parted lips, she mouths. "Please tell me we're actually here to steal a few paintings."

I suppress a laugh as Dominic gestures at the space.

"The house has quite a history," he remarks as we walk. "It was originally built in the 1920s for a silent film star. Rumor has it she used to host scandalously wild parties here." He winks conspiratorially.

Rowena's eyes widen. "Really? That's fascinating!" She's playing her part beautifully, showing just the right amount of interest but not being too obsequious.

We emerge onto a sprawling patio overlooking the beach. Preston is already lounging by the pool with his picture-perfect family. His wife, a blonde with a megawatt smile, waves enthusiastically.

"Adrian." Preston gives me a polite nod. Civil but not warm. We're each other's competition and we both never forget it. He'd cut me down at the knees if he could, and I'd do the same.

More introductions are made as Rowena charms the Harrises effortlessly.

"Why don't you two go get changed and join us?" Dominic suggests. "Let me show you to your room."

We follow him back inside and up a sweeping

staircase. He opens a door, revealing a spacious bedroom with a stunning ocean view. And a single, gigantic bed.

"I'll leave you to settle in," Dominic says, oblivious to the sudden tension in the air. "See you by the pool!" The door closes behind him with a muted click.

Rowena and I stare at the lone bed, then at each other. Her cheeks flush pink. "Um, I guess we should have expected this."

"It's fine," I assure her, though my pulse is inexplicably racing. "I can sleep on the floor."

Her hazel eyes widen with surprise before darting to the unforgiving hardwood. She shakes her head vehemently. "No, no way. I can't let you do that, Adrian. You'll wake up with knots the size of golf balls."

"I've slept on worse." In my early days as a trader, I once spent the night on the floor of my cubicle with a Bloomberg terminal as my pillow. This would be a definite upgrade.

Rowena crosses her arms, fixing me with a determined stare. "Absolutely not. I'd feel terrible knowing you were down there while I'm in this big comfy bed by myself." She plops down on the edge of the mattress as if to emphasize her point.

I arch an eyebrow. "What are you suggesting?"

"Well…" She tucks a stray strand of hair behind her ear. "We're both mature adults, right? I'm sure we can share the bed without it being weird."

My heart pumps too much blood in the wrong direction at the thought of lying beside her all night, our bodies mere inches apart. I swallow. "If you're okay with that, I'm fine, too."

She nods, biting her lip. "It's a big bed. We'll just stick to our sides."

"That is if you feel comfortable sharing with an international art thief." I attempt to lighten the mood.

Her bright smile is my reward. "As long as you don't also steal all the covers, we'll be fine."

"Deal."

Rowena springs into action, rummaging through her duffle bag. She grabs a bikini and slips into the attached bathroom. "Be right back!"

She closes the door behind her.

While she changes, I strip out of my suit and pull on my swimming trunks. I'm tying the drawstring when I hear the bathroom door open.

I turn expectantly, but nothing could have prepared me for the vision that emerges. Rowena is an absolute smoke show in a blush pink string bikini speckled with tiny blue flowers. The triangles of fabric barely cover her ample cleavage, and the low-slung bottoms reveal her toned thighs and flat stomach, not yet showing any signs of the baby.

My mouth is literally hanging open, and I'm blatantly staring at her incredible body like an ogling teenage boy. Quickly, I avert my eyes, heat rising up my neck. When I chance a glance back at her face, her cheeks are flushed pink. She definitely caught me gawking at her.

"You, um, you look great." Trying to recover, I give a small, awkward cough. "That color suits you."

She smiles shyly, her eyes flickering downward. "Thanks. I wasn't sure everything would still fit with the pregnancy." Rowena chuckles nervously. "I swear my boobs have already grown a size..."

I turn away and close my eyes briefly not to be tempted to stare at her chest again. "Oh yeah, definitely. Everything fits... snug, I mean, well." I cringe inwardly at how unsmooth I sound.

Rowena glides past, drawing a sheer blue sarong from her bag and securing it with a casual knot at her hip. The see-through fabric does little to conceal her long legs. "One of the many perks of pregnancy, I guess." Her tone is lighthearted but there's a glimmer of uncertainty in her eyes, like she's second-guessing bringing up her changing body.

She has nothing to be self-conscious about. I step closer and take her hand. "Rowena, you look beautiful. Pregnancy suits you."

Color blooms in her cheeks again but this time she holds my gaze. "You think so?"

"I know so. You're stunning, inside and out. Any man would be lucky to have you on his arm."

Including me, I realize with a jolt. I'm going to have zero problems playing the role of doting boyfriend this weekend.

"Oh, okay, because I don't know if you've noticed, but Preston and his wife look like life-sized Ken and Barbie dolls—so perfect it was almost creepy."

"I suspect Preston gets his hair highlighted."

"Maybe it's a wig," she jokes. "His mop looked so unflappable I wondered if it were a plastic helmet."

I laugh and I'm still smiling as we make our way downstairs to the pool area, where Preston, Ella, and Dominic are lounging on chaise chairs while the kids splash around in the water, their laughter mingling with the crash of waves beyond.

"Even their kids look unreal," Rowena mouths to

me as we cross the lawn. "I'm already getting comparative parent anxiety."

I lean down and whisper, "I'm sure you'll be an amazing mom." Then I guide Rowena to the last free beach lounger, my hand placed on the small of her back—its new favorite position. The warmth of her skin seeps through the thin sarong, sending tingles up my arm.

As we sit side by side, Ella turns to Rowena with a friendly smile. "So, Rowena, what do you do for a living?"

"I'm a software engineer," Rowena replies, fidgeting with the string of her bikini in a way that's too distracting. "You?"

"I work for a non-profit that promotes youth literacy."

"Oh, wow, that is an amazing mission." Rowena's hand unconsciously drops to her still-flat belly. "I'd love to also get more kids into coding from an early age."

"You work at a toy company?"

"No. I wish. I used to be on Wall Street." Her mouth twists into a line that, if not exactly disgust, is close. Then she looks at me and her face brightens —I'm not sure if it's part of the act or not. "Where I met this guy. But I recently left my job to focus on... other things."

Ella nods, intrigued. "Other things?"

She glances at me, as if asking for permission to... say she's pregnant? I give a subtle nod. "Well, we're expecting and I was exhausted all the time."

"Oh, wow." Ella congratulates us and as the women discuss pregnancy woes, I find myself distracted by the way the sunlight plays across Rowena's skin, highlighting the gentle curve of her shoulders and the swell of her breasts beneath the bikini top.

I force myself to pay attention to the conversation, chiming in with the occasional comment to back Rowena's story. But try as I might to focus on Rowena's words as she spins our well-rehearsed tale about how we met and fell in love, my attention is drawn to her lush figure barely concealed by that tiny bikini.

I'm not the only distracted party, though. I catch Rowena's gaze flitting over my abs and chest more than once as she talks.

I decide to mess with her a little. Flexing subtly, I make my pecs bounce. Rowena stumbles over her words mid-sentence. She quickly recovers but avoids meeting my gaze, suddenly very interested in the pool tiles.

I have to bite back a grin. So the attraction isn't just an act on her part. The discovery sends an unwise thrill through me. I shouldn't read too much into it. But I'd be lying if I said I wasn't pleased by her admiring glances.

Feeling reckless, I slip an arm around her bare waist and tug her against my side.

Rowena's breath hitches almost imperceptibly. She gazes up at me, her lips parted, eyes hooded. For a charged moment, I forget we're playacting. Forget the audience watching us. My mind is consumed by how badly I want to capture her lips with mine and—

Preston's boy dive bombs into the pool, splashing everyone and shattering the spell. We break apart, Rowena's face flushed, as Ella shouts after her son to be more respectful.

When Ella turns back expectantly toward us, Rowena seems dazed.

"What was I saying?" she asks.

Ella chuckles. "Oh, you were only about to tell us how Adrian proposed!"

I flash a grin, projecting ease I don't quite feel. What am I doing? I've no idea, but some devil must've possessed me because next, I switch position, sliding behind Rowena on the beach lounger and wrapping my arms around her waist. Her sun-kissed skin is warm under my palm, and the faint scent of her coconut sunscreen fills my nostrils.

I drop my chin onto Rowena's shoulder, our cheeks nearly touching. "Do you mind if I tell the story, Sunshine? You know how much I love reliving that moment."

Rowena turns her head to look at me, our noses almost brushing. For an agonizing instant, I'm positive she's going to pull away, to put some distance between us. But she doesn't. Instead, she leans into my embrace, a soft smile playing across her lips.

"Sure, Bunny," she teases in an intimate tone. "You tell the story."

Heat radiates from my hairline down to my thighs as more of her bare skin presses into mine.

I look back at Ella and go for a dramatic flair. "It was a dark and stormy night..."

Rowena laughs, the sound bright and musical. "Oh, come on! It was not!"

I grin down at her, tightening my arms around her waist. "Okay, okay. It was a perfect summer evening, with a sky full of stars and a gentle breeze blowing into the city from the ocean..."

As I launch into the fabricated tale of our engagement, there's a tiny part of me that wonders what it'd be like if the woman in my arms were truly mine, if the love shining in her eyes was real and not just a reflection of the setting sun.

18

ROWENA

This weekend is proving harder than I thought. First, there was the "only one bed with the 1,000 thread count sheets and romantic ocean view" situation. Which, if I weren't wearing blindfolds, I should've expected. Who would put an expecting couple in a room with two beds? No one.

Then there was the sight of Adrian in swimwear, his golden gladiator body on full display and missing only a thorough oiling to make all my Spartacus fantasies come true. Miles and miles of flat muscles and sculpted abs that could be used to grate cheese—and that I don't seem able to stop ogling.

Hello? Weekend at the beach house. I should've seen the partial nudity coming, too.

But I was unprepared for the wolfish way Adrian stared at me as I emerged from the bathroom in my bikini. He seemed particularly taken with my boobs specifically, which, admittedly, have never looked better—if only they didn't feel this achy. His heated gaze on me made me almost burst apart at the seams. I'm working as hard at keeping it together as my poor biking bra is struggling to keep my grown-out-of-size breasts contained. In short, there's too much skin on display on both sides.

Then there's the small matter of how much bare skin is currently pressed against my back or draped around my waist.

I'm not sure if Adrian has taken his method acting very seriously or what else, but as I lean back into his chest and listen to his deep voice narrate the concocted story of how he proposed, can I say that I don't care? That I'm just content being here for the moment, not looking too closely at the whys or hows.

My attention is evenly split. Half of it is trained on what he's saying and the other part on the so-lidity of him behind me.

"It was a perfect summer evening, with a sky full

of stars and a gentle breeze blowing into the city from the ocean..."

I lean my head back against his shoulder as he continues with our rehearsed speech. "The only problem was, we were both too busy puking our guts out from food poisoning to enjoy any of it!"

I can't hold back a grin. Genius, really, the way we mixed the mortifying true story of how we met, both retching in a public bathroom, with our fake proposal tale.

"There we were, sick as dogs," Adrian continues, "barely able to lift our heads from the toilet. And I just looked over at her and thought, there's no one else in the world I'd rather be violently ill with. So, I asked her to marry me, right then and there with no ring to show and in the least romantic place."

I smile because he did propose in a bathroom after all.

It's an act, I remind myself. No matter how tantalizingly real the heat of Adrian's skin is against my back, the way his arms engulf me. The rumble of his voice against my back.

I glance at Dominic, Adrian's septuagenarian boss. He's guffawing merrily, taken in by our little charade. If he only knew the truth...

Do *I* know the truth? I seem to keep forgetting.

As Adrian's fingers absently trace circles on my arm, raising goosebumps in their wake, it's a struggle to keep my breathing steady, to remember this is all for show. But with every passing minute, every casual caress and adoring glance, the lines between pretense and reality blur further.

Adrian goes on, his voice animated with mock excitement. "By the next morning, I was feeling right as rain. But she, my poor darling," he squeezes me affectionately, "she was still green around the gills. So we went to the doctor, only to discover her illness had nothing to do with bad shellfish."

I widen my eyes in feigned shock, playing along. "That's right. Imagine our surprise when the doctor announced I was pregnant!" I pat my flat stomach for effect.

Dominic lets out a hearty chortle. "Well now, I guess this isn't a shotgun wedding after all!"

Though he means it in jest, Dominic's comment serves as an implicit reminder. This weekend is a job interview for Adrian, and our relationship is part of the test. I'm acutely aware that how we portray ourselves as a couple could make or break his chances at this promotion.

Gazing up at Adrian with what I hope passes for unadulterated adoration, I turn the sappiness meter up a notch. "Even if you had proposed after we found out about the baby, I would've never doubted your love for a second." I bat my lashes for good measure, praying I don't look as ridiculous as I feel. "I know you're all in."

Adrian looks down at me, his eyes smoldering with an intensity I haven't seen before. He's looking at me as if seeing me for the first time, and it sends a jolt through my system. His voice drops to a soft, intimate pitch that trips my insides into a little dance. "Absolutely all in," he confirms, tilting my chin up so that our mouths are level.

There's a moment there, a beat in time where everything else fades away and it's just the two of us, lost in this risky game of pretend. I recognize the question in his eyes, the silent inquiry if this—what we're doing, what we're pretending to feel—is still okay.

Before I can make my mind up, Adrian cups my cheek, his palm warm and slightly rough against my skin. Without hesitation, he leans in and kisses me, his lips soft yet demanding.

The world explodes with sensation, a blast of colors bursting behind my eyelids.

It's just a chaste peck, a brief meeting of lips, but it leaves me wanting so much more. My pulse pounds in my ears, my skin sizzles as if I've been hit by lightning and the current is still discharging all over my body.

Adrian pulls back, his dark eyes unsettling in a way I can't quite define.

Is it just acting on his part, or did he feel a spark too? The same overwhelming need for more?

I lick my lips, tasting him there and it doesn't help to gather my scattered thoughts.

"Woo-hoo guys, get a room!" Ella hoots. "There are minors around."

We spring further apart and Preston's wife asks, "When's the wedding?"

With my mind still reeling from Adrian's kiss—the searing warmth of his lips lingering on mine—I can't seem to form words. I just blink dazedly at Ella, my cheeks burning.

"We haven't picked a date yet." Adrian's breath tickles my ear as he replies. "Still working out the details."

Ella snaps her fingers. "You *must* have an engagement party."

My stomach feels hot and uneasy. "Oh, I don't know... I've only just gotten past the morning sickness. I haven't had the energy to do much of anything lately."

"Nonsense, it'll be no trouble at all. I'll give you the contact of my fabulous event planner, Sophie. She'll take care of everything—you won't have to lift a finger!" Ella beams at me expectantly.

I glance back at Adrian uncertainly. He nods, dark eyes gleaming with reassurance.

I turn to Ella and muster a smile. "Well, I guess... looks like we're having an engagement party!"

"Marvelous! I'll call Sophie first thing Monday when we get back to the city." Ella claps her hands gleefully.

When the sun begins to dip behind the trees, painting the sky in brilliant streaks of orange and pink, Dominic stands and stretches.

"Alright everyone, time to head in and change for dinner," he announces.

As we gather our things, I'm dizzy with the events of the afternoon—the surprising twists of this fake engagement... and the very real sparks igniting between me and Adrian. We walk back into our room and there it is, the made-for-sex bed ready to mock me. It's only two nights, I tell myself, I can do it.

19

ADRIAN

I shouldn't have kissed her. The thought consumes me as I enter the bedroom Rowena and I are sharing. I lost control out by the pool and made the only-one-bed situation so much worse. But with the adoring way she was gazing up at me, her hazel eyes sparkling in the sun, I couldn't resist capturing her lips with mine, even if just for a fleeting, perfect moment.

What was I thinking? I lost sight of what we're doing here.

"Mind if I shower first?" Her cheeks are still flushed, loose strands of chestnut hair clinging damply to her neck.

"No, go ahead." I nod, struggling to keep my

voice even. She disappears into the bathroom and I stare at the closed door, mentally kicking myself. I'd like nothing more than to strip off my swim trunks and join her under the warm spray, soap up her curves, kiss the water from her skin.

But that's not the plan. The plan is not to screw this up, to keep things professional, to maintain the boundaries that are getting hazier by the second. This arrangement is supposed to be strictly business. Faking a relationship to win a job title. That's it. No kissing involved. That would be crossing a line I've already smudged today. I plop onto the side of the bed, run a hand through my hair, and focus on regaining some semblance of self-control. But the sound of running water is a tormenting reminder of her nakedness just a few feet away.

Deep breaths.

An eternity later, the bathroom door opens in a billow of steam. Rowena emerges, now wearing a stunning maxi dress that hugs her figure and flows elegantly to the floor. The floral print complements her glowing skin and sets off the golden flecks in her eyes. My mouth goes dry.

I stand up, grabbing my toiletry bag and a change of clothes.

As I brush past her, I catch a whiff of her fruity

shampoo and it takes all my willpower not to bury my nose in her damp hair and inhale deeply.

Closing the bathroom door behind me, I strip off my trunks and step into the shower. I crank the handle all the way to cold and let out a hiss as the icy water hits my overheated skin.

Think of spreadsheets, I tell myself. Profit margins. Anything but the gorgeous woman on the other side of that door. I soap up quickly and rinse off, refusing to let my mind wander.

Teeth chattering, I shut off the water and towel dry. After donning a crisp white button-down and navy slacks, I style my hair and brace myself for the night ahead. Impress Dominic. Do not act like a perv.

Showtime.

I exit the bathroom to find Rowena perched on the edge of the bed, slipping on strappy sandals. She looks up and smiles, easing some of the conflicted anxiety knotting my stomach. She's good, we're good.

"Ready to dazzle?" I ask.

"As I'll ever be."

I offer my arm. "Shall we?"

She takes it and we descend to the dining room.

Dominic greets us jovially, ushering us to our seats. As the first course is served, I place my hand over Rowena's on the table, interlacing our fingers. She jolts slightly but then relaxes into it. I squeeze, give her a nod, and let go.

Soon, the conversation drifts to market trends and summer plans. I throw in the occasional insightful comment while keeping a keen eye on Rowena. She's handling the casual chatter like a pro, jumping in when the topic shifts to tech, her insights as sharp as her curves are soft. Her dry humor earns more than a few genuine laughs from Dominic. And she seems more at ease.

But as the evening wears on, the tension between us ratchets higher again the closer we get to bedtime. I couldn't keep my hands or my mouth to myself while we were in public by the pool, what am I going to do now that we'll be alone in a room sharing a bed?

By the time the evening ends, my nerves are stretched taut.

Rowena's voice as she bids everyone a good night is light and breezy, but I catch a glint of something else in her eyes when she turns to face me. Is it eagerness? Dread? Both?

We climb the stairs, the quiet between us holding an edge. As soon as we enter the bedroom, we both stop awkwardly, eyeing the king-sized bed like it's a battlefield. For a moment, neither of us speaks. Finally, Rowena breaks the silence. "Should we put some throw pillows in the middle?"

I grab some from the settee in the corner and start building a makeshift barrier across the mattress.

"Fort West." I let out a forced chuckle, hoping to ease some of the tension. "No trespassing."

She squints at me. "We'll see how long your fortifications last against my invading forces."

We take turns in the bathroom, orbiting each other skittishly like asteroids on the verge of collision until we slide under the covers and settle at the opposite ends of the mattress.

Despite the distance, the scent of her lotion wafts over, vanilla and jasmine, and I clench my fists against the urge to roll over and pull her close. But we're both lying at the edges of the bed only a hair's breadth away from falling off.

I stare at the ceiling, counting my breaths. This is going to be a long night...

* * *

I wake slowly, the tendrils of sleep still clinging. Disoriented, I blink against the sunlight filtering through gauzy curtains. Where am I? Then it hits me—Dominic's Hamptons house.

Reality comes rushing back as I register the warm weight pressed along my side, the tickle of hair beneath my chin.

Oh, fuck.

In the night, Rowena and I gravitated toward each other like magnets. Now our limbs are tangled, her head on my chest. The barrier between us obliterated. I peek over the edge of the bed and spot the valiant soldiers lying on the floor, decimated.

She stirs and nuzzles deeper into my neck with a contented sigh. Parts of me twitch involuntarily. I should extricate myself, restore a respectful distance before she wakes up. But I'm frozen, hyperaware of every place where our bodies touch, her soft curves molding to my angles. It feels too right.

Rowena's lashes twitch and I panic. Carefully, I ease out from under her, sliding my arm from the sweet dip of her waist. She makes a disgruntled noise and burrows into the space I vacated, seeking my warmth. I watch, enchanted and aching, as she settles back into sleep.

Scrubbing a hand over my face, I pad to the bathroom.

Remember the rules. You don't need complications.

I splash cold water on my cheeks and behind my neck.

When I re-emerge, Rowena is awake, adorably rumpled with pillow creases on her cheek. Our eyes meet and lock with awareness.

"Sleep well?" I strive for nonchalance.

A pretty flush stains her skin. "Like a baby. You?"

"Same." I glance down, pretending to check my watch. "I'm heading down to breakfast. Take your time getting ready."

Escape. I need to clear my head before I do something foolish, like crush her to that mattress and—nope, not going there. Because fuck, do I want to. Falling into bed with Rowena would be easier than breathing. But I'm not even sure it'd be just mere physical attraction, and that's dangerous.

No, best to ignore the part of me that whispers it's already too late. I'm not relationship material. Rowena deserves better than the few spare hours my job allows for my personal life. And she's vulnerable now, jobless, pregnant, completely dependent on me... I can't.

I head downstairs to join the others, determined to keep my distance. But I can still feel the phantom warmth of her touch like a brand on my skin.

20

ROWENA

Nine weeks pregnant

I survived two days and two nights of extreme proximity with Adrian West. My spine still hasn't recovered from all the tingling, and I don't think my shoulders have ever been so wrung with tension—frustrated *sexual* tension—but I made it.

And now I have an engagement party to organize. True to her word, Ella has put me in contact with her event planner—apparently all investment bankers' wives have one to plan soirees for their husbands and the occasional party. Since the party needs to be soon, Sophie offered to come to the house to meet me in person right away.

She arrived just after lunch, and now we're sitting in Adrian's living room, discussing the details. The first question she asks is what my budget is. I text the query to Adrian and turn the phone to Sophie to let her read the answer directly as it pops in.

ADRIAN

Don't make me look skimpy

She smiles. "That should give us plenty of room to accommodate all your wishes."

The following question is what those wishes are, prompting me to be careful not to replicate my ideas for the actual wedding. At my blank expression, she inquires if I have a wedding planner and gets hired for the job immediately. Next, Sophie rolls me through options for both the wedding and the engagement party. We agree on a sunset event at the beach on 12 July for the party. And for the wedding, I give in to all my *Gossip Girl* fantasies and ask for a Central Park ceremony on 20 September.

Sophie assures me she has the perfect location at the Hamptons already in mind and a backup in case that one is taken and that she'll apply for the ceremony permits through the New York City De-

partment of Parks and Recreation right away to secure the best spot.

From venues, we move on to the invitations. Sophie tells me not to stress and that from the past
parties she threw for the Harrises she has a list of all
the important banking people that must be included in the participations, but to give her an addi-
tional list of family and friends on both sides.

That last statement leaves me in a slight panic.
I'm not sure what to do with my family. Do I tell my
parents the truth? No, I can't. It'd be better for them
to think that I got married, had a baby, and got divorced than to know I'm faking the whole thing and
the baby daddy is not even in the picture. Liam. Just
like that, another thought I've been shoving at the
back of my mind barrels down on me.

Cold sweat pools under my armpits as another
thought I can't cope with creeps in. Sophie leaves
the house with a promise that we'll start planning
the wedding soon. As soon as she's gone, I text my
best friends to see if they can meet me after work.
We've texted a few times since I moved in with
Adrian, but I've been kind of avoiding them. Sometimes it's easier to fully get on board with this new
life and pretend even with myself that I'm happily
engaged.

Hunter is the first to reply.

> HUNT
>
> If you've changed your mind, we
> can kick Dylan out of the third
> bedroom, he hasn't set up the
> office yet

Right there. It's difficult to be around people who try to be supportive but who clearly disapprove of my choices. I text back that I haven't changed my mind but still need to talk to them.

* * *

A few hours later, I stare at Adrian's buzzer, finger hovering over the lobby button. Asking his personal driver to chauffeur me around Manhattan feels so pretentious. But exhaustion drags at my limbs and the lingering morning sickness that gets past the new medication makes the idea of navigating the subway seem insurmountable. Sighing, I buzz for Sam to bring the car around even if I feel like an impostor putting on airs after a mere week into this extravagant life of luxuries.

I grab my purse and a light cardigan—for the air conditioning in the car, which Sam keeps to polar levels. He is already waiting by the curb by the time I get out, dapper as always in his black uniform. Sam opens the rear door with a smile. "Good afternoon, Miss Taylor. Where to?"

"Please, Sam, just call me Rowena." I slide into the backseat, rattling off the cross streets.

As we weave through traffic, I stare out the darkened window and let my mind wander. It's been only a week since I've seen Nina and Hunter. But after years of sharing a house, it feels like an eternity. I miss the easy intimacy of our friendship, the way we used to talk about anything and everything curled up on the couch with ice cream and wine. Now there's this huge, invisible barrier between us. And it's my fault. I've barely texted them, and only to give them proof of life. My excuse has been that between the ring shopping and the weekend at the Hamptons I've been too busy. But really, I sense their disapproval and it makes me pull away.

"Here we are," Sam announces, pulling up to the curb. "Just call when you're ready to be picked up."

"Thank you so much, Sam." I open the door myself before he can come around and do it for me, and exit.

A heartbeat later, the car merges back into traffic. I watch it disappear from the sidewalk, suddenly feeling awkward and out of place in my old neighborhood. The summer weather is perfect—hot and sunny but dry for once and not sticky. I should enjoy it, be excited to see my best friends and catch up. Instead, nerves twist in my stomach.

Tugging self-consciously at my skirt, I make my way around the corner.

Nina and Hunter are already seated at one of the small outdoor tables of our favorite café, heads together as they talk. At the sight of them, looking so wonderfully familiar, a bit of the tension eases from my shoulders. I'm still me. They're still them. We'll figure this out.

"Rowena!" Nina spots me first, leaping up to envelop me in a tight hug. "Oh my gosh, look at you! You're glowing!"

"Hey mama." Hunter grins, stepping in for her own hug as soon as Nina releases me. "Growing a tiny human looks good on you."

My eyes mist over at their enthusiastic welcome. For a moment I just cling to Hunter, so damn grateful to have them in my life.

"I missed you guys," I mumble against her shoulder.

"Missed you, too," Nina says, guiding me into a

chair. "We want to know everything. How are you feeling? How's the baby? And Adrian?"

I draw in a lungful of steadying air, letting it out slowly as I answer in the cheeriest voice I can muster. "I'm good. Better. Adrian got me the best OB in the city, so that's been great. I'm just tired a lot. But less... stressed, I guess?"

They frown at my interrogative tone so I reassure them that the pregnancy is going well and that Adrian has been nothing but considerate and helpful. I'm purposely leaving out the part where my pulse skyrockets out of control whenever I'm near him.

Once the typical catch-up chatter dies down, I broach the subject I've been both dreading and desperate to discuss. "So, I wanted your advice on something." I fiddle with a paper napkin, not quite meeting their eyes. Still feeling their expectant gazes on me. "Do you think I should tell Liam about the baby?"

Nina's eyebrows shoot up and Hunter makes a choking sound.

"Absolutely not!" Nina declares. "That jerk lost all rights to know anything about your life the second he started manipulating and gaslighting you."

Hunter nods in fervent agreement. "Winnie, that guy is bad news. All he ever did was make you doubt yourself and feel small. What if Liam were the same with the baby? Don't invite that toxicity back in."

I worry at my lower lip, conflicting emotions warring in my chest. "I hear you, and I mostly agree. It's just..." I pause, trying to articulate the nagging sense of unease. "Some part of me feels like the baby deserves a chance to have their father in their life. Not for me, but for them. Is it selfish of me to unilaterally decide Liam doesn't even get to know he's going to have a kid?"

Nina's gaze softens, and she reaches across the table to clasp my hand. "Oh, honey, no. You're not being selfish, you're being a good mom. And good moms protect their children from people who could hurt them. Liam's already proven he has no qualms about crushing your self-esteem. Do you want to risk him doing that to your child, too?"

I flinch at the thought, my free hand instinctively reaching for my still-flat stomach. "No, I don't." I sigh. "You're right, both of you. It's not fair to my baby to willingly expose them to a manipulator when they're too little to protect themselves."

Hunter raises her coffee mug in a mock toast. "Here's to deadbeat dads staying dead and gone!"

We all laugh, dispelling the somber mood. Inside though, a small, niggling part of me still isn't entirely convinced. Is it really my place to decide Liam never even finds out he's a father? I tamp the doubt down and paste on a bright smile that doesn't quite reach my heart.

There's a beat of silence that Nina quickly fills. "Tell us, what's it like living with Mr. Tall, Dark, and Loaded?" She wiggles her eyebrows suggestively.

"Oh, you know." I blush. "He's always busy working, so I have the place to myself a lot. But when he is around, he's just..." I fumble with my hands, blushing some more. "Like a walking, talking *GQ* magazine cover. But with spreadsheets. And he's got this intensity about him that can be overwhelming. But there are moments, like when he's just talking about something he loves or when he looks at me like..." I trail off, realizing I'm getting into dangerous heart-fluttering territory.

Hunter leans forward, her eyes alight with curiosity. "When he looks at you like...?"

My cheeks warm even more.

Nina and Hunter exchange a meaningful look. "Ooh, sounds like someone might have a crush on her dashing fake fiancé," Nina teases in a singsong voice.

I toss my crumpled napkin at her. "Oh shut up, it's not like that! I just meant he's been a surprisingly good friend, that's all."

Hunter snorts. "Sure, a friend."

"I swear."

The sun glints off Nina's oversized sunglasses as she leans across the table, a glint of mischief in her eyes. "The only way to know if you've got it bad for your fake boyfriend is to introduce us."

"Yeah," Hunter agrees. "We have to meet and vet the guy."

I roll my eyes. "Nothing is going on," I repeat. "And I'll guess you'll meet him soon."

"How soon?" Nina seems unconvinced.

"We're hosting an engagement party, and of course you'll be invited."

"An engagement party?" Hunter gasps, her eyes wide as saucers. "When did this happen? I need details, woman!"

Nina chimes in. "Did he buy you a ring?"

I fumble for my phone. "Yes. It's gorgeous but I'm too afraid to wear it. Don't want to get mugged."

I swipe to the photo and hold it out for them to see. The large, canary yellow diamond sparkles even in the digital image. Their jaws drop in unison.

"Holy shit, is that thing real?" Hunter grabs the phone to get a closer look.

"The diamond yes." I lower my voice and hiss, "But the engagement is still fake."

"But the ring is stunning," Nina adds, peering over Hunter's shoulder. "Do you think you can keep it after you break up?"

"I don't know." A jolt buzzes through my core at the memory of Adrian sliding it onto my finger. Somehow the idea of keeping it after everything will be over feels wrong.

"When's the big engagement bash?" Hunter asks as she hands my phone back.

"In about three weeks." I take a sip of my iced latte, the condensation cooling my hot palms. "We're hosting it at the Hamptons."

Hunter slams a palm on the table, rattling our coffee mugs. "Three weeks? Oh, hell no, we can't wait that long to meet the mysterious Adrian West! It'll be way too awkward if the engagement party is the first time we're introduced."

I shift in my seat. "Well, he's really busy with work and I don't want to spring too much on him at once—"

"Please, you two are engaged," Nina cuts me off with a dismissive wave. "If he's willing to put a rock that big on your finger, he can handle meeting your best friends."

"The ring is just for show," I tell them.

Nina low-whistles. "Regardless. Hunter is right. If you have to fake being in a serious relationship, he has to meet us at some point."

I chew my lip, considering the idea. It would be nice to have Adrian meet Nina and Hunter in a more casual setting before the craziness of the engagement party. But will he be up for it? I know how consumed he gets with work...

"Earth to Rowena!" Hunter snaps her fingers in my face. "When can we meet him?"

I fiddle with my straw, feeling so nervous about the prospect of the two worlds colliding. "I have to check with Adrian, but maybe over the weekend? I'll text you guys once we figure out a date."

"You better." Nina points an accusatory finger at me. "I need to see this 'thoughtful' side of Adrian for myself."

I laugh, shaking my head. "I promise you will. Just... go easy on him, okay? He's not used to being interrogated by overprotective best friends."

Hunter grins. "No promises, babe. We've got to make sure he's good enough to fake-marry you."

As we stand to leave, excitement and apprehension about the upcoming dinner bubble in my chest. Will they see what I see in Adrian, or will they think he's just an overworked hotshot with no scruples?

I push the thought aside, reminding myself it doesn't really matter what my friends think of Adrian. He's not my real fiancé.

21

ADRIAN

On Monday night, I arrive home late on purpose, pushing beyond my already crazy schedule. I unlock the door as quietly as possible, hoping not to wake Rowena. After spending the weekend together at my boss's house, I've been intentionally avoiding her today, getting up at the crack of dawn and sneaking in past midnight like a thief. It's not that Rowena did anything wrong—quite the opposite, actually. She's been perfect. Too perfect.

I feel the pull, the temptation to let myself get close to her. But I don't do relationships, not anymore. They never end well, always crumbling apart no matter how good things seem at first. So I have to maintain a safe distance.

Easing the door closed with a faint click, I slip off my shoes and loosen my tie. But when I step into the living room, I freeze. Rowena is curled up on the couch, fast asleep, with the flickering light of the TV playing across her serene face.

Damn, she's beautiful. The way her long chestnut hair spills over the cushion, her dark lashes fanned out against her cheeks. That familiar tug pulls at my heart, a string drawing me to her.

I debate carrying her to bed, but I don't want to risk waking her. Instead, I grab the soft throw blanket that has half slipped off and drape it over her, tucking it around her shoulders. Her glasses have fallen to the floor, so I pick them up and settle them on the end table.

As I straighten up, Rowena stirs. Her hazel eyes flick open and meet mine, still hazy with sleep. My breath hitches.

"Hey," Rowena says, her voice adorably husky. "I was waiting for you."

There's no accusation or annoyance in her tone, just a simple statement of fact. She rubs at her eyes and tucks her long legs underneath her as she sits up. The urge to gather her in my arms, to bury my nose in her hair and never let go, is nearly overwhelming.

Rowena glances around, seeming to get her bearings. She spots the glasses and puts them on. "What time is it?"

"Midnight." I shove my hands in my pockets to keep from reaching for her.

A tiny smile curves her lips. "You really do work late, huh?" Then her expression turns more serious, almost hesitant. "Are you too tired? Or can we talk for a bit?"

I scream at myself to make an excuse, to tell her we can chat another time and then go back to keeping my distance. But whatever she wants to discuss has to be important for her to wait up this late.

She shouldn't be relying on me like this. We need to maintain separate lives, I firmly remind myself. No getting too tangled up.

But instead of heeding my own advice, I sit on the couch right next to her, close enough that our thighs almost brush. Too damn close.

I angle myself to face her, giving Rowena my full attention even as I silently curse my lack of willpower. "What is it?"

In the shadowy light, Rowena stands straighter. "Well, there are two things," she begins, nervously twisting her fingers together in her lap.

I nod encouragingly, determined to at least not

screw this up since apparently I've made myself available to her tonight. "I'm listening."

"The first one is pretty easy." Her eyes find mine. "My best friends want to meet you." She raises her hands before I can respond. "I know it's not how our fake relationship works. But they said it would look weird, maybe even suspicious, if they just showed up at the engagement party without having met you."

I stifle a smile, shaking my head. "Sounds like you've got some pretty ingenious friends, Rowena." The way her name rolls off my tongue feels dangerously intimate in the dimly lit room.

She grins back at me, and that invisible string around my heart constricts, pulling me deeper into her orbit. "Oh, you're right. They're also super overprotective and will grill you harder than a steak at a summer barbecue." Rowena tucks an errant lock of hair behind her ear. "So, it's up to you if you want to meet them. No pressure."

I should say no. Keep those boundaries firmly in place. Instead, I nod like the fool I am. "Sure, let's do it. I'm game for a little friendly interrogation." I flash her a grin, trying to ignore the sinking feeling that I'm digging myself deeper and deeper into a hole I might not be able to climb out of.

Our lives, which were supposed to stay neatly separated, are getting more entangled by the minute. Rowena seems to take my agreement as a cue to launch into a quick update about the engagement party, rattling off details about the venue and the guest list.

"Oh, that reminds me." She taps her forehead. "I'll need a list of your friends and family to invite. How many people do you think you'll have on your side?"

I shuffle my feet on the rug, feeling a twinge of guilt. "Just my mom," I admit. "And I'll be telling her the truth about our arrangement. I can't let her believe she's going to have a grandchild when it's not real. It would break her heart when she found out."

Rowena's expression softens, and she reaches out to give my hand a gentle squeeze. I fight not to respond. Not to pull her into my lap and do unspeakable things to her.

"I understand," she says quietly. "That's thoughtful of you, Adrian."

I work air down my nose, ignoring the tingles where she touched me.

Rowena's shoulders slump. "I wish I could be as honest with my parents, but they'd never understand a marriage of convenience. I'd rather let them think we got divorced down the line than have them know the truth from the start."

Another wave of guilt washes over me. Our arrangement may be mutually beneficial, but maybe I should've tried harder to find a different way to help her, expecting nothing in return. The thought of Rowena lying to her family because of me doesn't sit well.

Instead of voicing my doubts, I reach out and gently tilt her chin up, so her hazel eyes meet mine. "Hey, it's going to be okay. Your parents will have a grandbaby to love and cherish." I'm such an asshole right now. "By the time they find out the truth, they'll be so head over heels for the little one, the rest won't matter."

Rowena manages a small smile, but it doesn't quite reach her eyes. She nods, seemingly trying to convince herself. "You're right. They'll love the baby no matter what."

Her fingers fidget with the hem of her T-shirt. I can sense she has something else on her mind. What more could there be?

"There's one more thing I wanted to talk to you about..." Rowena hesitates, confirming my suspicions that she kept the hardest topic for last. "I... I don't feel right about not telling the baby's father he's going to be a dad."

My eyebrows shoot up in surprise. I wasn't expecting that. "I thought you said he was a jerk?"

She nods, her eyes downcast. "He is. And honestly, I'm scared to face him. But I keep thinking that my kid might never forgive me if I don't at least try to let Liam know."

Liam—I instantly despise the name.

Rowena's next words come out in a rush, as if she's afraid she'll lose her nerve if she doesn't get them out fast enough. "You probably prefer as few people in the know as possible, but I just don't think I can—"

"It's your call," I interrupt politely. "I'm with you whatever you decide."

I shouldn't. This is madness. Her douche ex could expose us out of spite. Blackmail me. Even so, I don't care.

Her eyes widen in surprise. Then, slowly, a genuine smile spreads across her face, lighting up her features in a way that cuts deep.

"Thank you, Adrian." Her voice is thick with emotion. "That means more to me than you know."

I nod, dismissing my racing pulse. I'm doing the

opposite of what I should, making myself available, taking risks to do what's right for her and potentially disastrous for me, but when Rowena looks at me like that, I can't bring myself to care about the downsides.

"When are you meeting him?"

"That's the thing." Rowena readjusts her glasses. "When I talk to Liam, I was wondering if you might come with me? And pretend to be my, uh, mean and scary new boyfriend?"

I grin wide. "Isn't that already what we're doing? Minus the mean and scary part, I hope."

She grins. "Yes, but I need you to really sell it. I want Liam to know in no uncertain terms that this baby isn't some ploy to get back together with him. And that he can't use it to manipulate me again." Her eyes are pleading as they meet mine. "I just... I want him to see that I've moved on. That I'm not the same naïve girl he used to control."

Words leave my mouth before I even have a chance to second guess them. "I'll be there. Whenever you need me. I promise."

The relief that washes over her face is palpable. Without warning, she leans forward and wraps her arms around my neck, crushing me into a tight embrace.

For a moment, I'm frozen, unsure how to respond. But then, slowly, I allow myself to relax into the hug. My arms come up to encircle her waist, pulling her closer. I breathe in the scent of her shampoo, relishing the softness of her curves pressed against me.

It's a dangerous indulgence, I know. But just for a minute, I let myself savor it. This feeling of being needed. Of being wanted.

Reluctantly, I pull back. "We should get some sleep." My voice sounds rough to my ears.

Rowena nods, her cheeks flushed as she stands from the couch. "Right. Goodnight, Adrian."

"Goodnight, Rowena."

I watch her walk down the hall and turn just her head over her shoulder, whispering, "Thank you," before she disappears into her room.

Later, lying in the darkness of my bedroom, I stare up at the ceiling and let out a heavy sigh.

"Man," I mutter to myself, "what the fuck are you doing?"

22

ROWENA

Saturday morning I lace and unlace my fingers in an anxious dance as I pace back and forth in the living room. Liam has agreed to see me in an hour, and now I have to tell him I'm pregnant with his baby. I focus on my breathing to steady the nerves knotting in my stomach. We're meeting him in Brooklyn where he lives, and the only thing keeping me from totally freaking out is knowing Adrian will be by my side.

As if summoned by my thoughts, my fake fiancé emerges from his bedroom looking like he stepped straight off a runway in Milan. Even in a simple navy button-down and dark jeans, he screams money, power, status. I'm standing on solid ground, but I might as well be free-falling as I drink in the sight of him.

Still, I frown with worry.

Adrian arches a brow at my unusual reaction, his full lips quirking up in amusement. "Do I not look intimidating enough? I was going for rugged and menacing." His tone is playful but laced with genuine concern.

Warmth blooms in my chest. Adrian is so different from Liam—open, caring, never making me feel small or stupid. And going along with my weird requests on blind faith. I can be honest with him. I smile, shaking my head. "Trust me, you look plenty intimidating. Like you could buy and sell Liam ten times over." I circle a hand to point at his designer ensemble. "But could you dress down? I don't want Liam getting any ideas if he thinks you're loaded."

Adrian's brows knit together. "You think he'd try to take advantage?"

I shrug, rubbing my arm. "I just have a bad feeling, call it women's intuition. Better to be safe than sorry, you know?"

"I get it. Give me five minutes, I'll Clark Kent myself into something more low key." Adrian flashes me a charming grin and disappears back into his room.

If, for any reason, I'd asked Liam to change clothes or even criticized one little thing, he would've blown up in my face, yelling and belittling me.

Adrian is so understanding instead, so quick to put me at ease without a hint of condescension or annoyance. The total opposite of how Liam always made me feel—small, stupid, crazy. *Extra*.

I so wish I didn't have to see him again. I've prepared a speech, to antagonize him as little as possible. But there's no way to know how my ex will take the news, what his reaction will be.

I'm still rehearsing what I'm going to say to Liam in my head when Adrian reappears, now in faded jeans with a rip in one knee, scuffed-up black Converse, and a wrinkled black T-shirt that looks like it's seen better days. He spreads his arms, doing a little spin. "How's this? Broke enough for you?"

My lips twitch, eyes raking over him. Damn. Leave it to Adrian to make shabby look chic. "It's an improvement. But you're missing one detail."

"Oh?" He quirks an eyebrow. "What's that?"

I point to the gleaming Rolex on his wrist. "You might want to leave the fifty-K watch at home, Richie Rich."

Adrian barks out a laugh, unclasping the metal

band and tossing the watch on a side table. "Good call."

He winks, causing reactions better left un-analyzed.

"Alright, Miss Taylor." He offers me his elbow like a gentleman. "Your carriage awaits."

I tuck my hand into the crook of his arm. "Why, thank you, good sir."

We exit his penthouse, the heavy door thudding shut behind us with an air of finality. No turning back now. My stomach curdles but I'm bolstered by the solid strength of Adrian beside me. Together, we step into the elevator, ready to face whatever the day may bring.

The car ride to Brooklyn feels endless, even with Sam expertly weaving through the city traffic. I fidget in my seat the entire time. Adrian reaches over and takes my hand, his touch warm and reassuring. His dark eyes filled with compassion. "I'm right here with you. We've got this."

I exhale shakily and nod, trying to absorb some of his calm confidence. "I know. Thank you, Adrian. For everything."

He rests his hand on my forearm in a silent reassurance.

As we near the coffee shop, I turn to Sam. "Can

you please drop us off a couple blocks away? I don't want Liam to see us getting out of a fancy car."

"Of course, Miss Rowena," Sam replies, smoothly pulling over to the curb.

Adrian and I step out onto the bustling sidewalk. My legs feel unsteady as we walk toward the meeting spot.

"Deep breaths." Adrian keeps hold of my hand. "You're one of the strongest women I know. You've got this."

His words embolden me, pushing back the fear threatening to overwhelm me. I can face Liam. I have to, for the sake of my baby.

As we round the corner, I spot my ex sitting at an outdoor table, impatiently checking his watch. He probably arrived early only to call me out about being late, even if I'm on time.

My stomach plummets to my toes. Even seated, Liam exudes a cocky air of self-assurance. He looks just as handsome as ever in a crisp button-down and designer jeans, his light hair artfully tousled. But now, I see past the polished exterior to the cruel, manipulative man beneath.

Liam glances up, a calculated gleam in his ice-blue eyes as he meets my gaze with a smug smile spreading on his lips. He must think I've asked him here to beg him to take me back.

That arrogant confidence slips as Liam spots Adrian's tall figure next to me. My ex frowns, his face already betraying that quiet rage and meanness that made me feel so fearful when we were together.

I steel myself, gripping Adrian's hand like a lifeline as we approach the table.

"Hi, Liam."

"Who is this guy?" my ex asks, not even bothering to say hello first. His tone is accusatory, as if I've done something wrong by bringing someone with me.

I will my voice not to shake. "This is Adrian, my boyfriend."

Liam's perfect features contort in a sneer, and his face goes red. "What's the meaning of this? I don't appreciate wasting my time to meet your new fuckboy."

I wince at his rudeness, my cheeks burning with humiliation. He's even worse than I remembered. All the weeks I spent building up my self-esteem after our breakup seem to evaporate in an instant, leaving me feeling small and worthless again.

Before I can say anything, Liam stands up abruptly, his chair scraping against the concrete.

"I'm outta here. Whatever you have to say, I don't want to hear it. You're a loser, Rowena, and you've always only dragged me down."

His words hit me like a physical blow, paralyzing me. I stand there, mouth agape, unable to form a coherent response. But Adrian steps forward, giving me a nod before turning a menacing glare on Liam.

"You should sit down and listen to Rowena." Adrian's deep voice is calm but firm. "It's important."

Liam scoffs, looking Adrian up and down with disdain. "And who the hell are you to tell me what to do?"

Adrian doesn't back down, meeting Liam's gaze unflinchingly. "Someone who cares about Rowena and who won't stand by while you disrespect her."

The two men stare each other down, the air between them almost vibrating. I hold my breath, half-expecting Liam to throw a punch. But to my surprise, he breaks eye contact first, dropping back into his chair with a huff.

"Fine," Liam spits out, crossing his arms over his chest. "Say what you have to say, Rowena. But make it quick."

The sounds of the busy street fade to a muffled hum as we sit opposite Liam and I blurt out, "I'm pregnant." Feeling like the world is slowly being drained of oxygen, I add, "And the baby is yours, Liam."

My ex just stares at me, his ice-blue eyes wide with shock. Then, a harsh laugh erupts from his throat, cutting through the air like a knife.

"You've got to be kidding me." Liam shakes his head in disbelief. "You expect me to believe that? For all I know, you've been spreading your legs for every guy in town, including this joker right here."

I flinch at his crude words, my eyes glassing over with tears I don't want to give him the satisfaction to see. Under the table, Adrian's hands curl into fists. He looks about ready to pummel my ex into the ground for every venomous word Liam spat my way. But I find his hand with mine and subtly shake my head. Adrian's fists unclench, and his fingers intertwine with my own in a quiet show of solidarity.

"It's the truth," I insist, my voice wavering but determined. "I wasn't with anyone else before I found out I was pregnant. This baby is yours, whether or not you want to believe it."

Liam leans back in his chair, a smug smirk playing on his lips. "Right, because you're just the picture of honesty and fidelity, aren't you, Rowena? I mean, look at you—running around with this guy mere weeks after we broke up. How do I know he's not the real father, huh?"

Adrian tenses beside me, his jaw clenching with barely restrained anger. I give his hand a squeeze, silently pleading with him to keep his cool.

"He's not..." I trail off, my cheeks flushing with embarrassment. "I swear to you, Liam, this child is yours. I would never lie about something like this."

Liam studies me for a long moment, his gaze calculating and cold. Then, he stands up abruptly, fishing a few crumpled dollar bills from his pocket and tossing them carelessly onto the table. "I'm not paying for your mistakes. If you and your fuck-buddy here thought you could shake me down for money, you've got another thing coming."

Adrian rises to his feet, his imposing figure towering over Liam. "Watch your mouth," he growls, his voice low and threatening. "Rowena's not asking for your money. She just thought you deserved to know the truth."

Liam scoffs, waving a dismissive hand in our direction. "The truth? Please. I don't owe either of you a damn thing." He stares me down next. "If you're stupid enough to get knocked up, that's your problem, not mine."

He jabs a finger at the measly bills scattered on

the table. "That's all you're getting from me—enough for a coffee, and you're not even worth that. Don't contact me again, Rowena. We're done."

With that, Liam turns on his heel and stalks away, leaving me staring after him dazed, emotionally drained. Tears well up in my eyes, the crushing weight of his last humiliation pressing down on my chest.

"Adrian..." My voice trembles. "Please don't judge me for having dated him. Liam... he wasn't always like this. It took a long time for his true colors to show."

Adrian's expression softens, and he reaches out to pull me up into his arms. As the first sob rips from my throat, I bury my face against his chest, my body shaking with the force of my tears.

23

ADRIAN

She's crying in my arms and I don't know what to do. Rowena trembles against my chest, her body wracked with sobs. I stroke a hand over her silky hair, unsure what else to do or say.

Her ex is lucky my hands are occupied comforting her, or I'd chase after him and beat his sorry ass into the curb.

"Shhh, it's okay," I murmur against her hair. "You're safe. I've got you. And I don't judge you one bit for dating that scumbag, I promise."

Rowena shakes her head slightly where it's nestled against my shoulder. Her tears dampen my T-shirt but I couldn't care less.

"Hey, what is it? Why are you crying?"

She pulls back and looks up at me. Even with her eyes bloodshot from crying, she's still so beautiful it strikes me dumb.

"I'm okay, I swear. I'm just so fucking relieved that I'll never have to deal with Liam again." Her statement catches me off guard. "He's finally, truly gone from my life."

I blink back my surprise and let out a short, nervous chuckle. "Okay. So these are happy tears?"

"They're fuck-off tears," she says fiercely as a tentative smile appears on her beautiful face. The tension melts away from her frame, and it's like I can physically feel the weight lifting off her. A knot in my chest I didn't even know was there loosens, too. She doesn't still harbor feelings for that asshole. Thank fuck. I will not examine too closely why that makes me so damn happy. I pull her more firmly into my arms and rub soothing circles on her back.

We stay like that for a long time as her tears slowly subside and her breathing evens out. I don't let myself think about how right she feels in my embrace. How much I want to keep holding her and never let go.

She lets out a watery chuckle. "Gosh, what was I thinking, wasting so much time on him?" She wipes at her eyes, straightening up and away from me. I reluctantly let her go.

"Hey, no judgment, remember? We all make mistakes." I tuck a strand of hair behind her ear. "But you're free now."

Rowena pulls further back and I feel the loss of her warmth in my bones. She rummages in her purse, fishing out a tissue to blow her nose. "Yes, I'm free." The words sound momentous. "I did the right thing, telling Liam about the baby. His reaction was horrible, but my conscience is clear now." She gazes at me, her eyes shining with newfound resolve. "The baby and I will be better off without him. That was always the case, but now it won't be because I lied or hid the truth. It's Liam's decision to walk away, not mine."

I nod, admiration ballooning inside me. "I'm proud of you, Sunshine."

She fully grins now. "Thanks, Bunny. I couldn't have done it without you."

"You would've managed just fine. But I'm glad I could be here for you." I glance toward the café, then back at her. "So, what do you want to do now? Still up for that coffee, or would you rather just go?"

Rowena's smile turns devilish. She reaches for the table, snatching up the two ten-dollar bills Liam dropped in his dramatic exit. "Oh, we're having coffee. It's on that asshole, after all."

I laugh. "That's the right attitude."

"Damn straight." She tucks the money into her pocket, then tilts her head. "What's your poison, Bunny? Let me guess, black coffee?"

I grin, shaking my head. "Cappuccino, actually. With a sprinkle of cinnamon, if they have it."

Her eyebrows lift in surprise. "Really? I pegged you for a straight-up espresso kind of guy."

"What can I say? I've got a sweet tooth."

"A sweet tooth, huh? Well, in that case, you can have all the sugar in the world." Her smile is blinding, it could send me flatlining.

"I'll hold you to that," I manage, and she grins.

"Be right back." She turns and heads into the coffee shop, an extra sway in her step.

I watch her go, my chest tight and expanded all at once. Pride, affection, admiration and something deeper, something I'm not quite ready to name, swirl inside me like a whirlwind.

* * *

That evening, I walk into the kitchen and almost backtrack at the sight of Rowena bent over the oven, pulling out a tray of mini quiches, her pert butt sticking up in the air. Instead, I freeze on the threshold, savoring the aroma of spinach and feta filling the air and the view.

I suck at keeping my distance. I haven't worked a single hour today. Just this morning I was helping her handle the train wreck with her ex, and now we're playing house prepping appetizers for a dinner party?

Rowena must sense my arrival because she peeks over her shoulder, saying, "These smell amazing."

Her hair is piled in a messy bun, a few errant curls framing her face, oven mitts dwarfing her delicate hands.

"One of Rosa's specialties," I reply, stepping into the kitchen and helping her transfer the golden pastries to a platter. A task so domestic I can hardly believe I'm a part of it. "Along with the stuffed mushrooms and bacon-wrapped dates."

"You weren't kidding about going all out." Rowena surveys the spread with an impressed whistle. "I hope my friends are hungry."

"About that..." I raise an eyebrow. "Remind me again why I'm subjecting myself to this inquisition?"

"Oh hush, they just want to meet you." She

swats me with an oven mitt. "Make sure your intentions are pure and all that."

"My intentions? I'm a perfect gentleman," I deadpan, earning an eye roll.

Truth is, my intentions are becoming less gentlemanly by the minute. Especially after our brief excursion this morning—the ex-boyfriend confrontation, the long, spontaneous walk home across the Brooklyn Bridge with the Manhattan skyline glittering in the distance. All it was missing for us to look like a full-fledged couple was to hold hands.

I'm in over my head, and I know it. Rowena has stormed past all my carefully crafted walls as if they were made of tissue paper.

"Well, the table's set, the wine's breathing, the food's ready..." She ticks off a mental checklist. "We're in good shape."

I follow her gaze to the living room table set for six.

"Why is your best friend bringing her boyfriend and her brother? Are they supposed to be the muscle in case I misbehave?" I muse, only half-joking.

"We're a tight-knit group." She side-steps the

question. A chime from the second oven timer saves her from having to elaborate.

I watch her bustle around the kitchen like she belongs here.

With me.

I shake off the dangerous thought and grab the platter of quiches. The sooner we get this dinner party started and over with, the better. Because right now, playing house with Rowena is feeling far too real—and far too tempting.

Rowena sets down a tray of crab cakes next to the quiches and turns to me, her head tilted quizzically. "Can I ask you something?"

She says it casually, but I'm afraid she's about to ask something deeply personal. I could say no, but there's no point in pretending we're not at least friends—if not already more.

"Sure." I nod, bracing myself.

"You said it'll just be your mom at the engagement party? What about your dad?"

I straighten the forks beside each plate, trying to sound casual. "He passed away a while ago."

But Rowena's too perceptive to miss the discomfort in my attitude. Her hand comes to rest on my arm, delicate and warm. "I'm sorry, Adrian. I didn't mean to pry."

I shrug, still not quite meeting her eyes. "It's fine. It was a long time ago."

She examines me intently, seeing right through my practiced nonchalance. "You don't have to tell me the story. But just so you know... I'm here to listen. You already know my deepest, darkest secrets, after meeting Liam. And I don't judge either."

I fiddle with the cutlery, my thoughts churning. She trusts me. I saw it this morning. And there's a part of me that desperately wants to reciprocate, to let her in.

But old habits die hard. I've spent years keeping people at a safe distance. Opening up, being vulnerable... it goes against every instinct I have.

Rowena seems to sense my internal struggle. She pats my arm, then steps back, giving me space. "No pressure, though. Just know the offer stands."

I nod, not trusting myself to speak. She's already seen more of the real me than anyone else has in a long, long time. But Rowena has been so open and honest with me. With a sigh, I decide to trust her back.

"Well, I'm an only child. And everything was pretty good early on—I had a happy childhood. But then when I was fourteen, my dad lost his job. After that, things got... difficult."

I stop fidgeting with the already perfect setting and stare at her, memories flooding back.

"He couldn't keep a job for long after that. He got bitter and angry. Kept saying the system was rigged against the common man, that regular people like us could never get ahead. Mom had to take on a second job, and we had to move to a smaller house." My chest tightens as I recall that stressful time. The guilt. "When I was ready to go to college, I was so torn. Even though I'd won a scholarship and knew getting a degree would help the family in the long run... part of me felt like I should stay home. Get a job to help Mom out, you know? It felt wrong leaving her."

Rowena steps closer and rubs a comforting hand on my arm. "Adrian, you shouldn't have felt guilty. Going to college was the right thing to do for yourself and your family."

"Maybe. I don't know." I shrug. "I took a bartending job while I was in school. Sent whatever money I could back home to Mom."

"Is that why you chose finance? Because of everything your family went through?" Rowena asks kindly.

"Yeah. I knew I wanted a high-paying career. Didn't have the stomach to be a surgeon or the time for law school. So banking it was. Even with my very first job out of college, I was making more than both of Mom's salaries combined. She could quit that second job. I thought my dad would be proud of me. I'd proved to him we could make it without outside help. What I didn't understand at the time is that the only thing I'd accomplished was to dispel the lies behind which he hid not to sort himself out. And he resented me for it. Besides growing more bitter over the years, he was also a proud man," I continue, pausing briefly as I gather my thoughts. "He flat-out refused to accept any of the money I tried to give him and Mom."

"I'm sorry, that must've been hard." Rowena sighs. "So what did you do?"

"I wanted her to leave him, but she never did." I let out a humorless chuckle. "I had to resort to secretly slipping cash to my mom whenever I could. She'd use it to pay the bills behind his back, put food on the table." My brows furrow at the memory. "Then when I was twenty-six, Dad passed away suddenly from a heart attack. Fifty years old."

"Oh, Adrian, I'm so sorry," Rowena says softly.

"It's okay. Honestly..." I don't know what compels me to admit a truth I've never said out loud to anyone. "When he died, part of me felt... relieved.

Like I could finally give Mom the life she deserved without his stubbornness and pride getting in the way. Move her out of that run-down house into a decent place."

I brace myself, waiting for Rowena to recoil in disgust at my admission. What kind of heartless son feels relief at his father's death? Instead, she wraps her arms around me, snuggling close.

"Adrian, I understand," she mutters against my shoulder. "You don't have to explain or justify how you felt. Emotions are complicated, especially in situations like those." Her words echo through me, soothing the gnawing guilt that's been my secret companion for years. I hug her back. "You're not heartless. You were looking out for your mom. Wanting her to have a better life doesn't make you a bad person." She draws back to watch me with such tenderness my chest feels like it's been hit with a sledgehammer. The sensation is unnerving and comforting at the same time. "Now I see why your career is so important to you. Your mom must be incredibly proud of you."

Emotion clogs my throat, but I force my vocal cords to cooperate. "Thanks. That... means a lot."

Just then, the doorbell chimes, startling us both. Her friends, if nothing else, have impeccable timing.

Another minute alone, and I'm not sure what other confessions I might've started making.

"I'll get it." She smiles, smoothing her hair down.

As I follow her to the door, I marvel at how easily she can read me. This fake engagement is getting more complicated by the minute. But as I watch Rowena greet her friends with warm hugs and uninhibited laughter, I'm in no rush for it to end.

Even if it means facing a few more uncomfortable truths along the way. Or a firing squad of worried friends—two of them juggernauts.

Rowena neglected to mention that the "guys" are a pair of six-foot-five giants who look capable of bench pressing a compact car—or tearing me apart limb from limb if they chose to.

Tonight is going to be so much fun.

24

ROWENA

A nervous thrill runs through me as I open the door, revealing Hunter, Nina, Tristan, and Dylan waiting on the front step. I want them to like Adrian. Despite telling myself I shouldn't, I am as anxious as if they were meeting my true boyfriend.

Adrian greets them warmly, but both him and my friends keep at a safe distance as if they are mutually studying each other.

I make the introductions. "Adrian, this is Hunter. Nina, her boyfriend, Tristan, and her brother, Dylan. Guys, this is Adrian."

There's an awkward pause as they size each other up. The air stills in my lungs as I pray for them to hit it off. After what feels like an eternity but is only seconds, Dylan breaks into an easy grin. "Great to meet you, man."

They shake hands, a firm grip that seems to break the ice, and Adrian responds with equal enthusiasm. "Likewise."

The initial tension dissolves into a round of handshakes and half-hugs that has me exhaling in relief as I usher everyone into the living room.

"The house looks amazing," Nina remarks as we head inside.

"Thanks! I can't really take credit, my designer did everything. But I'm happy with how it turned out." Adrian is being the perfect host—gracious, charming, putting everyone at ease.

As the others move forward, Adrian gently tugs me back. He edges in, his lips grazing the shell of my ear. "You didn't mention your friends are straight out of an NFL lineup," he whispers teasingly.

I smirk. "Actually, Dylan and Tristan are only NCAA-basketball tall. No big deal. They won't tackle you."

Adrian shakes his head as he gestures for me to please proceed ahead. We join the others at the beautifully set table, and I hope the get-together will be as smooth as the place settings.

As we pass around the plates of appetizers, an

awkward silence falls over the room. Nina and Tristan exchange a glance. Hunter drums her fingers against her wine glass. I rack my brain for a conversation starter.

Adrian wipes his mouth before asking, "So, how do you all know each other?"

"We met in college," Hunter says. "On a tragic Halloween night where we all ended up ditched by our dates, soaked in a diner, and wearing the same Elle Woods costume." She sighs, looking at us. "It was love at first sight."

"I think I saw a picture." Adrian smirks at me. "Nice costumes."

I flush, remembering how I'd abandoned my office stuff in his car because I couldn't cope yet. And how candidly he told me he'd snooped through it.

"We all used to live together," Nina adds. "Until, well, recent events."

I want to avoid the fake marriage topic, so I deflect. "You mean since you moved in with that guy." I point at Tristan. "And Dylan leaped at the chance to turn my old room into a home office, right?"

Dylan grins. "Guilty as charged. And the company's not bad either." Dylan shoots a sly look at Hunter, who suddenly seems very interested in her

salad. I hide a smile behind my glass of non-alco-
holic cider. If Dylan only knew about Hunter's not-
so-secret crush on him. Nina's brother turns to his
old roommate. "Sure better than living with him."
Dylan throws bed crumbs at Tristan, who blocks the
flying projectiles with his hand.

One flies straight at Adrian's nose. Without
flinching, Adrian picks it up and tosses it right back
at Dylan.

Laughter erupts around the table, a welcome
reprieve from the earlier tension. Dylan pretends to
be outraged, his hand over his heart in mock hurt.
"Man, you've got some arm there. Did you play any
sports?"

Adrian grins and leans back in his chair. "Varsity
baseball, but I gave that up in college because I
didn't have time for athletics." He shoots me a look,
and I know that he's referring to him wanting a job
to send money home.

Knowing I'm the only person in the room—
probably the only person in his life—that can understand him from just that one look fills me up
with rainbows.

Adrian smiles and turns back to Dylan. "Rowena
told me you two played basketball in the NCAA?"

Once the topic is moved on to sports and Dylan

and Tristan recount the epic tale of how they won the national championship their senior year, the conversation flows more easily. They move from sports to other topics. Tristan talks business with Adrian, while Hunter and I subtly interrogate Nina on how she finds living together with a boyfriend for the first time.

As we listen to her loved-up tale, I feel a twinge of... something. I wouldn't call it envy, more like a wistful curiosity.

I glance subtly at Adrian, who's now animatedly discussing some tech start-up with Tristan. He turns my way as if sensing my gaze on him and gives me a quick nod of encouragement. *We've got this*, he seems to say.

I nod back and he returns to his conversation, leaving me in a cozy tangle of emotions: warmed that the night is going so well, that he fits in my world, but still unsatisfied. Hopeful at the same time as doubtful. Reassured yet vulnerable. Comforted but also longing for more.

If this is what being his fake girlfriend feels like, I can't imagine what the real thing would do to me. And in a moment of sudden clarity, it dawns on me that I'd be more excited than scared to find out.

When the time comes to say goodbye to my

friends, I discreetly walk them out onto the landing, closing the front door behind me so we can talk without being overheard by Adrian.

"What do you think?" I whisper.

There's a general murmur of praise for Adrian, but then Nina walks toward me with an expression I can't read. "He's a great guy," she says, then she hugs me tight. "Just not *your* great guy. Don't get confused, honey." She pulls back, staring at me. "Promise?"

I nod, feeling strangled. I walk them to the elevator and once they're gone, weariness takes me over. I'm suddenly bone tired.

I get back into the house where Adrian is clearing the table. When he sees me, he drops the plates he's moving into the kitchen sink and folds his arms over his chest. "Did I pass the test?"

Despite myself, I smile. For some inexplicable reason, I can't keep sad around him. "With flying colors and you know it."

"We're pleased you were satisfied with our service." Adrian detaches from the counter and follows me into the dining room, brushing past me. He picks up the last of the dessert plates. His voice is playful yet earnest as he glances my way. "Tell me where I should leave the tip jar."

The moment he mentions tipping, I get a mental image of him dancing shirtless in low-hanging leather pants and me sticking one-dollar bills down the waistband of his boxer briefs.

Good thing he's already heading the opposite way and doesn't catch the ferocious blush on my cheeks.

He comes back from the kitchen five seconds later, flipping off the lights. "Ready to call it a night, Sunshine? It's been a long day."

I nod. Even if, when he looks at me like that—his gaze lingering on me, thick with unvoiced thoughts—and calls me Sunshine with his sexy, raspy voice, I don't feel tired anymore. In fact, adrenaline pumps through me as we walk down the hall to our separate rooms.

And as we say goodnight, shutting our doors on another day, I wonder what he'd do if I knocked back on his door. Would he laugh in my face or take me into his arms until I dissolved into a world made only of us?

25

ADRIAN

I'm scanning through the quarterly earnings report on my tablet, sipping a strong cup of heavily sugared coffee, when Rowena pads into the kitchen. The sight knocks me off balance as I take in her attire—if you can call it that. She's wearing a flimsy cotton slip, the thin fabric clinging to her curves and the hem barely reaching below her butt. My grip tightens on the tablet until my knuckles turn white.

"Morning," she mumbles, stifling a yawn as she gathers her tangled waves into a messy bun atop her head. The motion makes the hem of her slip ride even higher up her smooth thighs.

"Morning," I croak out, quickly averting my gaze back to the mind-numbing spreadsheets and charts on the screen. I need to focus on finishing this report. And it's safer not to let my eyes linger on my dangerously sexy fake fiancée.

But as Rowena putters around the kitchen, crooning to herself while she spoons yogurt and granola into a bowl, my traitorous senses stay acutely attuned to her every move. The clink of the spoon against ceramic. The gurgle of coffee pouring into a mug. And the padding of her bare feet on the tiles.

"Thanks for making coffee."

Rowena flashes me a sleepy smile. My heart thuds in response.

I grunt an acknowledgment, unable to muster actual words, still pretending to be engrossed in the financial data even as I track her in my peripheral vision. She settles into the chair next to me, her fruity scent and warmth permeating my space, scrambling my thoughts. I'm debating making an excuse to escape to my home office when my eyes flick over just as Rowena cups her breasts and starts massaging them through the thin fabric.

Holy fucking hell. All the blood rushes from my head in the opposite direction. And I'm pretty sure my bloodless brain short-circuits.

I can't pretend anymore. My eyes are glued to

the mesmerizing motion of her hands as they knead and caress her breasts. She makes these little sounds in her throat, somewhere between sighs and whimpers, that shoot straight to my groin. I'm simultaneously horrified and aroused, knowing I shouldn't be watching but unable to look away.

"What are you doing?" I blurt out, my voice strangled.

Rowena turns to me, blinking innocently, as if she's not currently groping herself mere inches from me. "Pregnancy makes my boobs hurt," she says matter-of-factly. "My nipples have been hard and achy since I woke up. Touching them is the only thing that helps."

"Please stop talking," I beg, feeling heat crawl up my neck. I don't need the audio description as well as the visuals.

She frowns at me, perplexed. "You're the one who asked."

I nod jerkily, swallowing hard past the desert that has become my throat. "Can you please stop... handling yourself like that?" I meant to keep my tone even, but it comes out slightly desperate.

Her brow furrows. "Why?" She seems genuinely clueless as to how her actions are affecting me.

Frustration mingles with the pounding desire in

my veins. "Rowena, I'm a man with functioning eyes," I grit out. "You can't just parade around in next to nothing and start fondling yourself and making those little moans in front of me."

Her mouth drops open in outrage. "I wasn't moaning!"

As she processes the rest of my words, a slow, wondering smile spreads across her face. "You find me attractive." She sounds awed. A pause, then she clarifies unnecessarily, "Sexually, I mean."

She looks simultaneously amazed and delighted by this revelation, as if the thought had never occurred to her before. As if she didn't know she's the most beautiful, seductive woman I've ever seen. I can only nod mutely, not trusting my voice.

Rowena's smile brightens as if I just paid her the highest compliment. "Thank you." She looks me dead in the eye. "We should definitely have sex, then."

I nearly choke on air. Pinching the bridge of my nose, I say, "We should most definitely *not* have sex."

She takes a casual sip of her coffee, unbothered. "Hear me out."

I adjust my posture, ready to shut this ridiculous idea down, but she barrels on.

"I find you attractive, you find me attractive."

Again, she says this last part as if it's a novel concept. Wasn't she there at my boss's house when I basically groped her by the pool, or when I spooned her in bed? "And we agreed ours is a monogamous fake marriage, right? So technically, we can only sleep with each other." She ticks off her points on slender fingers. "You can't go to your secret sex dungeons while we're pretending to be committed."

I sputter indignantly. "For the last time, I do not frequent sex dungeons!"

Rowena waves a dismissive hand. "Semantics. The point is, it would be mutually beneficial to fool around a bit. And frankly, I'd like to enjoy sex again before my vagina is ripped apart like an over-ripe watermelon by this tiny human." She pats her belly affectionately.

Cringing, I hold up a hand. "I could have gone my whole life without that visual, thanks."

She shrugs, unrepentant. Then she pins me with a look, one brow arched. "So? What do you say? Wanna be fake spouses with benefits?"

"Absolutely not. We're not having sex." I purse my lips.

She frowns. "Why not? Is it because I'm pregnant? Everything still works fine down there. Better than fine, actually, with all the extra hormones, I'm basically horny all the time and—"

"Please stop talking," I beg, holding up a hand. "It has nothing to do with you being pregnant. It's because sex would complicate an already confused situation. We need clear boundaries."

"Ah." Her eyes narrow and she sets down her yogurt bowl with a clatter. "Got it. Message received, attractive but not *that* attractive." She stands abruptly, snatching up her mug.

"Rowena, that's not what I—"

"It's fine," she cuts me off, voice clipped. "I'm going to put on something more *decent*, since apparently my current attire is so repulsive to you."

She stomps off toward her bedroom. I drag a hand down my face, cursing under my breath. I handled that terribly. Pushing back my chair, I follow her, rapping my knuckles against her door.

"Rowena? Can we talk, please?"

Silence. Then the door flies open, revealing a still seething, still scantily dressed Rowena. Her cheeks are flushed from the argument, tendrils of hair escaping her bun, and damn if she doesn't look even more tempting all riled up. I want to run my thumbs along the arch of her collarbones and lower to—

Focus, West. "I'm sorry, I didn't wish to offend you. Believe me, I find you incredibly attractive. Sexy as hell, even. I just... I'm trying to maintain some self-control here." I scratch an imaginary itch on my arm. "Things are already complicated enough between us without adding sex into the mix."

She props a hand on her hip, glaring up at me. "Wow, a man exercising restraint around me, how flattering. Really living the dream over here."

I wince. "That's not what I meant. I'm just saying—"

"No, you know what? It's fine. I only want to sleep with a man who *can't* control himself around me, anyway. One who wants to rip my clothes off, consequences be damned." She gives a careless shrug. "You're off the hook. Don't worry, I won't proposition you again."

And with that, she slams the door in my face. I stand there blinking at the hardwood paneling, wondering how the hell I'm going to survive the next several months living with this maddening, intoxicating woman without losing my fucking mind.

26

ADRIAN

I'm hiding in my room on the bed, throwing a stress ball and catching it, feeling equally wise and stupid for having rejected her. The instinct to walk down the hall and do exactly what she asked—rip that damn slip off her golden skin and go feral on her— is so strong, I might have to lock myself in here. She accuses me of being too much in control, if only she knew my control is hanging by a thread so thin it could snap at any second. It nearly already fucking did over breakfast.

But it can't snap. And that's why, in the following days, I go back to avoiding Rowena as much as possible. I succeed in not seeing her at all until

Wednesday morning when a text message lands on my screen.

ROWENA

Can you meet me for lunch near your office?

Say no. I should say no. I'm definitely saying no. Instead, I type back a short:

ADRIAN

Why? Something happened?

ROWENA

No, I'm fine. I just need advice

Can't she go to her friends for advice? As if reading my mind, her reply comes in pronto.

ROWENA

Financial advice

I could tell her we can discuss it at home later, but we both know I won't be there until she's gone to sleep. And it might be better to talk while we're in a public space and not alone. At least she'll be dressed and hopefully not touching herself, so I should be fine. I pick the most unromantic place I can think of near the office and text her the address.

* * *

I glance at my watch for the fourth time in ten minutes as Dominic drones on about tightening our risk management parameters. The numbers and projections blur together in my mind, overshadowed by thoughts of Rowena waiting for me at the restaurant, and me being late, letting her down, which will happen soon if Dominic doesn't wrap this up.

"Am I boring you, Adrian?" Dominic's sharp voice cuts through my distraction. "Got somewhere else you'd rather be?"

I snap my attention back to my boss, an apologetic smile plastered on my face. "Sorry, Dominic. I'm supposed to meet Rowena for lunch in ten minutes, but if you need me to stay I can reschedule..."

A knowing grin spreads across the old man's face, his eyes twinkling with mischief. "Ah, yes, your beautiful fiancée. Far be it from me to keep you from her enchanting company. We can finish this later."

Relief washes over me as I rise from my seat.

"Thanks, Dominic. I shouldn't be gone more than an hour."

"Of course, of course. Enjoy your lunch, no hurry. And give my regards to the lovely Rowena."

I nod gratefully and make a beeline for the door. A long ride down in the elevator, and the stuffy office air gives way to the bright July sunshine as I step outside, shrugging off my suit jacket. The heat is oppressive, but it does little to dampen my spirits. At the mere idea of seeing her, I feel instantly better than I've felt in the past three days avoiding her.

The restaurant I picked is one of those sterile, upscale places frequented by bankers and businessmen, all sleek lines and minimalist décor. Definitely nothing intimate about this place. But as the hostess leads me to the outdoor courtyard, a sharp, unexpected tension seizes my muscles. There, at a table bathed in sunlight, sits Rowena, a vision in a flowy lilac sundress. Her hair is half up, half down, the soft tendrils framing her face like a halo with the sun casting a golden glow on her skin.

My choice of a sterile place is already proving futile. She could be sitting in a pigsty, and she'd still transform it into a paradise.

"Hey," I greet her with a tentative grin, drinking in the sight of her. "Thanks for waiting."

Rowena looks up at me, her eyes drifting away almost immediately with an emotion I can't quite decipher. "Of course. I'm glad you could make it. Thank you for coming." She sounds more formal than I'm used to. Not the easy vibe we'd been having before Sunday's we're-not-having-sex gate.

I reach for the menu as Rowena fidgets with her napkin, but before I can even flip it open, she blurts out, "Adrian, I need to apologize for Sunday morning."

Heat creeps down my spine, and I lower the menu, meeting her earnest gaze. "Oh?"

"I know that servicing me sexually isn't part of our deal," she continues, her cheeks flushing an adorable shade of pink as she fumbles with her hands. "I shouldn't have propositioned you like that."

In my peripheral vision, I catch a server approaching our table, only to do a one-eighty upon hearing Rowena's words. Despite the awkwardness of the situation, I chuckle. "Well, now you've traumatized that poor server."

Rowena's eyes widen, and she covers her mouth with her hand. When she lowers it, her smile is genuine, most of the strain gone, and I swear the summer sun pales compared to her beauty. "Oh my gosh, I can't believe I just said that out loud!"

"Hey, no worries," I assure her. "It's all good. I'm sorry I wasn't—"

She interrupts me with a raised hand. "Please, can we never speak of it, like, ever again?"

I nod, suppressing a smirk. "I'm just glad that we can move past it."

She nods, visibly relieved. "Me too."

As we place our orders with the slightly flustered server, I wonder what else Rowena has on her mind. She seems nervous, almost uncertain, and I wish to put her at ease.

Once our food arrives, Rowena picks up her fork, then sets it down and says, "So, the reason I asked you to meet me today is that I need your advice to plan for the future."

I lean forward. "I'm all ears. What's on your mind?"

She takes a bite of her caprese salad, letting out a soft moan of delight that stirs something primal and deep-seated within me. I brush an invisible speck of dust off my sleeve, trying to focus on what she's saying and not the enticing way her lips wrap around the silver fork.

"So after I finished everything on Sophie's massive to-do list for the engagement party and wedding planning." Rowena gestures animatedly with a cherry tomato speared on her fork. "I found myself just... sitting there in your house. Alone. With nothing to do." She pops the tomato in her mouth and chews thoughtfully. "And now that the morning sickness has mostly passed, I'm feeling restless, you know?" She takes a sip of sparkling water, the bubbles fizzing. "I've already read all the guides on the first trimester—it feels like tempting fate to peek ahead. And it's way too early to start on the nursery..."

Rowena trails off, sighing wistfully. She takes another big, appreciative bite of her mozzarella and lets out a little hum from the back of her throat. Jeez. How can eating a salad be so sexy? I mentally shake myself.

"So in short, I'm bored out of my skull and in desperate need of career advice from my brilliant fake fiancé."

She grins at me, eyes sparkling with a hint of... flirtation? No, surely, I'm imagining that. We've just closed that door. I force myself to ignore the way my pulse picks up at her proximity. I'm supposed to be giving sage counsel, not ogling her like a barbarian.

But damn if those little food-gasms aren't killing me by degrees.

I drum my fingers on the table. "What exactly about your career?"

"Well, I've been thinking a lot about what I want to do with my life after we..." She hesitates. "You know, get divorced."

Her casual mention of our divorce stings for no valid reason. Heck, I haven't even married her yet. So why the fuck do I feel like this? "Of course," I say as diplomatically as I can. "What are you thinking? Are you considering going back to software programming? Or something else?"

Rowena tilts her head, a strand of her silky hair falling across her face. "Yes and no. I mean, it's the only valuable skill I have, but..." She trails off, her eyes filled with uncertainty.

I want to tell her she has an abundance of valuable skills, that she's one of the most brilliant women I've met, but after the awkwardness of Sunday morning, I hold back. I don't want to lead her on or create any more ground for misunderstandings. Instead, I nod, encouraging her to continue.

"The thing is, even if I got a job like my old one or got a promotion, the salary wouldn't be enough to raise a child alone in New York City. I've run the numbers, and it's just not feasible." Rowena's voice wavers, and my heart aches for her.

"Rowena, you'll always have my support. The alimony—"

She cuts me off delicately, her hand resting on mine. "I know, Adrian, and I'm so grateful for that. But at some point, I want to be independent again, to stand on my own two feet. And I just don't see that happening with a job like my old one."

Her touch sends electricity coursing through my veins. I remain still, paralyzed by a prehistoric freeze response. I barely have enough motility to move my mouth and respond. "I understand completely. So, what other options are you considering?"

Rowena leans back in her chair, her brow furrowed in contemplation. "That's just it. I don't know. I'm at a crossroads, and I have no idea which path to take. I was hoping you might have some insights or advice. Is my only option to move somewhere cheaper? How do I make more money to stay in New York?"

If there's one thing I'm good at discussing, it's money and how to make more of it. I wipe my mouth with the napkin, giving myself a moment to think. I want to help her pursue her dreams without sacrificing her financial stability.

"Well, if a higher salary is the main concern, you could always apply to more established companies, banks or larger corporations with software development departments. They pay better than fintech start-ups like the one you were working at."

As soon as the words leave my mouth, I notice a flicker of disappointment in Rowena's eyes, a bit of her light dimming. I study her closely. "But something tells me that's not a path you'd enjoy."

She shakes her head, a wistful smile on her lips. "No, you're right. In my old job, I felt like it was sucking my soul away, bit by bit, every single day. I can't imagine going back to that, especially not in a more rigid corporate environment. I'll be alone raising a kid; I'm going to need flexible hours on top of a higher pay." She grimaces. "Easy, right?"

I lean forward, my eyes locked on hers. "Then don't go back to a job you hated."

Her eyebrows raise. "But how?"

I let air fill my lungs, knowing that what I'm about to suggest might sound unconventional. "I want you to forget about money for a moment. If salary wasn't a factor, what would you do? What's your dream job?"

Rowena bites her lip, hesitating. "I... I don't know."

"Close your eyes," I instruct her, my voice gentle. "Try to picture it."

As she lets her eyelids flutter shut, a dreamy expression settles on her face, and I'm struck by the sudden, overwhelming urge to lean across the table and kiss her. The desire is so strong that I have to grip the edge of the table and snap my thoughts back to her conundrum. I'm here to help not ogle.

"Imagine your ideal career, Rowena. What does it look like?"

A smile plays at the corners of her mouth as she speaks, her voice soft and wistful. "For starters, I'm my own boss."

"That's great. So you want to be an entrepreneur." I smile back like a fool. "Any field or products in your dream pipeline?"

She scrunches her face even more adorably. "I've always dreamed of helping young girls get into coding."

"What about boys? Don't they deserve that too?"

She squints one eye open, fixing me with a playful glare. "Yes, of course they do. But in my dream, I'm building this pink, girly console designed to appeal to young girls. It's my vision, and if a camouflage console for early boy coders isn't included, you'll just have to deal with it. Plus, boys need little encouragement to pursue careers in tech."

Her sassiness makes me chuckle, and I hold up my hands in mock surrender. "Fair enough. Your dream, your rules."

As Rowena opens both eyes, excitement is dancing in their depths, gears turning in her brilliant brain.

I lean forward, resting my elbows on the table. "If you're serious about making coding toys for kids, there's one crucial thing to keep in mind from a business perspective."

She tilts her head, curiosity etched on her face. "What's that?"

"To succeed in a niche market, you need to either be first, which might be already too late, or you need to be better than the competition."

Rowena's smile is a burst of sunshine, warm and radiant. "Be better," she repeats, her eyes set with determination. "I like the sound of that. How do I get to be better?"

"Can't tell you that. It's where your technical expertise comes in," I continue. "But the usual strategy is to look at the coding products currently on the market. Read the reviews, see what people are complaining about. Heck, go out and buy all the top competitor toys, play with them yourself, and figure out what you'd change, what you could improve."

She nods, absorbing my words like a sponge. Then, a mischievous grin spreads across her face. "You know, usually when a guy tells his fiancée to go shopping for toys, he means—"

I hold up my hands as a shield, cutting her off before she can finish that thought. "Please, don't even go there."

"Too soon?" Rowena mimes zipping her lips, her eyes twinkling. "Fine, fine. I promise you'll never hear the word 'sex' from me ever again."

I groan inwardly, because damn it, sex with her is still all I can think about after Sunday. If I'm being honest with myself, it's been on my mind even before that.

The server providentially appears with our check, and I automatically reach for my wallet, only to realize that I don't have it. I pat my pockets, confusion turning into understanding. "I don't have my wallet." I must have left it in my office as I came straight from Dominic's. "Do you have the credit card I gave you for expenses?"

"Sure, I've been meaning to inaugurate it eventually anyway," Rowena chirps as she pulls out the sleek black card from her wallet.

My eyes widen in surprise. "Wait, you haven't used it yet?"

She shakes her head. "No, Rosa handles all the grocery shopping, and you gave Sophie your details for the party expenses. My clothes still fit. I just haven't needed to use it yet."

I lean back in my chair, stunned. That Rowena hasn't touched the credit card at all in the nearly three weeks we've been living together, hasn't spent a single penny despite having free rein, throws me for a loop. It destabilizes my resolve to keep my distance, to remember that this is just a quid pro quo.

Rationally, I know she agreed to this deal for the money—but it's clearly not about that for her. She's not some gold-digger out to bleed me dry—or even take a little advantage. No, Rowena is an incredible woman who found herself backed into a corner, devoid of other options. And I've always known that, deep down.

But with each passing day, I discover new facets of her that make me like her a little more. And if I'm brutally honest with myself, it's not even just a purely sexual attraction at this point, though hell knows I'm so hung-up on her it physically hurts.

No, what I feel for Rowena runs under the skin and terrifies me. It's like nothing I've ever experienced before, and a part of me fears that exploring it could lead to my undoing.

The real kicker? I have no clue what she feels for me in return. Is it simply physical attraction on her end? Could there be something more between us?

I desperately want to ask, but I stop myself from broaching the subject. I can't go hot and cold on her like this. I said no to exploring anything different from a business arrangement only three days ago, and I must stick to it. Because either way, pursuing something real with Rowena is strictly off-limits. We can't go down that road, no matter how badly I may want to. I know what's at the end: disappointed expectations, resentment, bitterness...

But damn, what I wouldn't give to discover what's in her heart...

27

ROWENA

Ten weeks pregnant

I sign the lunch bill with a flourish, feeling very Carrie Bradshaw. Just as I snap my wallet shut, my phone buzzes with an incoming text. It's from Nina, asking if I'm still down to spend the long weekend at her parents' house.

I look up from the screen to stare at Adrian. "Do we have plans for the Fourth?"

He cocks an eyebrow. "Plans?"

Oh my gosh, now he probably thinks I'm trying to cling to him. "Yeah, like do you have any work commitments or an appearance you need to make with your boss?"

Adrian shakes his head, his chiseled jaw catching the sunlight streaming through the tree branches overhead. "No, we're good. The next event with Dominic is not for another three weeks."

"Oh, okay. Because I'd forgotten Nina had invited me to go to her parents' house, we're all going..." Should I invite him to come? Would he want to? "What about you, any fun plans for the long weekend?" I ask breezily, hoping I sound casual and not desperately fishing.

"I'm visiting my mom upstate."

"Oh, that's nice," I reply, trying to keep the disappointment out of my voice. The silence grows more awkward as I wait for him to break it. To invite me along. To ask me if I want to join him instead of going to Nina's... But Adrian just smiles politely and takes a sip of his water.

Of course he doesn't ask me to go, I scold myself silently. Seeing his mom is not a work event, so no need to parade the fake fiancée around. And unless he absolutely has to, Adrian is not interested in spending extra time with me. He made that crystal clear on Sunday morning when I clumsily threw myself at him and he firmly shut it down.

Nina's words after they met float into my mind: *He's a great guy... Just not your great guy.*

And she's right, as much as I hate to admit it. Yes, Adrian is giving me financial advice and even came with me to confront my toxic ex. He's an amazing friend.

But that's all he wants to be—just friends, or supportive roommates. A "mutually beneficial business arrangement," to use his words. Nothing more. I need to get that through my hormone-addled brain already and stop hoping for something that's never going to happen.

A pang of longing lodges in my throat. I hope Adrian can't see it as I plaster on a bright smile and text Nina back that I'm in for a besties weekend lounging by her parents' pool...

Fake thirty-two-teeth grin still in place, I turn to Adrian again. "All settled. I'm leaving tonight."

"Yeah, me too, I'll go straight from the office."

Would he have even told me he was going if I hadn't invited him to lunch? Or would he just have been gone for four days with no warning? To be fair, he was probably just embarrassed about Sunday. And Adrian doesn't owe me explanations on how or where he spends his time.

Whether he was going to tell me or not, the thought that I won't see him until Monday—or even later if he keeps up his ungodly schedule—plunges another little spear into my heart.

"I'm sure your mom will be thrilled to see you." This conversation is turning excruciatingly polite.

"Actually." Adrian seems oblivious to the wistful thoughts swirling in my head. "I'll use this weekend to let her know about our arrangement. Explain the whole fake marriage and pregnancy situation so she's not blindsided at the engagement party."

His words yank me firmly back to reality. Right. Our sham relationship.

Adrian leans forward, his dark eyes searching mine. "Have you told your parents? About the baby and everything?"

A flush creeps up my neck. "No, not yet. I was planning to do it this weekend, too." A lie, but one I should probably make come true. It's not like I can invite my parents straight to the wedding when I'll already be showing with no forewarning.

Picking at the tablecloth, I avoid his gaze. "I'll stick to the story we agreed on—pretend you're the father and we're getting married." The lies taste sour on my tongue. "I won't have them come out for the engagement party," I add hastily. "It's a long trip from Nebraska. Better to have them fly over only once for the actual wedding."

Adrian nods. "Makes sense. Whatever you think is best."

He stands. "Ready to head out? I should get back to the office."

"Sure." I gather my purse and follow him out of the courtyard through the bustling restaurant.

Outside, on the sunbaked sidewalk, Adrian turns to face me. "Well, have a great weekend with your friends." He flashes me a polite smile.

"You too," I reply flippantly, determined not to let him see how much his casual dismissal stings. "Enjoy your trip home."

As he strides away, an inexplicable tightness seizes my lungs. I want to call out, to tell him...

Tell him what exactly? That somewhere along the way, my stupid heart started wishing this pretend relationship was real? Yeah, that'd go over well.

Shaking my head at my foolishness, I call Sam to come pick me up instead, determined to go home and pack and forget all about handsome men who only want to be respectful to me.

* * *

The next day, I'm floating lazily on my back in the cool blue water of Nina's parents' pool, my oversized sunglasses shielding my eyes from the bright July sun. It's only been a few weeks since Adrian suddenly catapulted into my life, but already his absence leaves a hollow ache in my chest. Ridiculous, considering he's made it clear he wants nothing more than a strictly platonic friendship.

Still, I miss our playful banter on the rare occasions we bumped into each other at the house before I made it awkward or just existing in the same space as him. Somehow, he makes everything feel lighter, better.

"Hey party pooper, what's with the long face?"

I startle at the sound of Nina's voice. Lost in thought, I didn't notice her slipping into the pool with me. She splashes me playfully before swimming over, her blonde hair darkened by the water and slicked back from her face.

"Nothing, I'm fine," I lie, forcing a smile. "Just nervous about telling my parents about the baby, I guess."

Nina raises a skeptical eyebrow. But if she has doubts, she doesn't voice them. "You're calling them today?"

I avoid her probing green eyes. "Yep, I should go call them now and get it over with."

"I'm sure they'll be thrilled about the baby."

Nina gives me a tentative smile that tells me she's reading straight through the things I've left unsaid.

I give her a nod—a silent thanks for not forcing me to face my bullshit—and splash her back before hauling myself out of the pool and wrapping up in a soft towel. Water pools at my feet as I pad across the patio and into the house, phone in hand.

The call with my parents goes surprisingly well. Of course, me telling them I'm taking time off work to have a baby while in a stable relationship with a man who loves me and whom I'm marrying is easier to accept than if I'd told them I got fired, knocked up and left to fend for myself by my dickhead ex. After the initial shock wears off, Mom squeals about finally getting a grandchild while Dad is engrossed about meeting "this Adrian fellow." By the time we say goodbye, they're on board, eager to help in any way they can and booking their plane tickets for the wedding in September.

Wedding. The word sends a pang through my heart.

I end the call and reflexively check my messages, hoping against hope to see Adrian's name pop up. Even just a simple "Happy 4th" would lift my spirits at this point. But there's nothing, of course. I toss my phone on the couch and drag my hands through my wet hair, suppressing a frustrated scream. He doesn't owe me anything.

The rest of the long weekend drags by in a haze of forced smiles and half-hearted celebrations. Nina shoots me concerned glances when she thinks I'm not looking. I pretend everything is fine.

But nothing is fine, as evidenced by my plummeting mood when I return to New York and Adrian remains as scarce as ever over the next couple of nights. The penthouse echoes with emptiness. I've given up waiting up for him. If it weren't for his dirty cereal bowl in the sink each morning and the lingering scent of his cologne, I'd wonder if he still lived here at all.

At this rate, it seems the stupid engagement party next weekend will be the first time I'll lay eyes on my fake fiancé again. The irony is not lost on me as I curl up alone in my cold bed at night, the shadows on the ceiling my only company.

I've also stopped trying to get up before him. So, on Tuesday morning I'm still in bed half asleep at nine thirty, wallowing in apathy as I fidget with the engagement ring that I've put on because I'm *that* pathetic. An impulsive urge to yank it off and flush it down the toilet seizes me. But I don't, of course.

As if on cue, my phone pings with a reminder, jolting me out of my sulking.

Dress shopping with Sophie for the engagement party.

Great. Because that's what I need—to play pretend princess bride when my pride feels like it's been stomped on by a herd of elephants.

I drag myself out of bed with a groan, cursing my life choices as I get ready and bemoaning some more for the entire car ride downtown.

The upscale boutique is a dizzying whirlwind of sparkles and silk, a stark contrast to the storm clouds brewing in my head.

"Rowena, darling!" Sophie air kisses my cheeks, her megawatt smile blinding. "You look... tired. Late night?" She winks suggestively.

I force a weak smile. If only she knew the half of it. "Something like that."

"Well, nothing a virgin mimosa and the perfect dress can't fix!" She claps her hands, nodding at a waiting attendant who promptly appears with a tray of shimmering flutes.

I accept one gratefully, the cool citrusy liquid a small comfort as Sophie whisks me further inside, prattling on about designers and silhouettes. She holds up dress after dress for my inspection, but I can barely muster more than a half-hearted shrug at any of them. Each gown is gorgeous, but the churning mix of emotions raging inside me mutes any enthusiasm I might have had.

Longing. Rejection. Anger. Frustration. Want. They're all balled up in a tangled knot in my chest that makes me strangely vengeful toward a man who has done nothing to earn such a sentiment.

Sophie pauses, lowering the beaded monstrosity in her hands to eye me quizzically. "What's with the doom and gloom? This is your engagement party, not a funeral. What kind of dress are you looking for?"

I meet her gaze, lips pressed in a grim line as the swelling resentment boils over. "You know what, Sophie? I want a dress that would feel like a giant raised middle finger to an ex. One that would show him what he's missing out on and make him regret ever letting me go."

"So sexy as hell, if I'm reading the mood correctly?"

I let out the first genuine smile of the day. "You are."

The words taste like vindication on my tongue,

even if they're not entirely true. Because I can't tell her that the finger I want to raise is for the man who put a ring on it. The same man who wants nothing to do with me unless it's for show.

"Subtle, virginal sexy or in-your-face sexy?"

I smirk. "Let's go with the innocent but irresistible vibe."

The smile Sophie gives me in return is anything *but* innocent. "Adrian is going to lose his mind."

I down the rest of my mimosa in one long gulp, embracing the petty thrum of outrage pulsing through my veins. If Adrian wants to play the indifference game, fine. But I'm sure not going to make it easy for him.

I'll find a dress that'll blow his fucking mind. And when he sees what he's missing, he'll regret turning me down and disappearing on me.

If Adrian won't fight for... whatever this is between us, then I'll just have to fight harder.

And what better battleground than a party where he has to pretend he's in love with me.

28

ROWENA

Eleven weeks pregnant

I get the first proof of life from Adrian as a new text message flashes on my screen late on Thursday afternoon. I read the preview on the lock-screen without even picking up the phone.

ADRIAN

Hey. I just wanted to give you a heads up. Sam is picking up my mom tomorrow and won't be available to you in case you needed to go somewhere.

I drop the console in my hands to the floor. Over

the past couple of days, I've put my irrational, unjustified rage to productive use. After my revenge shopping on Tuesday, I left the fancy boutique and went to a massive toy store, buying every toy even vaguely related to coding I could find, and I've been testing them non-stop in my room since then.

I pick up the phone and type a quick reply.

ROWENA

Sure, no problem

Pettiness wafts off me in waves.

ADRIAN

I was wondering, if you're free tomorrow night, would you like to meet her? Have dinner together?

My heart soars, at least until the next text arrives and the poor organ plummets to the bottom of my ribcage.

ADRIAN

So it won't look like you just met each other on Saturday at the party

ROWENA

Makes sense. Do you want me to ask Rosa to make something special?

ADRIAN

No, thank you. I've already texted her. She knows what my mom likes

Right. Because his housekeeper knows him better than I do. I roll the bitter notion over in my brain. Adrian shouldn't be so pervasive in my thoughts. If he wants to ignore me, I should ignore him right back. Or at least not let him distract me from my console idea. He's the best at putting work first and I should do the same.

I nod to myself with this new resolution and resume testing my toys. I've already individuated a few key functionalities missing and ways to improve the teaching experience, making it more fun. And I'm only 15 to 20 per cent bitter that this brilliant strategy was Adrian's selfless suggestion.

* * *

The following evening, I stare at Rosa's neatly penned instructions—reheat at 375°F for fifteen minutes—as my mind races ahead to tonight's impending introduction. I'm about to meet Adrian's mom. My soon-to-be mother-in-law. The woman who birthed the man I'm about to marry... for purely financial reasons.

With a sigh, I slide the tray of lasagna into the oven, setting the timer. Just as I straighten up, my phone buzzes to life, Adrian's name flashing across the screen. My traitorous heart leaps in my chest. Fucker of an organ.

"Hey," I answer, aiming for casual and missing by a mile.

"Hey yourself," he replies, his voice a warm caress that sends tingles dancing down my spine. "Listen, I'm really sorry but I'm stuck at the office. I won't make it back before Mom arrives."

"Oh." My stomach performs an Olympic-worthy gymnastics routine. "So... I'll be meeting her alone?"

"I feel terrible springing this on you. I know it's awkward." He pauses and I can picture him rubbing the back of his neck, his brow furrowed with concern. "You sure you're okay with this?"

"Oh, totally." I lean against the kitchen counter for support. "I mean, what's there to be nervous about? It's just the woman who carried you in her womb for nine months, who loves you more than anyone else in the world, and who you recently informed that I, a complete stranger, will marry you for your money. No biggie!"

Adrian lets out a surprised laugh and the rich sound wraps around me like a boa constrictor. "Rowena, I promise it won't be that bad. Mom's pretty cool about the whole thing. She gets it."

"Right. Of course she does." I nod vigorously even though he can't see me. "I don't know why I should be worried. We'll be braiding each other's hair and gabbing about boy bands in no time."

"I'm sure. You only got one detail wrong." His tone is wry but I can hear the smile in his voice. "With my mom, it's more likely that she'll try to dye your hair some weird color and discuss that time she *met* a rock star in the seventies."

"And by 'met' you mean..."

"Things a son shouldn't know about his mother."

I laugh.

"But you'll see, it's like she lost thirty years overnight when my father passed, she's a completely different person now from the woman I knew growing up."

There's so much affection in his voice that I'm actually jealous of his mother. Could I sink any lower? But after what he told me about how his father was, I can also hear the small tangle of regret and guilt mixed in, so I try to lighten the mood with a joke. "Any woman who partied with rock stars in the seventies and lived to tell the tale has my utter respect."

"*One* rock star," Adrian specifies. "That I know of."

The line goes quiet on his side and the awkwardness of us not having spoken in over a week creeps back in. I break the stillness with a hesitant cough. "Well, I should go... get ready for my future mother-in-law's arrival and all that. See you when you get here?"

"Count on it." Another weighted pause. "And Rowena? Thank you for doing this. It means a lot to me. I have to go, see you in a few."

The line goes dead and I lower the phone, staring at the darkened screen. Adrian's words linger in my mind as I struggle to ignore the pesky fluttering in my chest.

The oven timer startles me out of my slippery thoughts awhile later. I grab a potholder and extract the bubbling lasagna, savoring the heavenly aroma of melted cheese and Italian spices. At least Rosa's culinary skills will allow me to eat all my stupid feelings tonight.

I'm just setting the garlic bread on the counter when the doorbell chimes, sending my heart racing into overdrive. I smooth my hair, breathing in and out slowly, and march to the front door.

When I swing it open, I'm stunned into momentary silence. The woman standing on the threshold is nothing like the matronly grandmother I'd imagined. Adrian's mom is tall and slender with a bob of straight hair, the top half a pearly natural white and the bottom half dyed midnight black. Her outfit is simple but stylish and she's rocking this vintage-chic vibe with a pair of oversized sunglasses perched on her head and wearing tight black pants and boots.

"You must be Rowena," she says, her tone friendly. "I'm Claire, Adrian's mother."

"It's wonderful to meet you," I manage, stepping back to let her inside. "Adrian is still at the office, but he should get home soon. Can I get you something to drink in the meantime?"

Claire's assessing gaze sweeps over me, and I fight the urge to fidget like an errant schoolgirl. "A glass of water, thank you. The air conditioning in the car parched me."

I smile. "Yeah. Sometimes I think Sam is preparing us for the next ice age. I've started carrying a cardigan just for our rides."

As I pour her water with unsteady hands, I can feel the weight of Claire's stare between my shoulder blades. The urge to fill the silence is overwhelming.

"I hope the ride was otherwise comfortable," I say inanely, handing her the glass.

"Yes, Adrian's cars are so fancy. I'll never get used to it." Claire takes a sip, her eyes never leaving mine. "And I wouldn't have missed this engagement party for the world. It's not every day one's only son gets married."

I almost swallow my tongue. "About that... I know the circumstances are unorthodox—"

Claire waves a dismissive hand. "No need to explain, my dear. Adrian has already filled me in on the details."

I blink at her, nonplussed. I'd expected disapproval, maybe even outright hostility. But this simple acceptance is even more unnerving.

Before I can plan a response, the front door swings

open and Adrian strides in, his tie loosened and his hair endearingly mussed. The moment he steps into the room, I unconsciously straighten my posture, then our eyes meet for the first time in over a week and the air between us shifts; it's subtle but undeniable.

He drops his gaze right away.

Coward, I want to scream.

"Mom." He crosses the room to embrace her. "I see you've met Rowena."

"Yes, indeed." Claire smiles, cat-like. "And I must say, darling, she's even lovelier than you described."

My cheeks heat at the compliment, and I summon a smile as if my fake fiancé hasn't ghosted me for the past two weeks—if you exclude our lunch last Wednesday. "Dinner's ready whenever you are."

Adrian looks at me again, his expression softening into something that makes my helpless heart tumble. "Smells delicious." He nods a silent thank you at me and turns to Claire, tucking her neatly against his side. "Hungry?"

"Starving."

They walk together into the dining room, making me feel almost like a third wheel.

But as we settle around the table, I feel more involved. Claire regales us with stories from Adrian's childhood, painting a picture of a precocious boy with a penchant for mischief and a heart of gold.

"He was always bringing home stray animals." She laughs, her eyes twinkling with fond memories. "I never knew what I'd find when I opened the front door. Puppies, kittens, even a baby squirrel once."

Adrian groans good-naturedly. "I couldn't help it," he defends himself. "They needed me."

Tender warmth unfurls in my chest at the thought of a young Adrian, but I also wonder if I'm the stray in this scenario that he brought home to rescue.

Catching the contemplative look on my face, he turns to me with a soft smile. "What about you, S—" He stops and he'd better not fucking dare to call me Sunshine. Adrian coughs. "Any childhood misadventures to share?"

I shrug. "Oh, you know. Just the usual stuff. Skinned knees, questionable fashion choices, the occasional ill-advised haircut."

"Oh. Do you have pictures?" Adrian smirks.

"Yes, but I'm not showing them to you."

"Darn." Adrian mock-pouts, the corners of his eyes crinkling in amusement. "And I was hoping for some grade-A blackmail material."

"You already have all the dirt you need."

Claire chuckles, her gaze bouncing between Adrian and me with the sharpness of a hawk. "You two seem to have a natural rapport. I mean, despite the situation. If I didn't know, I wouldn't be able to tell this is all make believe."

"It's not, Mom. I told you we've become friends."

Adrian's words sting and soothe simultaneously. I'm honored that he considers me his friend and hurt that it's just that. Being near him is a roller coaster of high and lows. I should get off the ride. But every time I reach the finish line, I go for another round instead. Am I repeating the same cycle I had with Liam, of being with a person who isn't good for me? No. With Adrian, it's different.

Because where Liam was manipulative, mean, and controlling, Adrian has been nothing other than kind, open, and supportive. In moments like this, I don't know if I should push things between us or follow his lead and pull away.

* * *

The next day, as I stare at my sexy dress hanging in our shared room at the beach resort where we're hosting the party, I decide I want to push.

29

ADRIAN

The warm, late afternoon sun envelops me as I stroll through the lush gardens of the Hamptons beach resort. Golden light glimmers off the ocean in the distance, creating a picturesque backdrop for our engagement party. Everything has to be perfect. My gaze rakes over the placement of tables and chairs, the elegant centerpieces bursting with white roses and calla lilies, checking that all is in order.

Rowena is still getting ready in our room while I handle the last-minute details out here. But even when she isn't nearby, she consumes my thoughts— the complexity of our connection, the undeniable pull between us, I can't seem to resist no matter how hard I try. Today, there will be no hiding from her, no escaping away to the office, nothing to keep my mind off her.

Sophie alerts me that the first guests are trickling in, and I station myself near the entrance to welcome them. Rowena should get here any minute, sharing the hosting duties with me. I'm equally impatient and reluctant for that moment to come.

Charles, a colleague from the London office, claps me on the back, startling me from my reverie. I paste on a grin.

"Charles, great to have you here. Grab a drink, the bar's open." I gesture toward the white-clothed tables where champagne glasses glitter in the sun.

More guests arrive in a steady stream—coworkers, clients, Rowena's group of friends. I make the rounds, shaking hands, engaging in small talk, but my eyes keep darting to the resort's doors. Where is she?

Then Rowena emerges, and the world stops spinning. She's a vision in a pale pink silk slip dress that clings to her in all the wrong places, the thin straps leaving her shoulders tantalizingly bare. The dress is so simple, so barely there, she's practically naked. My mouth goes cotton dry. I want to memorize every dip and swell of her body beneath that whisper of silk and at the same time, forget I ever saw her in it.

Keep your distance, I warn myself sternly. But then her eyes meet mine and she smiles, radiant and heart-stopping, and I wonder how I'm supposed to survive the night with her looking like that.

Rowena glides toward me, a sensual smile playing on her lips. As she reaches me, she slips her hand into mine, intertwining our fingers as if it were the most natural gesture in the world. I go rigid instead, struggling to maintain my composure, to remember how to breathe.

"You look beautiful." I force the words past the tightness in my throat, my voice rough.

"Thank you, Bunny." She looks at me from under her long lashes, eyes sparkling with an unknown purpose. "You clean up pretty well yourself."

Before I can reply, Dominic strides in. He greets us with a broad smile and a nod of approval. "Rowena, lovely as ever." He bows his head at her. "And Adrian, my star. I heard the Johnson deal went through flawlessly."

I give a confident shrug as if closing the new investors had cost me nothing. No matter that I've spent every awake minute of the last two weeks focused on securing the funds, lest my thoughts drift to the forbidden woman currently standing by my side.

But Dominic somehow sees straight through the bravado. He turns to Rowena. "I hope you didn't feel too abandoned while he was working late."

"Never. Adrian is always there when I need him." Rowena half presses herself into me, her hand coming to rest on my chest, a feather-light touch that sears through my linen shirt. My heart pounds beneath her palm. Can she feel it? "I've never felt less alone than since we got together. And I'm the same when I have a new project. I lose myself in my work. We understand each other in that way."

"Great, it's important to..."

The rest of Dominic's reply is lost on me because with Rowena pressing herself against my side, half-turned into me, I have a clear view of the rear of her dress—or rather, the lack thereof. The same two thin straps that curl over her shoulders cross once over her otherwise bare back, exposing an expanse of smooth, tempting skin. I exhale shakily, my fingers itching to trace the path of those silken strips of fabric, to unravel them and uncover the hidden treasures beneath.

Dominic clears his throat, a knowing glint in his eye. "Adrian? Did you hear me?"

I want to say yes, but my mind was wholly pre-occupied with thoughts of peeling Rowena's dress off her shoulders, of trailing my lips down her spine, and I've no idea what my boss asked.

Heat crawls up my neck. "Sorry, Dominic. What was that?"

He chuckles, shaking his head. "Never mind. We can discuss it later. If I had such a beautiful woman on my arm, I'd be distracted, too." With a wink, he excuses himself to get a drink.

I keep my arms firmly by my sides, clenching my hands into fists to stop myself from reaching for Rowena. She's already touching me enough for the both of us, her fingers now casually curling over my biceps. Is she doing it on purpose, or simply playing her part?

After our conversation two weeks ago, I thought we were clear on not confusing things. But I'm not a saint, and my self-control is wearing thin. Why is she torturing me so sweetly?

Whatever she's doing, it has to stop. I step away from her, putting some much-needed space between myself and her soft curves. The reprieve is short-lived as the photographer we hired for the event appears not a minute later, asking us to pose for a photo.

Rowena closes the gap between us once more, her hand cupping my face as her lips brush against my cheek. My blood simmers at the innocent yet maddening gesture. She's pushing me to my limits, and I suspect she knows it. That everything she's doing is deliberate.

Once everyone has arrived, I slip away to get a strong drink, desperate to calm my frayed nerves. But as I down the amber liquid, I still sense the inevitability of her pull. The urge to be close to her.

Even if I had the strength to stay away today, I couldn't do it because we have to pretend we're a happy couple. At least, that's the excuse I give myself as I search for her in the sea of people again.

I find her talking to her friends, their laughter ringing out across the garden. There's a beautiful woman with them who I don't recognize. I greet them politely, and introduce myself to the stranger, Dylan's new girlfriend, it turns out.

Servers in crisp white uniforms bring forward trays of hors d'oeuvres, creating a distraction, and I steal Rowena away.

We move through the crowd together, her arm linked through mine, pulling me closer with every step. Desire battles with the need to maintain boundaries, a war raging inside me. As we chat with colleagues, Rowena's fingers find my shirt collar, gently straightening it. Each contact is a reminder of the attraction I'm trying to resist.

I'm losing the battle.

Excusing myself once more, I make a beeline for the bar. Another drink. Anything to dull the ache of wanting her. But even as the alcohol burns down my throat, I know it's futile. Rowena has me wrapped around her finger and all she has to do for me to unravel is pull a little harder.

As if she's heard me, I feel a prickle on my scalp a second before she sidles up to the bar. Her arm wraps around my lower back, turning my nervous system haywire. "Can you get me a virgin mimosa, Bunny?" she purrs, her breath tickling my neck.

I nod, barely able to focus on what I'm telling the bartender as I order her drink. Moments later, I hand Rowena her cocktail, grab some food, and sit at one of the many whitewashed tables with a few of my traders, hoping for a brief respite.

But my plan backfires when Sarah joins us and, immediately after, Rowena, noting the lack of extra chairs, settles into my lap, draping an arm over my neck as she sips her cocktail. The intimacy of the position drives me wild. I'm unhinged. As I attempt to keep up the conversation, Rowena plays with the hair at my nape, twirling it around her fingers. I close my eyes, briefly savoring the sensation even as I remind myself to stay in control.

The torture never ends. Rowena's hand trails over my shoulders, tracing patterns on my forearm. Each touch is a sweet agony, eroding my resistance a little further.

As the time for speeches and toasts approaches, I'm relieved I'll have to stand soon.

But just as I'm about to get to my feet, she tilts my chin up, forcing me to meet her gaze. "You've got this, Bunny," Rowena whispers, finally slinking off me.

With that simple encouragement, she sends me off to face the crowd, my body on fire. I shake my head to disperse the lust mist clouding my brain before I step up to the microphone, my voice steady despite the turmoil burning within me. As I speak, the words I've prepared about what a lucky guy I am to have found my missing half flow from my heart. And I'm not even sure where the fiction ends and the truth begins anymore. As I finish my toast, Rowena joins me on stage and, seemingly over-whelmed with emotion, she grabs the microphone and says, "What he just said."

Our guests laugh and clap. In response, she

drops her forehead on my chest, snuggling closer. To everyone watching, it must look like she's moved by my heartfelt speech.

I'm not sure what she's up to exactly, but I'm done pretending I don't crave whatever it is she wants to give me.

"Kiss her already!" someone in the crowd shouts, and my heart nearly stops.

Rowena's head snaps up. Our eyes lock. For a split second, a flicker of uncertainty dances across her irises, but then she gives me a tiny nod. Permission granted.

I lean down, brushing my lips against hers in a chaste kiss. The brief contact is not nearly enough, but it's all I can allow myself. But as I make to pull back, Rowena's arms wind around my neck, refusing to let go. She kisses me again—nothing chaste about it this time.

And that's when I lose it.

I tighten my grip on her waist, digging my fingers into her hips as I pull her impossibly closer, deepening the kiss. Her hands thread through my hair, tugging more frantically as our mouths grow more urgent, more insistent.

We are lost together, in a moment of absolute, unfiltered passion. Rowena's lips part beneath mine and I take the invitation, my tongue sweeping into her mouth to taste her fully. She tastes like the pineapple juice of her mimosas, sweet and intoxicating. Our breaths mingle, ragged and hot, as the kiss ignites.

Her body melts against mine. My hands roam her back, skimming the low edge of her silky dress —its plunging line not much higher than her tailbone. Her skin is warm under my fingertips even as she shudders. Rowena moans softly into my mouth, and the sound sends me spiraling. I forget we're standing in front of an audience full of people, my hunger for her insatiable.

All that exists is the taste of her, the way she fits in my arms. I'm lost, drowning and I never want to come up for air.

Catcalls and whistles finally break through the haze and someone shouts, "Get a room!"

We pull apart, both of us panting and wide-eyed. I stare at Rowena, shocked, marveling at the way she made me unravel—utterly, completely. She looks equally overwhelmed, but there's also a hint of smugness in her expression. That coyness makes me want to repay the teasing look with another kiss.

Thank fuck the moment is broken by a server announcing dinner is ready. The main meal is served in a different section of the resort, still facing the beach, but with elegantly decorated tables. The menu is a lavish affair, but I can barely taste the food. Rowena sits beside me, every accidental brush of limbs a distraction.

First she leans in, her fingers tracing the tense muscles of my shoulder. "You have a bit of lint," she breathes against my ear. She plucks at the invisible offender, her touch lingering longer than necessary.

I grind my teeth, trying to concentrate on the surrounding conversation, but it's impossible. Rowena's proximity is driving me to the edge, and after that kiss, I'm not sure how much longer I can hang on to the flimsy thread of self-discipline I got back.

All throughout the meal, she finds little ways to torment me. A whisper in my ear, a hand on my thigh under the table. Each touch is innocent enough, but the cumulative effect is maddening.

After dinner, the band strikes up a slow melody and couples drift to the spacious deck lit by string lights to dance. Rowena stands, holding out her hand to me. "Dance with me, Bunny?"

I hesitate, knowing that dancing with her is reckless insanity, but the stage is set. I take her hand and let her lead me onto the floor, my jaw working as she steps into my arms.

Rowena's hands slide up my chest, settling on my shoulders. She looks at me with those impossibly big eyes, a shy smile on her face. "I don't really know what to do."

Instinct takes over. I palm the small of her back, pulling her toward me, the startled gasp that escapes her lips my reward. With my other hand, I trail up her forearm, entwining our fingers. "Let me lead, then."

My darling fiancée swallows, suddenly not so smug anymore.

I lean forward, letting my voice hover just above a breath against her ear, "Don't worry, I'll be gentle."

She doesn't respond, but a tremble shakes her body.

Today Rowena started a risky game, and now I'm her willing pawn, captured into this match that can't have winners.

On my prompt, we sway to the music, our bodies pressed together. With every step, every touch, my resolve to keep away crumbles a little further. Halfway through the second song, I bury my face in her hair, inhaling the scent of her. I shouldn't let myself get caught up in the moment, but I'm helpless to stop.

When we step apart after a countless number of

songs, I'm a mess of tangled emotions. I want her so badly it hurts, but I can't have her. Not really. Not for long. My job is too demanding to allow space for a healthy relationship. And if Dominic picks me as his replacement, it'll only get worse. I can't do this to myself—not again. But especially, I can't do it to her.

But as Rowena slips her fingers into mine, leading me to the edge of the beach to watch the firework display, those thoughts fade into the distance. Her laughter rings out, clear and infectious, as the night sky explodes into a tapestry of color. Fireworks reflect in her wide eyes, as the guests ooh and ahh at the spectacle.

Rowena sidles in front of me, her bare back pressing against my torso as she shivers. "It's getting chilly." She reaches behind to grab my hands and wrap my arms around her waist. "Keep me warm."

My throat tightens as my body responds to her nearness, her touch, her scent. She fits perfectly against me, like she was made for me. I hold her close, relishing her warmth, even as I tell myself this is wrong—or too right.

The fireworks continue to burst overhead, but I barely notice. My focus on Rowena. The way she leans into me, the soft sigh that escapes her lips, the way her fingers lace with mine. It's all too much, too overwhelming, too real.

I'm teetering on the edge of a dangerous precipice, and if I'm not careful, I'll fall. Fall into a hole so deep I'll never be able to climb out.

The show ends, and, gradually, the guests disperse, heading back to the hotel or off to their own mansions. We linger on the beach; I'm reluctant to move, to break this spell we're under.

But then Rowena turns in my arms, her gaze on me almost challengingly. "Time for bed?"

I should say no. I should tell her to go ahead, that I'll join her soon and sleep on the sand instead, where it's safe. I should give myself a minute to clear my head, remember all the reasons this is a terrible idea. But when Rowena takes my hand, tugging me toward the hotel, I'm powerless to resist.

We reach our room and I close the door behind us. Rowena turns her back to me, reaching up to remove her earrings with a casualness that belies the tension crackling between us.

I watch her, transfixed by the dotted line of her spine. I want to reach out and lower those crossing strips, trace each knot with my fingertips, my lips, my tongue.

Something inside me snaps, the last threads of

my control fraying and breaking. I've fought this attraction for so long, denied myself what I want. But I won't fight it anymore. Not after tonight. Not after the way she's toyed with me, teased me, driven me to the brink of madness.

"You've been playing with me all day," I say, my voice thick with unspoken need.

Rowena meets my gaze in the mirror, her eyes dark and full of promise. And that's when I know I'm well and truly lost.

30

ROWENA

When we get to our room, I go in first, keeping my back to him. The door closes behind us with a sharp click.

I reach up to remove my earrings, trying to act casual, but inside, every nerve is buzzing.

I feel his eyes on me, a lick of flame on my back that's searing skin.

Tonight I've pushed his buttons, wanting to discover how far I could go before he snapped. And now, he's at his breaking point. I can sense it. The reckoning will all be mine. And I'm not sure if I should be thrilled or terrified.

"You've been playing with me all day." The accusation is rough.

I meet his gaze in the mirror, my eyes challenging, projecting a confidence I don't feel. I notice the struggle in his expression, the way he's holding back.

He undoes one of his shirt cuffs. No more skin than before is showing, but I still find the gesture incredibly erotic. His movements are slow and controlled. And I don't want him in control. I want to see him unleashed, however dangerous or unwise that desire might be.

I play dumb. "Have I?"

"You were all over me."

"I thought that was my part to play."

"Was it? You seemed pretty invested." Adrian moves on to his other cuff and raises an eyebrow at me. "Was it just for show or were you trying to get a rise out of me?"

"You've made it clear I *can't* get a rise out of you." I huff. "So, I don't see what the point of this conversation is."

"Come here," he tells me—*orders* me.

"Why?"

"Because now we're alone."

I don't move, still looking at him through the mirror. "Nothing to worry about then, you won't be *forced* to kiss me anymore."

When I don't go to him, he comes to me. Eyes dark, predatory. He drops his hands on my shoulders and spins me around, pulling me flush to his chest—one hand on my lower, exposed back, one tangling in my hair as he cups my nape. "No, this one is just for me." And then his mouth descends on mine.

Adrian's lips move with a raw urgency that makes my pulse thunder, every nerve in my body alive with a desperate, dizzying need.

A dam has burst, unleashing a flood of pent-up need. His mouth claims mine with such fierce urgency that it feels like he's drawing the very breath from my lungs, leaving me lightheaded and yearning for more.

I melt against him, my body melding to the hard planes of his chest as I lose myself in his kiss.

My head spins dizzily, unable to form a coherent thought beyond how amazing his lips feel moving over mine, how delicious he tastes. My entire being narrows to this single point of connection, electric currents zinging through my veins. I clutch at his shoulders, needing an anchor in this maelstrom of sensation threatening to sweep me away.

We break apart, gasping for air, chests heaving. But it's only a momentary reprieve. Like two magnets inexorably drawn together, our mouths find each other again, crashing in a tangle of lips and tongues and teeth. If the first kiss was an explosion, this one is an inferno, burning hot and bright, consuming everything in its path.

I pour every ounce of longing, every repressed flicker of want I've harbored these past weeks into the kiss, telling him without words how much I crave this, *him*. My fingers delve into his hair, tugging him to me in a claim of raw possessiveness I didn't even know I was capable of. He groans deep in his throat, the sound reverberating through me and igniting my nerve endings like a lit fuse. I gobble it, wanting more of these reactions for myself.

I nip at his bottom lip, dragging my teeth over it, sucking it into my mouth. The sound Adrian gives me in response is feral. And I relish it. Delight that I was the one to elicit such a reaction.

We stumble backward, still locked in our passionate embrace, until the backs of my legs hit the bed. Adrian tears his mouth away, chest heaving, pupils blown wide. He rakes his gaze over me, a slow, scorching caress that sets my skin alight.

"You have no idea," he rasps, voice rough with want, "how much torture it's been, seeing you in this dress all night. I've been dreaming of peeling it off you."

Acting on his words, he traces a fingertip along the thin strap on my shoulder, a barely there touch that has me breaking into goosebumps. With deliberate slowness, he eases the strap down, baring my skin to his heated stare. He dips his head, pressing a hot, open-mouthed kiss to the curve of my shoulder.

A whimper escapes me at the contact, the brush of his lips branding me. He lavishes attention on the sensitive spot, grazing with his teeth, soothing with his tongue. His reverence is at odds with the urgency from moments ago, each touch worshipful, achingly tender. Like he wants to memorize me with hands and mouth, imprint himself on my skin.

Emboldened, I reach for the buttons on his shirt. One by one, I slip them free, revealing a tantalizing slice of tanned skin and taut muscle. Adrian shudders as I push the fabric off his shoulders, his breath stuttering out on a groan when I run my palms over his chest, delighting in the warm, satiny smooth texture.

Unable to resist, I drag my nails lightly down the ridges of his abdomen, tracing the defined contours. The muscles of his stomach contract under my touch, and his control snaps again. With a low growl, he yanks me flush against him, sealing his mouth over mine in another wild, desperate kiss.

Behind my back, Adrian throws the covers away and lays me on the bed. The weight of him pressing me into the mattress is delicious, his body radiating heat, searing it into my already burning skin. My hands map the broad expanse of his back, learning the dips and planes of him, committing them to memory.

This is happening. After days of wanting and waiting, we're crossing that invisible line into uncharted territory. Exhilaration zings through my veins. I've imagined this moment countless times, but the reality blows every fantasy out of the water. Nothing could've prepared me for the sheer bliss of being in Adrian's arms.

I pour everything I'm feeling into the kiss—all the longing, the desire, the bone-deep yearning I've harbored. Adrian matches me breath for breath, touch for touch, the same desperation thrumming through him. There's no hesitation, no awkwardness like most first times. It's as if our bodies already know each other, like we were made to fit together just like this.

Everywhere he touches me, pleasure skitters across my nerve endings in bright sparks. I arch into him, craving more, needing to be closer. He obliges, aligning us so there's not an inch of space separating us. The delicious friction has me seeing stars behind my closed eyelids.

Adrian tears his mouth from mine to blaze a trail of feather-light kisses along my jaw, down the column of my throat. I tip my head back on a moan, my pulse jumping erratically beneath his lips. "Fuck, Rowena," he rasps against my skin, voice rough with want. "I've dreamed of this... of you... for so long."

"You should... have said... sooner," I manage breathlessly, dragging him back up to recapture his eyes with mine. "Why did you pretend you didn't want me?"

I almost don't recognize this woman who has the boldness to ask such questions.

Adrian puts all his weight on his elbows as he stares down at me. "I never said I didn't want you, only that this is going to turn messy. That we shouldn't do messy."

I caress the hair back from his face. "So what's changed?"

"I think you know." He drops his nose to mine, nuzzling, moving down my cheek to my neck, my ear. He drags my lobe between his teeth. "Everything you did tonight was a test to my resolve, and I failed. I'm not a saint."

Delicious as his butterfly kisses are, I cup his face and pull him up again. "I don't want a saint. I only want honest."

He rolls off me partly, staying closely pressed to my side. The shift in his eyes is clear; whatever self-control I had shattered, it's now reasserting itself.

Adrian grabs my hand and kisses my palm before interlacing our fingers. "Honest is that I've no idea what we're doing. You're pregnant and vulnerable and I don't want to take advantage of you." As I make to protest that I can make my own decisions, he presses a finger to my mouth. "Let me finish." I nod, and he lets go. "This thing we're about to do, won't be just sex. It'll complicate things, and I'm not relationship material." He anticipates my intention to argue again, silencing me with a look. "You might think you're okay with my crazy schedule at first, but in the long run, you won't be. Doing this tonight would mix things up"—he trails a finger down my sternum between my breasts over the silk of my dress down to my navel where he lays his palm flat—"for all three of us. Add that we'll be standing in front of a minister two months from now, vowing to love each other for the rest of our lives, and everything will be even more confused."

"W-what are you saying?"

"That I admire you and respect you and that I'm crazy attracted to you. But that I hope you understand it's with the utmost affection and consideration that I say we can't take this any further."

I smile despite the meaning of his words. I keep caressing the hair away from his face. "All that hard work, and then I ruin it by running my mouth. I should've taken you while you were in your lust haze."

He taps my nose. "Around you, I'm constantly in a lust haze."

"Nah, not anymore. I could undress now in front of you and you still wouldn't touch me." To demonstrate, I kneel on the bed next to him and lower the remaining strap of my dress. The silk flows down my torso, dropping to my waist. I'm not wearing a bra underneath.

Adrian's jaw snaps so tight, I'm afraid he might break a molar or two. His gaze is dark and intent as he follows my every move, but he keeps deadly still. I feel his eyes on me like a physical caress.

I lift up and shimmy out of the dress completely. I remove my strappy sandals next. From the floor, I collect Adrian's discarded linen shirt and pull it on.

He makes a strangled sort of noise that sounds like a cross between a groan and a whimper. "That's my shirt." There's a note of desperation in his voice that's almost funny.

Ignoring his comment, I button the shirt, leaving it open enough to be suggestive but closed enough to maintain a modicum of modesty. I straddle him next, but keep my thighs high so that we're not really touching. I undo his belt, unbutton his pants, and pull the zipper down. Throughout this, Adrian watches me, jaw tense, hands balled into fists at his sides.

I drag the pants down his legs and remove his shoes and socks, before pulling the trousers down completely. I stand at the foot of the bed and admire Adrian, in all his glorious semi-naked splendor. I can see he's not lying when he says he wants me.

I scoot back onto the mattress, settling down on my side to face him. "Now we're ready to sleep." I drop a soft kiss on his mouth. "Please hold me tonight."

I turn on my other side and curl up in a fetal position. There's a heartbeat of silence, then a heavy sigh as Adrian flicks off the lights and pulls the covers over us. For a short instant I'm afraid he's going to keep his distance, but then his arms pull me against him. One slides under my head as a sort of second pillow, the other protectively wraps over my waist.

There's still tension lingering between us. I'm keenly aware of every point where our bodies touch, the heat of him seeping into me. But also a different kind of warmth seeps in, soothing away the sparks of electrified air. His breathing is steady, a rhythm I sync with as the minutes tick by.

Sex or no sex, I'm already so far gone for this man that I wonder if I can find my way back. And I'm not sure I'd even want to.

31

ROWENA

I blink awake, my hand instinctively reaching across the sheets. Empty. My heart sinks. He's gone again. Adrian will probably go back to being a ghost, avoiding me at all costs. I pushed too hard.

I sag on the bed and facepalm myself. What got into me with the striptease? He must think I'm so desperate. And in a way, I am, because even now, I turn my chin and sniff the collar of his shirt that still smells like him—of a starry night.

The front door creaks open, and I let go of the shirt collar—caught in the act. Adrian strides in, gloriously shirtless and glistening with sweat, his T-shirt tucked into the back of his sporty shorts. I drink in the chiseled planes of his chest, the sculpted muscles of his abdomen. I prop myself up on my elbows to get a better view.

"I went for a run," he explains, still huffing as his eyes meet mine, unreadable.

"Oh. Good. That's... good," I stammer, flustered by his nearness, by memories of our bodies pressed close under the covers. Are we going to discuss last night?

He runs a hand through his damp hair, then looks away. "I'm gonna hop in the shower."

I guess not.

Adrian disappears into the bathroom, and as the shower turns on, I imagine rivulets of water sluicing over his naked skin, steam rising around his sexy, powerful body. Adrian with his head tilted backward as the jet hits his face, his hands lathering soap over his chest. I picture the way his eyebrows might draw together in concentration or relaxation—gah, what is wrong with me? I've turned into a full-blown preggo pervert. I blame the hormones.

My phone buzzes, jolting me out of the sensual fantasy. I grab it from the nightstand. A barrage of texts light up the screen—Nina and Hunter, demanding I meet them for breakfast. They also crashed at the resort after the engagement party.

Throwing back the covers, I pad to the bathroom door on shaky legs, still reeling from the intimate images playing through my head. I raise my hand to knock.

"Adrian?" I call out, trying to steady my voice.

The spray of water stops. "Yeah?" His deep baritone echoes from the other side of the door, rough and sexy.

"Um, Nina and Hunter want to meet up for breakfast, so I'm going to head down," I explain.

"Okay, sounds good," he replies easily. "I'll catch up with you later."

"Great. See you in a bit!" I wince at the overly bright tone. Could I be more awkward? Shaking my head, I regretfully slip his shirt off and throw on a sundress and sandals, determined to pull myself together. But as I leave the room, I throw one last glance at the bathroom door, wishing I was on the other side of it.

In the breakfast hall, I pile my plate high with fluffy pancakes drizzled in maple syrup and fresh berries. Perhaps I'm not eating my feelings but I'm definitely eating my lust. I spot Nina and Hunter at a table near the windows, overlooking the beach, and slide into the beachside chic chair—half wood, half rope—across from them with a carefree, "Hey."

I barely have a chance to dig in before they pounce.

"How were things in the honeymoon suite last night?" Nina asks too casually.

"Not a honeymoon suite," I deflect. "You're about two months early."

"Oh, come on. That kiss last night? You and Adrian set the sky on fire!"

Hunter nods emphatically. "Seriously, the fireworks had nothing on you two."

I squirm under their inquisitive stares, stuffing a forkful of pancake into my mouth to buy time. How can I explain the complexity of our evolving relationship when I barely understand it myself?

I shrug. "It was just for show. You know, keeping up appearances and all that."

Nina arches a disbelieving brow. "Riiiight. Because platonic fake-daters always kiss like they're reenacting the kiss-in-the-rain scene from *The Notebook*."

Hunter leans forward. "Are you sure the farce isn't running away from you?"

"Look, guys, I appreciate the concern, but I've got this under control," I assure them, even as my stomach twists—must be the metric ton of sugar I'm ingesting. "Nothing to worry about."

No matter my projected confidence, a traitorous voice whispers that I've already fallen deeper into this new life than I ever intended. Desperate to change the subject, I turn my attention to Hunter, noting the uncharacteristically blue circles under her eyes.

"Hey, you okay, Hunt? You seem a bit off today."

Hunter picks at her eggs, avoiding eye contact. "I'm fine, just tired. I've been having trouble sleeping lately."

Nina snorts. "Please. We all know it's because Dylan brought his new girlfriend last night. Probably has her over at your place often, too."

Hunter's head snaps up, eyes wide with shock. "How did you—"

"Oh, come on, babe. It's obvious you're into my brother," Nina says gently. "But he's clearly too blind to see what's right in front of him."

I nod in commiseration, secretly relieved that at least I don't have to witness Adrian with someone else—our monogamy clause a sudden, overwhelming relief. The thought of him bringing home another woman, of having to plaster on a smile while they *canoodle* just a drywall away... I shudder inwardly. Poor Hunter. I can only imagine how gut-wrenching that must be.

"Honestly, I give it two months tops," Nina declares, stabbing a sausage with unnecessary force. "Little Miss Perfect is not right for him. Even Tristan said so."

Hunter smiles weakly, but I can tell she's cheered by Nina's prediction. I'm about to add something encouraging when a shadow appears over the table. I recognize his scent before I even lift my gaze to look at Adrian. He asks us if we mind if he takes a seat, and of course, we reply not at all. He sits next to me, so close and yet so distant, making my brain short-circuit for the rest of breakfast, so much that I have to struggle to keep up with the conversation. The entire time, I'm hyperaware of his presence beside me—every movement, every breath throwing me off. It's a losing battle to stay focused, and by the time we say goodbye and head back to New York, I feel mentally drained.

* * *

As Adrian navigates the sleek Ferrari down the Long Island Expressway, only the purr of the engine fills the taut silence. After saying goodbye to his mom— Sam is driving Claire back to her home—we left early to beat the weekend traffic. Now, with nothing but open road ahead and a thousand unspoken words hanging in the air, I find myself second-guessing everything.

I steal a glance at his chiseled profile, the way his strong hands grip the steering wheel with quiet confidence. The same hands that held me so tenderly last night. He stares straight ahead, lost in thought.

I force my gaze back to the blur of passing scenery, mulling over the unexpected intimacy of the weekend. It should feel awkward. I barely know this man—we only met a month ago. And yet, being with him also feels oddly familiar. Comfortable. Right.

Adrian adjusts his grip on the wheel, but keeps quiet. My gut is full of tangled wires short-circuiting as I silently will him to speak, to say something, anything to break this deadlock. But he remains silent, eyes fixed ahead. The car vents hum, cool air washing over my bare legs. I shift uneasily, too unnerved to sit still.

Being with Adrian is a well of contradictions—thrilling and steadying, foreign and familiar, maddening and mesmerizing. When we're close, I'm constantly on edge, every nerve ending electrified and attuned to him. Yet there's also this inexplicable comfort, like coming home to a place where I never knew I belonged. It doesn't make logical sense. Then again, nothing about this bizarre situation does.

I chance another peek at him and find his eyes on me. Heat rises in my cheeks as he arches an eyebrow, the ghost of a smirk on his carved-from-a-dream face—and I'm talking the kind of sexy fantasy that would require a cold shower and a confessional. Busted. I glance away, pulse racing. That's where I keep my gaze for the rest of the journey—firmly ahead.

* * *

It's a relief and a disappointment when we pull into the underground garage of Adrian's building. I exhale slowly, bracing myself for his inevitable retreat, the wall of avoidance that always seems to slam down between us when there isn't a public engagement forcing us together.

As we step into the private elevator, Adrian turns to me, his expression cryptic. "I have a few emails to respond to," he begins, his voice gravelly. Here we go, now he'll say bye and disappear into his office forever. "But maybe later, we could watch a movie together? If you're not too tired."

I blink, taken aback by the unexpected offer. Oh, so he isn't planning to be MIA for a month. "Um, sure. That sounds nice."

His mouth twitches into a smile, gone as quickly as it appears. The elevator dings, and we enter the penthouse, the familiar surroundings doing little to ease the restless energy flowing in my veins.

I'm too tired to follow his lead and work on my toy console project—so far I've defined the improved functionalities, schematized the basic coding, but I still need to dig deeper into the specifications. Instead, I take a long bath, review my schedule for the week, noting a doctor's appointment I should tell Adrian about, and nap.

By evening, I'm waiting nervously on the couch, shuffling movies and wondering what Adrian enjoys watching. He emerges from his office ten minutes later, a drool-inducing vision in sweatpants and a tight white T-shirt.

He self-consciously passes a hand through his thick hair. "Still up for movie night?"

"Yeah. I'll make some popcorn," I offer, desperate for something to do with my hands. "You pick the movie?"

Adrian nods, already scrolling through the options on the massive flatscreen. I busy myself in the kitchen, the mundane task of popping kernels calming. By the time I return with a giant bowl of buttery goodness in my hands, he's settled on the couch, a Will Ferrell comedy queued up and ready to go.

I sink down beside him, careful to leave a respectable distance between us. But as the opening credits roll and the laughter begins, I inch closer, drawn to his solid warmth like a night-blooming flower to moonlight. We're not quite cuddling, but I savor every electrifying second of it.

When the movie ends, I tell him about the upcoming doctor's appointments.

"I have an ultrasound this week."

He raises an eyebrow at my out-of-the-blue declaration as if saying, *And you're telling me, why?*

"I made a calendar," I say, forwarding him the sheet I drafted on my phone. "Of all my check-ups and stuff. I figured you might need it, in case anyone asks about the baby and you want to appear... involved."

Adrian looks at his phone, his eyes scanning the dates and times. "Your next one is tomorrow," he notes, glancing up at me. "I'll go with you."

Pressure builds behind my ribcage. "You... you

want to come? I'm sure it's enough for you to know the basics for Dominic to..." I trail off under the narrowed focus of his stare.

He holds my gaze. "I'm coming."

The seed of hope I've been desperately trying to suppress blossoms like a rose in the desert, thriving where it shouldn't. He wants to be at my doctor's appointment. Why? What does it mean?

32

ADRIAN

I stare at my reflection in the full-length mirror as I button up my crisp white dress shirt. It's Monday morning and under normal circumstances, I'd be rushing out the door to make it to the weekly strategy briefing at the office. But today is different. Today, I'm skipping the meeting to accompany Rowena to her ultrasound appointment.

As I loop my blue silk tie around my neck, I rationalize my decision. Dominic has been clear that he wants a family man to take over the company when he retires. Missing work to accompany my pregnant fiancée to her doctor's appointment should score me some brownie points with the boss, right? It's the perfect excuse.

But deep down, that's not the real reason I'm doing this. After this weekend with Rowena, I'm a goner. Completely lost. Memories of our passionate kisses and the tantalizing way she undressed before me flash through my mind as I slide on my suit jacket. Even though we stopped short of taking things further, she has me under locks.

I'm not going to this appointment to impress Dominic or further my career. I'm going because I don't want her to have to do this alone. Because being near her, supporting her, has suddenly become the most important thing in my life. More vital than oxygen.

My entire world has shifted, and Rowena is now at the center of everything.

I check my reflection one more time, smoothing down an errant lock of hair, and, turning away from the mirror, I unplug my phone from its charger to send a quick text to Sarah.

ADRIAN

Sarah, I need you to take the lead in the strategy meeting today. I'm going to be late to the office

SARAH LOPEZ

Did someone die?

ADRIAN

No one died, I just have a personal matter to attend to

SARAH LOPEZ

Are you kidding me?

ADRIAN

No, I'm delegating to you

SARAH LOPEZ

OMG, then you're dying? Is it cancer?

ADRIAN

No one's dying

Or dead

SARAH LOPEZ

Stay strong. 81.2% is the average survival rate across various types of cancer when detected at an early stage

ADRIAN

Were you just carrying around that depressing statistic?

SARAH LOPEZ

No. I'm researching a new drug
for potential early investment

ADRIAN

Zylotrin?

SARAH LOPEZ

shocked-face emoji

How did you guess?

ADRIAN

cool-face emoji

I didn't guess. It's my job to know

Check the satellite imaging
surveillance of their research
facility parking lots, I smell smoke

SARAH LOPEZ

You scare me

ADRIAN

Make me proud at the meeting
today. If I get the top chair, you'll
be CIO

Then it'll be your job to know
these things

SARAH LOPEZ

Worry not, I'm going to whip those traders harder than a dominatrix in a sex dungeon

I smile, imagining the grief Rowena would dish at me if she read this message, and only type back:

ADRIAN

Now *you* scare me

I only get a smiley devil emoji in response.

Straightening my tie one last time, I compose myself and head out of my room to meet Rowena.

* * *

As Sam pulls up to the clinic entrance, I glance over at Rowena on the backseat beside me. She meets my gaze and gives me a small smile, eyes anxious as they crinkle at the edges with unspoken tension. I lean over, cupping her cheeks. "It's going to be fine," I whisper. "I'm right here with you."

She nods. "I know. Thank you for coming with me today, Adrian. It means a lot."

"Of course. There's nowhere else I'd rather be."

The words come out more earnest than I intended, revealing a deeper truth, but before I can dwell on it, Sam opens the car door for us.

The modern glass façade gleams in the morning sun, radiating a sense of sleek professionalism and efficiency. "Fancy." I try to lighten the mood. "Think they'll have cucumber water and those little sandwiches with the crusts cut off in the waiting room?"

Rowena laughs and bumps me with her shoulder. "No, sorry to crush your fancy snacks dreams. They only have vending machines."

Clinlada's doors swish open and, with a mock gallant bow, I gesture for Rowena to pass first.

The cool blast of air conditioning envelops us as we step inside, carrying the faint, astringent scent of antiseptic. I wrinkle my nose. I've never liked that medicinal hospital smell.

Rowena approaches the reception desk where a smiling woman greets her warmly and checks her in. I stand off to the side, hands shoved in my pockets, trying not to fidget. I don't know why I'm so nervous. It's not like I'm the one getting an ultrasound.

"The doctor will be right with you, dear," the receptionist says. "You can have a seat in the waiting area."

The receptionist points us to a row of blue padded chairs. I help Rowena sit with a hand under her elbow. There's no other word for it: I'm fussing. "Comfortable?"

She grins up at me. "Yep."

I settle into the chair next to her, our hands finding each other and interlacing almost on reflex, like it's the most natural thing in the world.

"So," I say after a moment. "Have any name ideas yet?"

Rowena smiles, a wistful, secretive grin. "A few. But I want to wait to decide until I meet them, you know? See what suits them."

I nod. "Makes sense. You wouldn't want to saddle the kid with a name like Elmo or Agnes still in the womb."

She laughs. "What if Elmo or Agnes were my top picks?"

I gape. "You wouldn't?"

Before she can respond, a nurse appears in the doorway with a clipboard. "Rowena Taylor?"

I stand, still holding Rowena's hand as I help her up. "Ready?" I ask, searching her face.

She nods, her fingers tightening around mine. "Ready. I can't wait for you to meet the baby."

The baby, but not *our* baby. Hers. The words ring in my head as we follow the nurse down the hall.

With every step closer to that ultrasound room, I wish things were different. That this were *my* baby. And I've never wanted kids.

The nurse leads us into a brightly lit room filled with unfamiliar equipment. A large screen dominates one wall, and in the center stands the examination table, complete with stirrups that cause my stomach to clench. Are those comfortable? Will Rowena have to undress? Maybe it was a mistake to tag along, I don't want to make her uncomfortable.

Rowena seems to sense my unease, giving my hand a last squeeze before letting go to greet the doctor. He's younger than I expected, with a friendly smile and a firm handshake. "Ms. Taylor, great to see you again." Turning to me, he adds, "I'm Dr. Raikes. And you must be the father-to-be?"

I start to correct him, but Rowena beats me to it. "This is Adrian, my..." She hesitates, glancing at me uncertainly.

"Partner," I finish for her, the word feeling right as it leaves my mouth. "I'm her partner."

Dr. Raikes nods, unfazed. "Nice to meet you, Adrian. Rowena if you could lie down and lift your shirt for me."

As Rowena settles onto the bed, I hover nearby, unsure of my role. Dr. Raikes must notice my nervous energy because he gestures to a chair beside the bed. "Why don't you have a seat right here? You'll have a perfect view of the screen."

As I sink into the chair, Rowena reaches for my hand again.

Dr. Raikes explains the NT scan procedure, his voice calm and reassuring. "We'll be using ultrasound to measure the fluid at the back of the baby's neck. This, along with a blood test, helps us assess the likelihood of certain chromosomal conditions."

I nod, trying to take it all in, but my mind is racing. Chromosomal conditions? Risks. Today isn't just a cute photo opportunity. It's about the health and future of the baby. Of Rowena. Their lives could be crushed today—mine too.

As if sensing the direction of my thoughts, Rowena catches my eye, her gaze steady and sure. "It's going to be okay," she mouths silently. I'm supposed to be the one helping here, and instead, I'm the one needing encouragement.

I press my lips together, vowing to keep my cool and not become another thing she has to worry about.

Dr. Raikes squirts gel onto Rowena's belly and

she inhales sharply. I watch in fascination as the doctor places the probe on her skin, moving it in slow, deliberate strokes.

A grainy, black-and-white image flickers to life on the screen. I stare in awe at the curve of a head, the delicate arch of a spine. Tiny arms and legs, waving and kicking in the amniotic fluid. It's a full body. Even if, at twelve weeks pregnant, Rowena told me this morning that the baby is only the size of a lime.

"There's your baby." Dr. Raikes points to the screen. "Looking nice and active."

Rowena's eyes are shining with tears as she stares at the monitor, transfixed. I swallow hard against the lump in my throat, overwhelmed by a dangerous need to claim both Rowena and the baby as my family.

Dr. Raikes takes measurements, the clicks of the keyboard punctuating the hushed reverence of the moment. I can't tear my gaze away from the screen, from the life growing inside Rowena.

A life that has started to feel inextricably tied to mine.

Rowena's grip on my hand tightens. I glance down to find her eyes trained on me, a tentative smile on her lips. "Pretty amazing, huh?"

"Amazing doesn't even begin to cover it." I lift our joined hands to press a kiss to her knuckles. "Thank you for letting me be here."

"Always," Rowena replies, her voice hushed. There's an unspoken promise in that single word, a future we're tentatively circling around, like satellites unsure of the gravity that tugs at us. The idea of a forever doesn't scare me anymore. But I have to earn it. A plan begins to form, but for now, I concentrate on the present.

Dr. Raikes's voice is a soothing backdrop as he continues the scan, pointing out the baby's features with a kind smile. "Would you like to hear the heartbeat?" he asks, glancing between us.

Rowena nods enthusiastically. "Yes, please."

I lean in closer, our shoulders brushing as the doctor adjusts a dial, and suddenly, the room is filled with a rapid, rhythmic thumping sound.

Thump-thump-thump. Fast and strong, the heartbeat echoes in my ears, resonating deep in my chest.

A fresh wave of emotions slams into me: love, protectiveness, a fierce sense of belonging. It's not my baby, not biologically, but in this moment, none of that matters. The only word pulsing in my mind is 'mine.' This precious life, this incredible woman

—they're mine to cherish, to protect... to love? Could I?

Tears slip down Rowena's cheeks and I reach out instinctively, brushing them away with my thumb. She leans into my touch, her eyes never leaving the screen, and I press a tender kiss to her temple.

The heartbeat fades as Dr. Raikes turns off the machine, the sudden silence almost jarring. He hands Rowena some tissues to wipe away the ultrasound gel and I help her sit up, my arm around her shoulders.

"I'll give you two a moment," Dr. Raikes says kindly, stepping out of the room to compile the results.

As soon as he's out, I gather Rowena into my arms, holding her close as she buries her face against my chest. I kiss her hair, my eyes stinging.

"That was... incredible," I murmur, my voice rough. "You're incredible."

Rowena lifts her head, her eyes red-rimmed but shining with joy. "There's a baby in me, Adrian." She moves her palm to her stomach. "A perfect, healthy baby."

I cover her hand with my own, feeling the slight swell of her belly. "I know, I saw." I chuckle, keeping the mood light.

She smiles, that radiant, heart-stopping smile that never fails to take my breath away. I have to hold myself in check not to lean down and capture her lips in a kiss.

I will not kiss her. Not here. Not now. But I can no longer deny I want this, her, us, the baby. Nor can I forget how selfish these wants are. A deluge of breakup lines from my past relationships ring in my ears: absent... always distracted... emotionally unavailable... never felt so lonely... just an afterthought... ignoring my feelings... putting your career first... missing in action... never truly committing... failing to be there when I needed you... taking me for granted... making me feel invisible...

I never want Rowena to feel invisible or neglected or second to anything, but can I manage it? Can I change my ways?

Dr. Raikes returns, interrupting my churning thoughts, a blue folder in his hands and a reassuring smile on his face. He settles into his chair, opening the folder and spreading out a few papers on his desk. We sit opposite him.

"Alright, let's go over what to expect from here," he begins, his tone calm and professional. "The NT measurement looks good, and combined with the blood test results, it suggests a low risk for chromosomal abnormalities."

Dr. Raikes smiles, his eyes crinkling at the corners. "I'd like to see you back here in about a month for your next scan. If you have any concerns or experience any unusual symptoms in the meantime, don't hesitate to call."

"We will," Rowena assures him.

"And if you'd like, next time, we should be able to determine the baby's gender, if that's something you want to know," Dr. Raikes adds.

I glance at Rowena, raising an eyebrow in a silent question.

She bites her lip, considering, then smiles. "There are few happy surprises in life, and this could be one." She turns to me. "You think it's silly to wait?"

"No, if you want a surprise, let's make it a surprise," I tell her honestly. I hate surprises, but this could be the one exception.

Dr. Raikes chuckles. "You don't have to decide now." He stands, extending his hand. "If you don't have any more questions?"

I stand as well, shaking his hand firmly. "You covered everything. Thank you, Dr. Raikes."

"You're very welcome. Stop by the front desk to

schedule your next appointment, and you'll be all set."

With a final warm smile, he escorts us back to the reception area. As Rowena settles into a chair, lost admiring the ultrasound pictures, I approach the desk to make the appointment.

The receptionist smiles at me, all friendly professionalism. "Four weeks from today work for you?"

I nod, committing the date and time to my planner as she enters it into the system. Task complete, I turn back to Rowena, only to find her holding out one of the ultrasound pictures to me.

"For you." Her eyes are still shiny. "I want you to have one."

I take the small black-and-white image, staring down at the fuzzy outline of the baby—her baby.

Holding that picture, reality hits me again, only this time more powerful—like a wrecking ball to the chest. This isn't my child, and if I stay on the path I've been on, chasing success and status, it'll never be. I'll never be a father, never have a family of my own.

And for the first time, that thought chills me to the bone.

Have I been wrong all this time? Have I been

chasing the wrong things, neglecting what really matters? I thought nothing could be worse than what my father did: giving up. But maybe I'm worse because I'm not even trying.

I look at Rowena, at the barely noticeable baby bump, and I know one thing with absolute clarity. I want this. I want her. I want the chance to be a father, a husband. The chance to build a life and a family with someone I love.

And I'm ready to do whatever it takes to make that happen.

33

ROWENA

Fourteen weeks pregnant

Two weeks after the ultrasound, at home, I nestle into the plush sofa cushions, my oversized T-shirt draping comfortably as I tuck my legs beneath me. Across from me, Adrian lounges at the other end, his gray sweatpants and faded college T-shirt the epitome of casual. But his gaze is laser-focused, all his attention on me.

In the past fortnight, something has shifted between us. That first night Adrian asked me to watch a movie together after returning from the Hamptons wasn't just a one off. His presence in the penthouse has become a constant, no longer a fleeting apparition but a warm, tangible entity in my life. We've been sharing meals, swapping stories over late-night conversations, enjoying more movie nights curled up on opposite ends of the couch.

He still maintains some physical distance—if you don't count the occasional foot rub I sneak in as a pregnancy perk—but, emotionally, he's been there for me. Adrian has been around so much lately that I work up the nerve to ask him something I've been dying to share.

"Hey, I was wondering..." I fidget with the hem of my shorts. "Would you have time to listen to a presentation? For the interactive toy idea I'm working on?"

"Sure." He leans forward, smiling. "Lay it on me."

Excitement bubbles inside me as I go get my laptop and dive into my pitch.

"So, the idea is to build a programmable console that's leagues ahead of anything on the market," I begin, gesturing animatedly. "Designed specifically for kids, with a vibrant, intuitive interface that makes learning to code an absolute blast."

He nods, intrigued, fueling my enthusiasm. I describe the user-friendly interface featuring a touchscreen with colorful icons and simple commands tailored for young children, highlighting the integration of voice-activated controls to receive step-by-step guidance and troubleshooting tips just by speaking to the console. "No more frustration or feeling stuck."

Adrian's eyebrows shoot up. "And none of the competitors integrate voice commands?"

"No, it seems so obvious, but so far there's nothing out there with voice activation."

Adrian low-whistles.

Bolstered by his reaction, I forge ahead. "But vocal input isn't even the tip of the iceberg. The basic level is drag-and-drop programming blocks, making the concepts tangible and easy to grasp. As kids progress, they can transition to text-based coding, with features like spell check and autocomplete to aid their learning journey." I can't contain my excitement as I envision the console in action. "The entire experience will be gamified. Interactive challenges, rewards for completing tasks and solving problems. We'll keep them engaged and motivated every step of the way."

"Gamification, that's cool."

"Right?" I bounce on the couch cushion, the ideas tumbling out faster now. "Imagine the sense of accomplishment they'll feel as they level up their coding skills. And we can incorporate physical computing too! Connecting the console to robotic kits or wearable tech, so kids can see their code come to life in the real world."

Adrian leans back, a look of admiration on his face. "It's brilliant. The multimodal approach, the progression from blocks to text, the physical integration."

I swell like a balloon at his praise. "But it's not just about the coding itself. I want to foster a sense of community, a place where kids can collaborate and learn from each other."

Adrian cocks his head. "How so?"

"Picture an online platform integrated with the console, a safe space for kids to share their projects, work together on coding challenges and celebrate each other's successes. But I want to take it a step further with virtual mentorships, with seminars from experienced coders who can offer guidance and inspiration."

He nods thoughtfully, his fingers drumming against his knee. "Building a supportive ecosystem around the product. Smart."

I grin at his validation. "And the kicker is—we make it interdisciplinary. Coding projects that incorporate math, science, art... showing kids how software connects to their everyday life. We'll have regularly updated STEM challenges, pushing their problem-solving skills."

The corners of his mouth curl up. "You basically want to empower the next generation of innovators."

"Empowering the next generation of innovators, that's the company's motto right there." I smile so wide my cheeks hurt. "I want every child to have access to this. No matter their background or abilities. The console will support multiple languages, include accessibility features like text-to-speech and adjustable settings for learning and other disabilities."

Adrian's eyes light up. "That's an amazing vision. I love it."

"Do you think I can pitch this to someone other than you? I mean, potential investors?"

Adrian's expression shifts, his brow furrowing as he bounces his knees. "Rowena, this is incredible. But we need to talk numbers. How much will the console cost to make?"

The question catches me off guard. "I... I'm not sure yet. I haven't calculated the production costs."

He nods, his gaze keen. "And where will it be

manufactured? That has a tremendous impact on overheads and logistics."

I frown, uncertainty creeping in. "I hadn't thought about that either."

Adrian's questions keep coming in rapid-fire. "What about profit margins? Expected sales volumes? Target demographics? Will your marketing be aimed at kids directly or at their parents?"

Each inquiry feels like a tiny pinprick, deflating my confidence. I stammer out half-formed answers, realizing just how unprepared I am.

And Adrian sees right through me. "Rowena, I'm sorry, but you're not ready to pitch to investors. The concept is brilliant but you need a business plan."

His words pierce through me like shards of ice. My stomach churns and sinks me back into my old insecure mindset, making me suddenly feel small.

All of Adrian's questions are valid, just as his assessment is: I'm not ready for investors pitches. Fair. But it still feels like he's tearing apart my project, sucking away all the enthusiasm and self-assurance I had mere minutes ago.

"I... I understand," I choke out. "I'll work on it."

"I can help if you need me."

"Maybe if you could send me a list of the things I need to figure out."

Adrian nods and we put on a movie afterward, but I don't really follow the plot.

He said he loved the idea, yet I feel like a total failure. Because I'm clueless about where to start with his million questions. A wonderful concept is nothing without a solid plan, and I don't have one. How will I be able to put all of this together? I lack the financial knowledge to do it. Will I have to hire someone? With what money? And how long will it take? Will the five and a half months I have left before the baby comes be enough? Could I still work on the console while caring for a newborn?

As we go to bed in our separate rooms, the doubts keep gnawing at me. I fall asleep to tired frustration and a million other unanswered questions.

* * *

Over the next several days, Adrian reverts to his old routine of working late most evenings holed up in his home office.

Doubt creeps in again from all sides, feeding on my insecurities. Did my half-baked business plan turn him off the whole concept? Does he think I'm an idiot who's in over her head? Has he lost all interest in me?

One night that the self-doubts are keeping me awake, I pad to the kitchen for a glass of water at 2 a.m. But on my way back, I notice a dim glow emanating from Adrian's office, the door slightly ajar.

Curiosity overtakes me and I push the door open all the way. Adrian is passed out in his desk chair, his head lolling onto his chest, while the blue light from his computer screen casts shadows across his face.

I hover uncertainly in the doorway, torn about whether to wake him and tell him to go to bed or let him sleep. If I leave him there like that, his neck will kill him tomorrow. I cross the room, deciding to rouse him, but then my eyes land on the screen, and I step closer to the computer to see what he's been working on so intently.

I gasp as I read line after line of a detailed business plan for my toy console. All the data points, market research, financial estimates and projections that I fumbled to provide, are laid out meticulously in neatly organized sections.

A spreadsheet has never looked more gorgeous —or more romantic.

Adrian has filled in all the gaps, fleshing out a robust, professional-grade proposal.

All these late nights he's been pulling, the time hiding away in his office... it was for me. To help bring my project to life, transforming it from a pie-in-the-sky dream to a viable venture. He believes in this. In me.

He's just being a good friend, I tell myself.

But friends don't kiss each other the way he kissed me the night of the engagement party.

An uncontrollable wave of affection floods me, so strong it nearly brings me to my knees. If he weren't conked out in that chair, I'd throw my arms around him and smother him in kisses.

I settle for gently shaking his shoulder. "Adrian," I whisper. "Wake up for a sec."

"Hmm?" He blinks at me groggily, disoriented. "Sunshine? What time is it?"

"Late. Come on, let's get you to bed."

I slip an arm around his waist and guide his sleepy, stumbling form down the hall to his bedroom. Adrian is so out of it, he's practically sleepwalking. Together we collapse onto his mattress in an uncoordinated tangle of limbs.

He passes out again within seconds, but I linger awake, studying him. His perfect features, resting so peacefully, his chest rising and falling with each breath. I can't resist the urge to brush back a rebellious lock of hair from his forehead to then press a hand to his chest and the steady heartbeat beyond.

Because as handsome and sexy as Adrian is, the best part of him is inside. It's in the man who'd come to meet my ex mere weeks after knowing me. The one welcoming my friends in his house for a not-so-secret interrogation. The man taking me to doctor's appointments for a child that is not even his. A person who, on top of an already demanding career, would pull all-nighters to help me reach my dreams.

And it's in this quiet moment, with him sleeping next to me, that a sudden awareness strikes me: it's not just lust that draws me to him or a passing infatuation. I've utterly, desperately fallen in love with my fake fiancé.

34

ADRIAN

Warmth envelops me as consciousness slowly seeps in. I draw in air, inhaling a hint of vanilla and jasmine—Rowena's body lotion? I blink in the soft morning light, finding her curled up beside me, her head resting on my shoulder. Confusion swirls through my sleep-addled brain. How did we end up like this? In my bed? I glance down. At least we're both fully clothed. I didn't cross any lines last night.

Careful not to disturb her, I lift my arm to check my smartwatch. Saturday, 8.07 a.m. glows on the screen. A relieved sigh escapes me. The markets are closed. No meetings, no deadlines looming. I can enjoy this unexpected moment a little longer. Gently, I pull Rowena closer, relishing her warm weight against me as I let my eyelids drift shut again.

Sometime later, she stirs, stretching languidly before turning to face me. Her chestnut hair is adorably mussed, her eyes heavy-lidded with lingering sleep. Gorgeous and irresistible, but still off-limits. Before even thinking about taking that step, I need to prove I can have a healthy work-life balance.

Before even saying good morning, Rowena trails a finger down the bridge of my nose, a playful smile flitting across her face. "You've been naughty, Bunny."

My heart lurches. Oh fuck, what did I do? Did I grope her while we were sleeping? "I... what? Naughty how?" I stammer.

"Working yourself into the ground making a business plan for me." She raises an eyebrow. "Ring any bells?"

"Ah. That." Relief floods through me, followed by a twinge of self-consciousness at being caught. "I wanted it to be a surprise. To help you bring your amazing idea to life." I trail a thumb over her hip where my hand is still resting. "So... is that how we ended up here? Not that I'm complaining."

"I stopped by your office late last night and found you passed out at your desk, head lolling."

She chuckles softly. "So I half-carried, half-sleep-walked you to bed. You were out cold."

No mention of why she stayed. Rowena must read the unspoken question in my gaze because color blooms on her cheeks. She doesn't say anything, though, and I don't ask.

"I can't believe you did all that, just for me. The business plan." Her voice softens. "I'm so grateful. Honestly. I'm pretty hopeless with the financial aspect of things."

I grin, giving her side an affectionate squeeze. "That's what I'm here for. To be your business-savvy sidekick while you focus on being the brilliant creative genius."

She laughs and burrows closer, resting her head on my chest. My heartbeat quickens. With Rowena in my arms, it's easy to picture this as my new normal. But I have more work to do, on myself and my workaholic tendencies, before I'm ready. For now, I'll savor stolen moments like these and keep working on becoming the man she deserves. And the best thing I can do for her is make sure she has her independence back. That this dream of hers becomes reality. So that if one day, she stays with me, it won't be because she has no other choice, but because she wants it.

"I've been thinking…" I absent-mindedly draw circles on Rowena's shoulder. "About the best way to bring your idea to market. Partnering with an established toy company might be the path to follow."

She tilts her head to look up at me, brows knitted. "Why's that?"

"Well, without an existing infrastructure, manufacturing and shipping costs could eat away all profit margins."

"So, it wouldn't be my company?"

"No, you'd be licensing the technology."

"Licensing? How does that work?"

"How about we discuss it over breakfast? I feed you first and then we talk shop."

Rowena's face lights up. "I like the way you think, Bunny."

Half an hour later, the late morning sun feels glorious on our faces as we stroll hand in hand toward the café where we first met to discuss how our fake marriage would work—I can't believe it's already been two months almost to the day since that awkward second meeting. A gentle breeze tempers the early August heat, making the walk to the café even more pleasant. Inside the coffee shop, the rich aroma of freshly ground beans envelops us. We order iced lattes and an assortment of flaky, sugar-dusted pastries before snagging a table by the window.

"Okay, so," I begin, after a refreshing sip of my latte, "your best bet is pursuing a Joint Development Agreement with Licensing Terms. Essentially, you'd grant a partner rights to manufacture and sell your console for royalty payments. No upfront costs to you."

Rowena's eyes widen. "Wow. So... I wouldn't have to pay for anything? That's... that's perfect. I mean, I have no savings."

I reach across the table and lay my hand over hers. "That's not necessarily the issue. If I genuinely believed going solo was the best choice, I'd happily invest in your project myself or help you find other investors. But a licensing deal will be better for you in the long run. You'll get to focus on what you love —developing kick-ass software and games to im-prove the console. Let the toy company handle the boring stuff like manufacturing and distribution."

Rowena's smile is incandescent. "That sounds amazing. I'd get to geek out and code all day without worrying about the rest? Sign me up!"

Chuckling, I raise my latte in a toast. "To you, nerding it out and conquering the world."

Giggling, she clinks her cup against mine before taking a giant bite out of a pastry. It leaves her upper lip covered in powdered sugar.

I reach across the table and wipe the smudge of white dust from Rowena's mouth with my thumb. Her breath hitches at the contact, and for a charged moment, neither of us moves. The air between us feels electric, the pull of attraction almost impossible to ignore. But I force myself to drop my hand and lean back, determined not to make things physical until I've proven I can be the kind of partner she deserves.

"How quickly could you have a prototype ready?"

Her jaw goes slack. "Do I have to build a console from scratch?"

"No, no," I assure her. "If we're aiming to license the concept, a demo on a tablet to showcase the software and functionalities will be more than enough."

Relief washes over her features. "Oh, um... I'm already pretty far along with the coding. I could have something ready in three weeks, tops."

"Great. I've narrowed it down to two potential

partners that would be a fantastic fit for your product."

"Adrian, you're amazing. I don't know how you found the time. I'll never be able to thank you enough."

Despite her words, she shifts uncomfortably. "But?"

"But what if they start asking financial questions and I botch it like I did with you?"

"Don't worry, I'll come with you and cover the business side of things. You just focus on being the brilliant inventor you are."

Rowena beams at me. "I... I..." She shakes her head as if too moved to speak. "Just, thank you."

My blood hums in response. I'm showing up for her—I'm doing it. Maybe I can really be the partner she needs.

35

ROWENA

Twenty weeks pregnant

Adrian has been true to his word, and exactly a month after our second discussion of my project, after I've completed the demo, he's accompanying me to meet the first potential partner: MC Toys.

With only ten days to go before the wedding, Adrian took time off work to be here with me. He's been taking a lot of time off lately, coming to cake-tasting appointments and floral consultations, acting like a man who knows the difference between peonies and petunias—which he doesn't, but bless his heart for trying. And a million other wedding-related errands I was sure he would have absolutely no interest in.

We're both terribly busy with work, me developing my demo and him, doing his obscure finance stuff, but we have dinner together most nights and spend time with each other on the weekends.

Tragically, we still sleep in separate beds and he hasn't tried to kiss me again. And as much as I'm not a prideful person, I lack the shamelessness to throw myself at him a third time. Two attempts to seduce him with zero success is a depressing enough score for me.

As we pull in front of MC's office building, I take in the faded brick façade and minimal signage. Not quite what I expected for the headquarters of a billionaire's new venture.

"This is it?" I turn to Adrian with a raised eyebrow as we climb out of the car.

He chuckles. "Don't let appearances fool you. I hear Thomas Mercer is determined to make this a grassroots start-up, despite his family fortune."

From what Adrian—*and Google*—have told me about Thomas Mercer, he's the billionaire son of a billionaire, who recently left the family multi-billion enterprise to found a toy company.

Intrigued, I follow Adrian inside. The lobby is

tidy but lacks any hint of extravagance—bare white walls, basic furniture, not a luxury fabric or gilded frame in sight.

"Whoa, when you said grassroots, you weren't kidding," I mutter, peering around at the minimalist space. "Not a penny wasted on décor, that's for sure."

"Exactly." Adrian grins. "From what I've gleaned, Mercer wants to build this company from the ground up, relying on hard work and innovation rather than family money. Gotta respect that."

So Thomas Mercer isn't another rich kid playing with a new toy—pun intended— but a driven entrepreneur willing to roll up his sleeves. "You know what? I like him already."

Right on cue, the man himself strides into the lobby to greet us. He is striking, tall and athletic with tousled dark-blond hair and a megawatt smile. The full force of his cheerful charisma hits me like a blast of warm summer air.

"Rowena, Adrian, welcome!" He shakes our hands warmly, guiding us inside an office. "So glad you could make it. I'd like you to meet my wife, Reese, the brains behind MC Toys."

Beside him stands a beautiful woman with long brown hair streaked with pink. Her curious eyes give an impression of deep intelligence. She opens her mouth to speak but is cut off by a whirring sound.

To my amazement, a small robot zips forward, tripod legs clicking, metal claws snapping. Radar eyes swivel beneath a transparent dome as an electronic voice pipes up. "She might be the brains but I'm the star here!"

I laugh in delight at the pesky bot. "Well, hello there! And who are you?"

The robot swivels to attention. "I am an advanced kinematics precision pneumatics service droid, ready to assist."

"He's incorrigible." Reese sighs in fond exasperation. "Please, just call him K2-P."

As Adrian shakes his head, chuckling, I grin back at our hosts, their easy-going attitude but clear brilliance already sparking my excitement.

For the pitch, we settle into a meeting room. My fingers fumble with the projector cord as I set up my presentation materials, hoping my console idea will fit right in.

I take a deep breath and launch into my pitch, walking them through the educational features, accessibility settings and imaginative games. "... and that's how this console will revolutionize playtime for kids everywhere," I conclude, the words tumbling out in a rush of enthusiasm.

Reaching for the demo tablet, I hand it to Thomas, but he waves me off with a self-deprecating chuckle. "Oh, you'd better give that to Reese. She's the one you need to impress." His effortless charm and humility catch me off guard, a refreshing change from the big egos I was used to at my previous start-up.

As Reese explores the demo, her brow furrows in concentration. Each tap and swipe ratchets up my anxiety. I study her face for any hint of a reaction. Seconds feel like hours.

Suddenly, her expression transforms, eyes widening with delight. "This is incredible! The perfect companion to our K2-P toy line. I've been researching how to teach coding skills in a fun, approachable way and your console nails it."

Pride surges through me at her effusive praise. I'm about to respond when, from across the table, K2-P lets out a sarcastic beep. "Excuse me, I believe I remain the superior product."

His comedic timing defuses my nerves, pulling a laugh from everyone.

Reese continues to gush, seemingly oblivious. "Seriously, Rowena, this blows every other idea out of the water. The accessibility features, the engaging gameplay... it's genius."

As I bask in the validation of my work, I marvel at the energy in the room. Thomas and Reese's passion for creating meaningful toys is infectious, their easy banter and obvious affection heartwarming. Even K2-P's snarky interjections feel like being part of a family.

I catch Adrian's gaze. His subtle nod and proud smile are the cherry on the cake.

Thomas's grin widens as he watches his wife's enthusiastic response. "Honey, we might need to work on your negotiation tactics. You're not supposed to let them know how much you love it right off the bat." His teasing tone is laced with adoration.

Reese laughs, her cheeks coloring. "I can't help it! When something is this perfect, why hide it?" She turns back to me, her eyes sparkling. "Rowena, I genuinely believe our visions align seamlessly. Creating educational toys that are inclusive of children with disabilities is a core value for us."

Thomas nods in agreement. "Absolutely. And what's great is that your console works brilliantly as a stand-alone product but can also integrate with our existing K2-P line as an add-on."

"Just ensure my magnificent design remains the

star attraction," K2-P interjects, his radar eyes swiveling between us. "I have a reputation to uphold, you know."

The robot's quip cracks me up. It's astonishing how this quirky invention has stolen my heart in mere minutes. Reese and Thomas must've poured their souls into its creation.

Thomas leans forward, his expression turning serious. "Rowena, I'll need some time to crunch the numbers, but I'm confident we can put together an attractive offer. A royalty agreement, coupled with a collaborative R&D arrangement. How does that sound?"

I'm floating on air with the promise of a dream coming true. I glance at Adrian, who gives me an encouraging smile before he addresses Thomas. "That sounds fantastic. In the interest of full transparency, we are taking meetings with other potential partners as well."

Thomas nods, unruffled. "Of course, I wouldn't expect anything less. But I assure you, we'll be able to table an attractive proposal. This could be the start of something incredible."

As the meeting concludes, handshakes are exchanged and smiles are mirrored all around. Adrian and I make our way out, a giddy excitement bubbling within me.

The last thing I hear as we exit the conference room is K2-P's indignant voice. "Wait a minute, do I get a cut of these royalties?"

"No!" comes their joint reply.

Angry beeps follow. Then Thomas's and Reese's laughter mingles with the robot's persistent grumbling.

This is where my toy console belongs—in the hands of creators who understand the power of play to change lives. I'm almost tempted to go back in and tell them I want to sign right away.

As if sensing my exuberance, Adrian turns to me as we exit the building. "Make sure you listen to the other proposal before you decide anything."

I nod while silently disagreeing.

Adrian sees straight through me, reinforcing his warning. "MC Toys is great, but they're just a start-up with limited distribution."

"Why? Who are we meeting next?"

His responding smile is dazzling. "Only the largest toy manufacturer in the country."

My jaw dangles open. "How did you manage that? I suppose they don't just take walk-ins."

Adrian shrugs, trying to diminish something

that surely took a lot of effort to pull off. "I have a few contacts."

"So when do we meet them?"

Adrian holds the door open for me. "Unfortunately, not for another three weeks. We have the wedding in ten days and they couldn't schedule us in until the following week. I already got the plane tickets."

I stop in my tracks. "Wait, where is the meeting?"

Adrian smiles casually. "California. I'm passing the time off as a mini honeymoon."

Honeymoon. Right. In ten days, we'll be husband and wife, and somehow, that's both exactly what I want and not at all. Funny how things can be both perfect and completely off at the same time. I just hope when the day comes, I'll have the strength to walk down that aisle, wearing the smile he expects as I plunge even deeper into a beautiful, cruel lie.

36

ADRIAN

Golden sunlight streams through the windows of the groom suite, illuminating the dust motes swirling in the air. I adjust my bow tie in the mirror for the tenth time, my fingers trembling. The tux fits me like a glove, crisp and perfectly tailored, but I feel more like an impostor than ever.

In just under an hour, I'll be standing at the altar with Rowena, pledging my life and love to her in front of everyone we know. It feels so right, as if fate brought us together for this very moment. And yet, the guilty pit in my stomach reminds me I'm still living a charade, that I haven't found the courage to bare my soul to her and confess my true feelings. I'm lying to her, to her family, to her friends...

Her parents arrived a few nights ago, and even though it was the first time they'd ever met me, they welcomed me with open arms, saying how happy they are to have me as a son-in-law. If they only knew the truth—that this whole engagement started out as a sham, that I'm letting their daughter believe today is still nothing more than a calculated trade-off.

I glance around the empty suite, feeling the absence of close friendships acutely. When it was time to pick my groomsmen, I realized my only "friends" were more work acquaintances than anything else. So today, I'll be borrowing Tristan and Dylan for the role. Great guys, but more Rowena's people than my own. No matter that I've gotten to know them better over the past few months.

A soft knock at the door startles me out of my brooding thoughts. My mother pokes her head in.

"Oh, honey, look at you! So handsome," she gushes, hurrying over to fuss with my lapels. "How are you feeling? Nervous?"

"Mm-hmm," I mutter, unable to meet her keen gaze. But Mom must hear what I'm not telling her because she places a hand on my cheek, gentle but firm, forcing me to look at her. "Adrian, listen to me. If you want this to be real—if you want *her*—then you need to tell her. Don't let fear hold you back from something wonderful."

I swallow rocks. "I don't know if I can. What if I'm not enough?"

"You are more than enough," Mom insists fiercely. "You *can* make her happy. But you need to give her that chance. Don't wait until it's too late and you lose her."

She pats my chest, right over my racing heart, and steps back. "It's time, sweetheart. Let's go get you married."

Adjusting my cufflinks, I nod and follow her out of the suite. My legs feel like jelly as we walk across the lobby and out into the warm, last-day-of-summer air. Central Park awaits, the trees swaying in the gentle breeze, calling me forward to my bride.

As we stride down the sidewalk, dodging the oblivious tourists and harried locals, Mom slips her arm into mine and pulls.

The sun-dappled path through Central Park feels almost ethereal as we make our way to the Bethesda Terrace for the wedding ceremony. A light breeze carries the scent of late summer blooms, and the distant sound of the fountain grows louder with each step.

As we approach the terrace, a strange stillness

overtakes me. It's like stepping into a fairy tale—the grand staircase adorned with cascading white flowers, the elegant arcade framing the iconic angel statue of the Bethesda Fountain. Rows of white wooden chairs line the terrace, filled with guests.

I spot Dylan and Tristan already in place next to the minister, looking sharp in their tuxes. They give me encouraging nods as I take my position near them.

As we wait for the bride, the mellow sounds of the park mingle with the delicate strains of classical music from the string quartet. It's picture-perfect. Almost too perfect.

My fingers twitch involuntarily as I scan the crowd, waiting for Rowena to appear. I should be over the moon, but unease churns in my gut, warring with the euphoria of what's about to happen. I paste on a smile, hoping it reaches my eyes.

The music swells and a hush falls over the assembled guests. The bridesmaids arrive. Nina and Hunter begin their procession down the aisle, radiant in flowing gowns the color of champagne and holding matching ivory bouquets. As they take their places opposite me, the string quartet shifts seamlessly into the bridal march.

There, at the end of the aisle on her father's arm,

appears Rowena. An angel in white, gliding toward me, her dress flowing around in the breeze. The subtle curve of her baby bump only adds to her glow.

All I can see is her. All I can feel is the overwhelming rush of love that sweeps through me, and suddenly, I'm fighting back tears. The guests rise in unison, every eye riveted on my stunning bride as she floats ever closer. I plaster on my most charming smile, praying it conceals the whirlwind of emotions threatening to blow my composure.

As Rowena reaches the altar, her father places her delicate hand in mine, giving me a warm nod of approval before taking his seat. Her eyes sparkle up at me, brimming with excitement and unbridled trust. I've never felt more worthless.

"Dearly beloved, we are gathered here today..." the minister begins, his rich voice resonating under the arcade.

The comforting weight of Rowena's hand grounds me as he waxes poetic about the power of love and the beauty of a lifelong commitment. I steal a glance at my radiant bride, she meets my gaze and her rosebud lips curve into a secret smile meant only for me. I've no idea how she feels today, and I'm too much of a coward to ask.

"And now, the bride and groom have elected to recite their own vows," the officiant announces.

Rowena insisted personal vows would make a better impression on my boss. My palms turn clammy as I fumble in my jacket pocket for the folded slip of paper. The earnest words I poured onto the page in the midnight hours are the singular honest thing about this charade of a wedding.

I risk one more glance at Rowena's beaming face before I begin. "Rowena, from the moment I laid eyes on you, I knew my life was changed."

A soft murmur ripples through the guests, some nodding as if they witnessed our first meeting—if only they could guess how unglamourous it was.

"You have a way of lighting up a room with your passion and determination. Whether it's your dedication to making a positive impact on the world through your work, or your fierce loyalty to your friends, you inspire everyone around you. Even when you're throwing axes better than me—which is both impressive and a little terrifying—I am in awe of your strength and spirit." Even if our first-date story is completely made up, it still feels like an inside joke. Laughter bubbles up from the audience, a few chuckles escaping louder than intended. Rowena is smiling, but is there also a veil of sadness in her eyes? I can't be sure, so I continue with my speech.

"I love how you collect fortune cookies but never keep the motivational quotes inside them, only the romantic and funny ones. I adore your zest for life, your love for the simple things—tacos, a good book, making popcorn on movie night." The bridesmaids exchange knowing smiles, Hunter dabbing at her eyes with tissues even if she's supposedly aware this isn't real. "Your attention to ensure inclusivity for children with disabilities in your new project is just an example of your boundless compassion. It's one of the many reasons I'm proud to stand by your side. Everyone who knows you loves you, and the loyalty of your friends is a testament to the wonderful person you are." A collective hum of agreement resonates from the rows behind us.

"And you do all this while also growing a tiny human inside of you. This baby is already the luckiest in the world because they have you as a mom." Rowena's hand instinctively goes to her bump.

"You make every day a discovery and make me excited to wake up and explore what lies ahead for us. I thank you for that. And vow to do my best to deserve it, to deserve *you*. I promise to always be

there for you, whether we're navigating life's challenges or simply enjoying a quiet moment. I vow to
support you in all your endeavors, to stand by you in
times of joy and sorrow, and to cherish the time we
share.

"I want to grow old with you. And if you'll let
me, I promise to love you, to laugh with you, and to
comfort you for all the years to come. I will always
be your biggest fan and your partner in everything.
Thank you for being my sunshine and for showing
me what true love is."

I gaze into Rowena's eyes as I finish my wedding
vows, after pouring my heart into every word. But as
I utter the last promise, I notice something off in her
expression. Tears stream down her face, but they
don't seem to be purely tears of joy. A swirl of emotions dances in her irises that I can't quite decipher.

For a suspended beat no one seems to even
breathe, only a few sniffles are audible from the first
rows.

Then the minister turns to Rowena. "And now
your vows."

She parts her lips but no words come out. Her
mouth works but she can't seem to form a coherent
sentence. After a moment, Rowena shifts her attention to the gathered crowd with a bright smile plas-

tered on her face. But I know her too well—she's hiding something beneath that grin.

"S-sorry everyone," Rowena says, gasping as if she's trying hard not to sob. "Already it's h-hard for brides not to cry at their weddings. But it's downright impossible when you're pregnant and the victim of raging hormones!"

The crowd lets out a collective "aww" of understanding. But I'm not fooled. I can tell she's masking her true feelings with humor. A sinking sensation grips my gut. Something is wrong, very wrong. What happened? Was it something I said? Something I did?

Rowena turns back to me, her smile faltering. She tries to speak again but stammers anxiously over the words. "I... I had an entire speech prepared, but..." She trails off and shakes her head, once more overcome with emotion. Her pleading eyes meet mine, silently begging for help.

My heart constricts with worry but I force a lighthearted grin onto my face. I don't want to make a scene in front of all the guests. "It's okay, Sunshine," I say soothingly. "I know you love me. You always let me have the last slice of pizza. I don't need a speech."

The tension breaks as the crowd erupts into

cheers and laughter. The ceremony continues, and, with shaking hands, Rowena and I exchange rings. And then in a blink, we're married. Husband and wife... so why does it feel like I'm losing her?

Throughout the reception, I plaster on a smile and try to play the part of the blissful groom. But inside, my stomach churns with unease as I watch Rowena flit between guests, her laughter ringing just a bit too loud, her grin stretching a little too wide.

I maneuver through the crowd, dodging well-wishers and attempting to catch my new bride alone. But there's always something or someone standing in my way.

Even when we do our first dance and are the only ones on the dancefloor, she barely meets my eyes and refuses to speak a word.

The rest of the night passes in an anxious blur. I go through the motions—cutting the cake, thanking everyone for coming. But always tracking her. Finally, the last guests depart. She walks her parents out; they have an early flight back tomorrow. And I follow her. Now we can go home and figure this out.

I walk out just as the car driving her parents takes off. Rowena is standing on the curb, in her wedding dress and fancy hair updo, her back to me.

"Hey," I call out.

Her shoulders immediately go rigid, and her expression when she turns chills my bones.

"I'm going to head home with Nina and Hunter tonight," she says, not quite meeting my gaze.

"Why?"

"I just need space to clear my head."

"Space?" I gape. "From what? Whatever's going on, let me help. Please don't shut me out." I reach for her hand but she pulls away.

"I'm not shutting you out. I'm just asking for a moment to process… this." She swats at thin air. "On my own."

Rowena glances over to where her bridesmaids wait by a cab. Then she looks back at me, her expression pained but determined. "I'll call you tomorrow, okay?"

Helplessly, I nod. What else can I do? I have no idea what's happening, but I can't force her to stay and talk.

I watch Rowena walk away with her friends, impotent, defeated.

Three months ago, spending my wedding night alone wouldn't have meant anything. Now, it threatens to destroy me.

37

ROWENA

Twenty-two weeks pregnant

I sit on the living room floor of my old apartment, the voluminous skirt of my wedding dress splayed around me like a deflated jellyfish. Nina and Hunter lounge beside me in their champagne bridesmaid gowns as we eat leftover treats from the desserts buffet. We sent Dylan home with Tristan and are having an emergency girls' night. It feels good to be back to being just the three of us. Even if my former roommates keep exchanging worried glances as I take a giant bite out of a chocolate cupcake.

The rich frosting coats my tongue and I let out a

heavy sigh. "You were right," I mumble through the mouthful of cake. "I'm in over my head."

Nina raises an eyebrow. "What do you mean, Winnie? Talk to us."

Hunter nods emphatically, leaning in closer. "We're here for you, always."

Tears prickle at the corners of my eyes and I blink rapidly. Not again. I've cried enough today to fill a small pond.

"Can we just... not talk about it right now?" My voice wavers. "I need a distraction. A night of silliness with my best friends and an obscene amount of sugar."

Nina and Hunter exchange another look, seeming to have an entire conversation with just their eyes. Finally, Nina grins.

Soon we're all up, twirling and leaping around the living room in our fancy dresses like sugar-high princesses. Our laughter reverberates off the walls as we dance to cheesy pop songs and stuff our faces with éclairs and cream puffs.

For a brief, shining moment, I forget about the heavy weight in my chest. I lose myself in the pure joy of being with my best friends, knowing that whatever comes next, I'll always have them in my life.

Hours later, we're watching the third *Scream* movie after starting a marathon. As Ghostface chases his next victim across the TV screen, I glance over at Nina and Hunter sprawled on either side of me. Their hair is wild, makeup smeared, bridesmaid dresses hopelessly wrinkled. Both out cold, snoring softly.

I smile, snuggling deeper into the couch cushions and letting my own eyes drift shut. Nineties slasher movies and a sugar crash—the perfect recipe to keep my spiraling thoughts at bay. At least for tonight.

Unfortunately, I can't exile Dylan for more than a night, so eventually, on Sunday, I have to creep back into Adrian's penthouse. I time my arrival with the hour of the day he usually works out, and I luck out —he's in the home gym. I grab provisions from the fridge and water reserves and hole myself up in my bedroom.

He knocks on my door later that evening, a hesitant rap of knuckles against wood. I bury my face in the pillow, waiting motionless until his footsteps retreat.

Over the next week, I keep up the same avoidance tactics. My phone buzzes with his texts. *Everything okay? Just checking in. Let me know if you need anything.* I type back quick replies full of forced cheer.

But we can't avoid each other forever. The following Sunday, we have to leave for California—together supposedly. So that morning, I slink into the kitchen, praying our first meeting after the day we got married won't be too awkward.

Adrian sits at the island, jaw tight, hands wrapped around a mug of coffee.

Our eyes meet and he quirks an eyebrow at me coolly. "Morning."

After a week of radio silence, even if it's my fault, his curt greeting cuts like a knife.

"Hey," I mumble, yanking open the fridge to avoid his penetrating gaze. I rummage through the shelves, not really seeing anything. Why does he have to look so irritatingly handsome even at this ungodly hour?

"Have you packed yet?" His clipped tone makes me wince.

I emerge from the fridge empty-handed. "Actually, I was thinking... you don't need to come with me to California. I'm a grown woman, I'll be fine on my own. I know how busy you are with work and—"

"Don't be ridiculous, Rowena." Adrian sets his mug down with a thud, his eyes flashing. "Of course I'm coming. Sam will be here in an hour to drive us to the airport."

I turn to argue, but his stormy expression makes me rethink. Shoulders slumping, stomach empty, I trudge back to my room, so looking forward to a long, awkward trip. Who wouldn't want to be trapped for six hours on a plane next to their infuriatingly gorgeous, emotionally unavailable, simmering-with-anger fake husband?

An hour later, I'm wedged into the backseat of Adrian's sleek car, wishing I could crawl out of my skin. Sam keeps glancing at us in the rearview mirror, clearly picking up on the icy vibes. I stare out the window, counting the minutes until we reach the airport.

The flight proves even worse—endless hours of suffocating silence broken only by the occasional rustle from Adrian as he types on his laptop. I bury my nose in a book, not really paying attention to the story but determined to survive this excruciating silence without talking first. By the time we begin our descent and the patchwork of landscape below draws near, I'm ready to hole up in my hotel room and cry myself to sleep.

* * *

In El Segundo, Adrian tersely checks us into the rooms he's booked. Separate, but adjoining. I can't meet his eyes as we ride the elevator up.

"Well, I'm pretty beat," I mumble when we reach our doors. "I think I'll just rest..."

I pass the keycard over the contact reader, eager to escape. The lock opens with a bleep and I walk in, flicking on the lights.

"See you tomorrow?" I move to close the door without waiting for an answer, but Adrian's foot blocks it from shutting.

I instinctively take a step back as he pushes in, brows furrowed. "What's going on? You haven't been the same since the wedding. You can't avoid me forever."

I avert my gaze, staring at the bland hotel artwork on the wall. "It's nothing. I'm fine."

Adrian sighs heavily. "Do you hate being married to me that much?"

Something inside me snaps. Tears sting at my eyes as I whirl to face him. "Yes! I hate it. I fucking loathe it."

His eyes widen. "What did I do?"

"Nothing. You never do anything. And I hate being married to you because it's not real!" The words explode out of me, my voice rising. "What you said in your vows... it was everything I've ever wanted to hear—*from you*. But you didn't mean a word of it, did you? It's all just an act to you."

For an endless moment, Adrian stares at me in stunned silence, his anger evaporating. Then he steps fully into the room, letting the door close behind him with a soft thud. In two long strides, he's right in front of me, cupping my face in his warm hands. His dark eyes bore into mine.

"Rowena, listen to me. I meant every single word I said in my vows. Every. Single. Word." He says this in that bring-you-to-your-knees voice. I stand no chance.

I search his handsome face, my mind reeling. "But then why do you always turn me down when I try to get close to you? Why do you keep me at arm's length?"

His jaw sets with determination. "Because before I let anything happen, I want to prove to you, and to myself, that I can be in a committed relationship without making my partner feel neglected or unimportant. I know I get caught up in work, but I never want you to feel abandoned because of it, like my past partners did. I need to show that I can be there for you, emotionally, before anything physical happens between us."

Tears spill down my cheeks but for the first time in weeks, they are tears of joy and relief. A smile tugs at my lips. "Adrian, you've been more present and supportive of me these past three months than Liam ever was in our entire relationship. Don't you see that?"

His thumbs swipe the tears from my cheeks. A soft smile plays on his lips as he gazes at me with an expression of pure adoration that makes my heart soar. And I feel horrible for the way I've treated him since the wedding.

"I'm sorry for bailing. My emotions got the better of me and I just couldn't cope."

"It's okay."

"No, it's not." I take his hands in mine. "Now I'm going to tell you something and I need you to listen to me."

He nods, so I go on. "I understand your commitment to your job, Adrian, and I don't resent it. Especially after what you shared about your father not being able to provide financial stability for your family growing up. I get it, because I can be the same way—swept up in my work, losing myself in a project for days on end." I reach up to caress his cheek, feeling the slight stubble beneath my palm. "And that's why we work so well together. We both need a partner who understands that drive and doesn't begrudge the long hours. Someone who encourages our ambitions but also reminds us to come up for air. You are enough, you're more than enough, you're everything I ever wanted."

Adrian leans into my touch, his eyes fluttering closed for a moment. When they open again, the naked honesty in his gaze, both fierce and vulnerable, makes time stand still. "Rowena, you're everything I never knew I wanted. Everything I never knew I *needed*."

A serene calmness envelops me. I rise on my toes, lacing my fingers behind his neck to pull his mouth down to mine in a kiss—no doubts in my mind that this time he won't push me away.

Adrian's strong arms band around my waist, crushing me against the hard planes of his body.

A whimper escapes my throat as my lips part.

Pulling back, Adrian scoops me up, carrying me to the bed wedding-night style.

I joke about it. "Trying to make up for a missing wedding night?"

A wicked smile parts his lips. "I've heard honeymoon sex is even better."

38

ADRIAN

The muted glow of the city lights dances across the ceiling as I lie tangled in the sheets, Rowena curled against me. Her soft, even breathing tickles my upper arm, making my skin tingle with each exhale. I never imagined I'd find myself here, in a quiet hotel room, raw and exposed in every sense of the word. The chaos that's defined our relationship seems miles away in this moment of tranquility.

I spoon Rowena from behind, draping my arm over the gentle swell of her waist. The warmth radiating from her bare skin is both soothing and electrifying, like plunging into a hot spring on a snowy day. As I pull her closer, I'm overcome with a profound sense of peace that's eluded me for years.

Making love to Rowena wasn't just a physical act; it was a soul-stirring connection, a merging of hearts that transcends the tangible.

"Are you still awake?" she asks, her voice heavy with sleep. Rowena shifts in my arms, turning to face me.

"Yeah, just... processing." I brush a stray lock of hair from her forehead, struck by her beauty as the streetlights illuminate her features. "That was..."

"Unexpected?" A playful smile tugs at her lips. "In a good way, I hope."

"In the best way." I chuckle softly, tracing the curve of her shoulder with my fingertips. "I feel like I've been wandering in the dark my entire life, and suddenly, you flipped on a light switch."

Rowena's eyes sparkle with amusement. "So, I'm your personal illuminator now?"

"No, you are my sunshine." I grin, pulling her into a slow kiss. As our lips meet, the carefully constructed walls around my heart crumble, brick by brick, and for once, I'm not afraid of what might pour in.

After a few more lingering kisses, we both sigh contentedly, our foreheads touching. I run my fingers through her hair, feeling the calm wash over us. My hand moves to her belly, cradling it protectively as we drift off. Just as I'm about to fall asleep, Rowena's soft gasp startles me awake.

My eyes widen as I feel a faint flutter beneath my palm, resting over her swollen belly.

"Was that... the baby?" I ask in awe.

Rowena looks at me, a radiant smile on her face. "Yes, that was the baby."

"Does it happen often?"

She shakes her head, her eyes bright, joyful, amazed. "No, this is the first time I've felt them move."

A rush of emotions overwhelms me—amazement, protectiveness, responsibility. This tiny kick symbolizes a future that could include not just Rowena, but her child as well. A fierce instinct to shield them from any harm rises inside me.

I tighten my arms around my wife and press a soft kiss to her bare shoulder. The baby kicks again, more insistently this time. I marvel at the strength in those tiny movements, already so full of life and personality.

"The baby is on board with us fooling around," Rowena jokes, her tone light and playful. "We should do it many more times."

I chuckle and nuzzle her neck, enveloped in her sweet scent mingled with hints of sweat and sex. "Is that your professional opinion as an expectant mother?"

"Absolutely. I've been a sexually frustrated, horny, pregnant woman for the past five and a half months. I've got some serious making up to do."

"What numbers are we talking here?" I ask jokingly.

"Ah, always the numbers guy." She sighs mockingly, adding, "I want to do this every day for the rest of my life." Rowena says this lightly, but her eyes search mine, seeking answers to unspoken questions. Beneath her breezy tone, I sense the weight of her words, the hint at a shared future that hangs in the space between us. All I have to do is reach out and grab it.

I run my thumb lightly over her cheekbone, memorizing the contours of her face. The depth of my feelings for her catches me off guard sometimes, a wave I never saw coming until it swept me under. It's more than just the heat of our bodies moving together, more than the practicality of our situation. It's the way she makes me feel whole, as if I've discovered a part of myself I didn't even know I was missing.

"Every day for the rest of our lives, huh?" I draw lazy circles on her hip. "I'm all in."

Rowena's eyes widen, her playful expression morphing into something more serious, more vulnerable. "You are?" Her voice is soft, almost hesitant, as if she's afraid to hope for too much.

I cup her face. "I am, Sunshine. We didn't plan for this, and there's a lot we still need to figure out, but... I want this, us."

Her eyes shimmer, and she presses her mouth in a tight line, nodding. "I want it, too, Adrian. More than anything."

The emotion in her voice, the raw honesty of it, hits me hard in the solar plexus. I capture her lips in a passionate kiss.

As I kiss her, I decide that labels and logistics can wait. Right now, we are where we're meant to be. A family, not in the traditional sense perhaps, but in every way that counts. *My* family.

We make love again, slowly, tenderly, savoring each touch and caress. It's different from before, more intimate somehow, as if each movement is an unspoken promise we're making to each other. The world outside the warmth of our sheets seems to fade into oblivion, leaving only the two of us and the undeniable bond growing stronger with every beat of our hearts.

Later, as she sleeps nestled against my chest, I lie

awake, almost afraid that if I close my eyes, I'll wake up to discover this has all been a dream.

The baby shifts again as if to remind me this is real. Another gentle nudge that brings a smile to my face. "You're right." I bend down to kiss Rowena's belly. "Time to sleep."

I get a tiny goodnight kick back.

39

ROWENA

Twenty-three weeks pregnant

The next morning, as Adrian and I walk through the revolving glass doors of America's top toy manufacturer, I'm struck by the grandeur of the lobby. Soaring ceilings, gleaming marble floors, modern art installations—it's like stepping into the pages of *Architectural Digest*. The contrast to the humble start-up digs of MC Toys couldn't be starker.

"Ms. Taylor, Mr. West, welcome." A tall man in an impeccable navy suit strides toward us, hand outstretched. "Franklin Davis, VP of Acquisitions."

I shake his hand, trying to project confidence

despite feeling out of my element. "Pleased to meet you, Mr. Davis."

No sooner have I let go than another hand is thrust into my face. "Rowena, Adrian, Vanessa Carlton, Director of Marketing." The redhead's grip is firm, her smile polished to a high shine. Three more suits descend on us in quick succession, a whirlwind of introductions and handshakes.

My head spins as I attempt to commit names and titles to memory. This is the major leagues, no doubt about it. I peek at Adrian, but he looks at ease, flashing his megawatt grin as he makes small talk. Of course—he's in his element.

"If you'll follow me, I'll show you to the conference room," Franklin says. "The rest of the team is eager to meet you both."

There's more of them?

As we fall into step behind him, I tug at my plain blouse, wishing I'd opted for something more befitting a corporate takeover. Adrian leans in close, his breath tickling my ear. "Relax, Sunshine. You've got this."

I shoot him a grateful smile, drawing strength from his nearness. In fact, despite the formal and somewhat intimidating environment, I can't stop smiling. Last night, we made love. It was intimate

and passionate and real. And he said he wants this, me, us. My mind is split in half, part having a celebration party, singing and dancing, and the other, trying to concentrate on the presentation I have to make.

We're ushered into a spacious conference room with floor-to-ceiling windows that offer a stunning view of the city with the ocean in the distance. The space is furnished with a long, gleaming table and ergonomic chairs that look like they belong in a museum of modern art rather than an office.

Before we even begin, an executive slides a stack of papers across the table. "Standard non-disclosure agreements," he says briskly. "We'll need you both to sign before proceeding."

My nerves spike at the formality of it all, but Adrian remains unruffled. He flashes me a reassuring smile as he reaches for a pen. "No problem at all."

I catch his eye and he gives me an encouraging nod, his quiet confidence steadying my fluttering nerves. We sign the documents, and I busy myself setting up my presentation.

As I connect my laptop to the projector, I rehearse the pitch in my head one last time, even if I've run through it a dozen times. But the stakes feel monumentally higher now with a room full of poised executives waiting expectantly. Having Adrian next to me, grounds me. I absorb his calm and let it flow through me as I launch into my spiel.

"As you can see"—I point to the interface on the screen—"our console offers a fully immersive experience that seamlessly blends the tactile nature of traditional toys with the interactivity of modern gaming."

I outline the innovative features, my voice growing stronger with each passing minute. The executives lean forward, their expressions morphing from polite interest to genuine intrigue as I demonstrate how the console fills a unique niche in the toy market.

Adrian chimes in occasionally, answering financial inquiries. And it's a wrap.

To my relief, the presentation goes off without a hitch. The executives nod along, jotting down notes and peppering me with insightful questions that I'm able to answer with confidence.

Until an older gentleman in a pinstripe suit speaks. "Ms. Taylor, this is all very impressive. However, would relocating to California and staying on as a co-developer be an issue for you?"

I blink, momentarily thrown by the question.

"I'm sorry, move? I wasn't aware that would be a requirement."

The executive smiles thinly. "If we're going to bring this to market, we'll need you to oversee the research and development here at our facilities. With toys like these, constantly coming up with newer, improved versions of the console is a must."

I smile tensely. "Isn't smart working a thing now?"

His lips thin. "We prefer our innovators in one place. It fosters creativity."

My mind reels at the thought of uprooting my life, of leaving behind everything and everyone I know. I glance at Adrian, trying to gauge his reaction, but his expression is inscrutable. Would he want me to go? Would this be the perfect excuse for a clean break once the marriage charade has run its course? Is our marriage still fake? How could it be after what he said last night?

An apprehensive sounding, "I... err," slips out of my mouth before Adrian smoothly interjects, "That's something we'd be open to considering," he says calmly, "but perhaps it's a discussion better suited for a later time, once we've ironed out the details of the potential partnership."

A beat of silence precedes murmurs of assent

from around the table. I exhale shakily, feeling like I've just dodged a bullet I didn't even know was coming.

We conclude the meeting with a round of handshakes and promises to be in touch soon. I'm collecting the presentation material, when Adrian pulls me into a quick, covert embrace. "You were amazing," he whispers fiercely. "I'm so proud of you."

I press my face into his chest, allowing myself a moment to just breathe him in, to revel in the warmth of his arms around me. But even as I savor his praise, my pasted-on smile fades.

A tiny seed of doubt has been planted now, the tiniest fracture in the fantasy I've been spinning since last night. And I wonder if I'm still deluding myself.

* * *

Those same thoughts churn in my mind as we make our way through the bustling airport terminal, my hand clasped tightly in Adrian's. I try to focus on the warmth of his touch, the comforting solidity of his body beside me, but my brain won't cooperate.

We settle into our seats on the plane, and as the

engines rev to life, my doubts only seem to grow louder. I stare out the window, watching the tarmac rush by in a blur, and suddenly it hits me—I have no idea what Adrian wants.

Sure, he said his vows were real and that he's all in. But for how long? Does "all in" mean forever? That he sees a future with me? Or am I just a fun diversion, a temporary escape from the stress of his high-powered career?

And then there's the matter of California. The prospect of moving is daunting. But what scares me even more is the possibility that Adrian might want me to go. He said we only needed to stay married six months, and the countdown has started. Does he still plan to end everything in March?

I sneak a glance at him out of the corner of my eye. He's typing away on his laptop, brow furrowed in concentration.

I blink back the sudden sting of tears. I want to believe in us, in this crazy, wonderful, unexpected thing we've found together. But I'm terrified. Of getting my heart broken. Of being left behind.

As the plane lifts off, soaring up into the endless blue sky, I can't shake the feeling that everything is about to change. And I'm not sure I'm ready for it.

As if sensing my eyes on him, Adrian pulls his

gaze from the screen and looks at me. My face must give some of my inner turmoil away because his hand covers mine, stable and reassuring, just as the plane veers in a U-turn.

"Hey, what's on your mind?" His voice is soft, concerned. I wonder if I should tell him, when he adds, "If you're worried about the pitch, you nailed it." He flashes me a proud smile.

I nod, but the knot in my stomach doesn't ease. It's not the presentation that bothers me. It's us. Our future. The uncertainty of it all.

But I know Adrian. His brilliant mind is always fixated on work first. On closing the next deal, tackling the next challenge, climbing one more rung up the corporate ladder. It's how he's wired, and he's never tried to hide that from me. I've insisted it doesn't bother me. And really, it doesn't... except in vulnerable moments like this, when I desperately crave the reassurance that I'm just as important to him as his career. That we're on the same page about our future.

I wish I had the boldness to give voice to my doubts and needs instead of having fears and uncertainties tangling my tongue. But as the plane stabilizes, I simply stare out the window at the quilt of fields and towns below, wondering where Adrian and I will be a year from now. Or five. Or ten. Wondering if happily ever after is in the cards for us.

I keep these qualms to myself as I always do, and give Adrian's hand a reassuring squeeze. One corner of his mouth ticks up. For now, I suppose that small sign of affection will have to be enough.

40

ROWENA

Thirty-eight weeks pregnant

The winter morning light filters softly through the expansive windows, illuminating the penthouse in a balmy glow. Outside, the city sparkles under a fresh blanket of snow, like an endless sea of diamonds catching the sun's pale rays. I sit alone, my swollen belly throbbing with a persistent ache that radiates through my core. At thirty-eight weeks pregnant, the weight of the life growing inside me is an ever-present reminder of the monumental changes to come.

A sudden hot flush washes over me and I wrap myself in a cozy cardigan before stepping out onto the terrace for some crisp January air. The remnants of holiday decorations still linger on the city below —colorful lights twinkling amidst the snowy rooftops, clinging to the festive spirit for a few more fleeting moments. But the brisk breeze carries with it the promise of a new year that's just started, a fresh chapter waiting to be written.

Cooled and refreshed, I walk back inside and settle at my desk, the two offers for my gaming console spread out before me. As I sift through the proposals from MC Toys and the Californian behemoth, my mind drifts to thoughts of the past three months with Adrian.

Since that night in a hotel room at the end of September, life has been an exhilarating whirlwind. Adrian's unwavering support has exceeded all my hopes and expectations. Together, we've shopped for tiny onesies and baby blankets, giggling like teenagers as we debated the merits of ducks versus dinosaurs. We've spent weekends assembling cribs and changing tables. Adrian meticulously painted the nursery himself, refusing to hire help to do it, his dedication shining through each brushstroke. Even with his demanding job, he's made time for birthing classes and doctor's appointments, holding

my hand and beaming with pride at every ultrasound.

Our days have been filled with the busy prepara-
tions of pending parenthood, but our nights—oh,
our nights have been pure magic. The separate bed-
rooms are but a distant memory. We fall asleep
every night wrapped in each other's arms, we
whisper dreams for the future and promises of forever between passionate kisses and sighs of pleasure. The love we share pulses with an intensity I
never knew possible.

As I run my fingers over the offers on my desk,
I'm amazed at how far I've come since the day I met
Adrian puking my sorrows out in a public restroom,
jobless and hopeless. He's given me the strength and
confidence to pursue my dreams while giving me
space to lose myself in lines of code when inspiration strikes, just as I step back when he needs to an-
alyze the rises and falls of the financial markets.

And here in my hands is the concrete proof that
everything is possible. It's taken so many hours of
hard work and negotiations, but now I have two
stellar offers to choose from.

Staring at the two proposals spread across my
desk, I bite my lip, my mind swirling with the weight
of the decision before me. The MC Toys offer, with

its promise of focused attention and creative control, tugs at my heartstrings. They seem to understand my vision, eager to nurture my console as their second flagship product.

But the sleek folder from the Californian behemoth is hard to ignore, the numbers jumping off the page and dancing in my head. The sheer scale of their distribution network is mind-boggling, and the financial projections make my pulse quicken. This could catapult my passion project to heights I never dared imagine.

And yet, there's that clause. The one stating I'd have to move to California, 6,000 miles away from everything I know and love. Away from Adrian.

I think back to our conversation last week, when I first brought up the Californian offer. Adrian, ever the pragmatist, methodically laid out the pros and cons, his voice steady and measured.

"The reach and financial backing they guarantee is unparalleled," he said, his eyes serious as they skimmed the pages. "It's an incredible opportunity."

I'd waited, my heart rug-burned, for him to say more. To tell me he didn't want me to go. That he couldn't imagine building a life with me so far away. But he said nothing. He just swapped folders, continuing his analysis of pros and cons without factoring any emotion into it. "But MC Toys clearly believes in your vision. They'd give you the creative control to make this console shine, and you wouldn't be just another number on a spreadsheet."

He laid out the facts, giving me no other input, making it clear it's my decision. That I should do what's best for me and the baby. But what is that?

The doubts echo in my mind as I absently rub my belly, feeling a flitter of movement within. My vision glistens as a wave of fierce adoration swells in my chest. I never knew it was possible to love someone so completely before they've even entered the world. In a little over a week, we'll have a tiny new person depending on us. The thought of navigating those first precious months alone in California sends a chill scratching down my spine. But do I want to stay in New York just because of Adrian, or because it's the best thing for *me*?

I glance at the clock, my heart rate spiking with the conviction that I need to decide. Today. Before this baby makes their grand entrance and turns our world upside down in the most wonderful way.

I pick up the two folders, not really needing to read the fine print. By now, I know both proposals almost by heart. I close my eyes and hug one stack of papers to my chest, leaving the other down on the desk.

With trembling fingers, I pick up my phone and dial the familiar number. It rings once, twice, three times.

"Hello?"

"Hi, yes, this is Rowena Taylor," I say, my voice sounding far steadier than I feel. "I'm calling to let you know I've made a decision regarding your offer..."

As I relay my choice, a sense of peace washes over me, intermingled with a thrill of excitement. This is it. The start of a new chapter. They send me a virtual contract to sign, and I do it right away.

As I save the signed contract on my laptop, a sudden, sharp pain lances through my belly, knocking the wind out of me. Initially, I dismiss it as another bout of Braxton Hicks contractions—I've been having a few in the past two weeks, but the intensity catches me off guard. Slowly, I walk to the living room and ease myself onto the couch, hoping a change in position will provide some relief.

But the pain only surges, each wave more powerful than the last. I fumble for my phone, pulling up my pregnancy app with shaking hands. My due date is still ten days away, but as I start timing the contractions, a sinking realization takes hold.

Five minutes apart. Lasting nearly a minute each time.

This isn't a false alarm.

Excitement wars with trepidation as I struggle to my feet, one hand braced against the base of my spine. I need to get to the hospital. I need Adrian.

I dial his number, but it goes straight to voicemail. Of course, he's in a meeting with some high-powered client, his phone off. I leave a rambling message, my words punctuated by stuttering gasps as another contraction seizes me.

"Adrian, it's me. I think... I think the baby's coming. I'm heading to the hospital now. Please, please call me back as soon as you can."

Next, I dial his secretary, relaying the same message and trying not to let the rising panic bleed into my voice. She assures me she'll track him down, and I thank her profusely before ending the call.

My final lifeline is Sam, Adrian's unflappable driver. He answers on the first ring.

"Sam, I need you to take me to the hospital. I think I'm in labor."

"I'll be right there, Miss Rowena."

I smile, thinking how I never got him to drop the Miss.

True to his word, Sam appears at the penthouse door in record time, his normally stoic face creased with concern. He grabs my overnight bag and helps me to the elevator, his reassuring arms a welcome clutch as another contraction nearly buckles my knees.

The elevator descends at an agonizing slow pace, each jolt sending a fresh wave of agony radiating through my body. I try to focus on my breathing—using the pain management techniques they taught in birthing class—and on the new person I'm about to meet, but all I can think is how desperately I need Adrian by my side.

As the doors slide open and we step into the lobby, a fierce determination settles over me, tempering the chaos of my thoughts. I'm about to become a mother and I'm going to rock at childbirthing.

41

ADRIAN

As I settle back into my chair in the sleek meeting room at Fulton, the glass and steel table gleams under the soft, ambient lighting, complementing the panoramic view of the New York skyline.

I can't suppress the surge of satisfaction that courses through me.

I did it.

Across the table, the NY police pension fund manager regards me with a stern yet engaged expression, clearly impressed by my pitch. Securing Fulton the management of five billion in assets will be our most significant deal ever. I can already see Dominic, my boss, shaking my hand as he finally gives me that promotion I've been chasing.

Our risk manager takes the floor next, launching into a droning spiel about volatility management and safeguards.

My attention drifts to the glass wall behind the investors, where my secretary is frantically trying to catch my eye. I subtly wave her off, not wanting to disrupt the meeting's flow. But she persists, pressing a sheet of paper to the wall. Big black letters jump out at me:

Rowena is in labor

My heart seizes in my chest, the words blurring before my eyes. I blink, and Wendy adds a second page:

Sam took her to the hospital

In one swift motion, I shut my laptop and rise to my feet, cutting the risk manager off mid-sentence. The room falls eerily quiet, all eyes fixed on me.

"I apologize, but I have to leave. My wife has just gone into labor," I announce, my voice sounding distant to my ears.

Shocked faces stare back at me—my colleagues, Dominic, the investors. I turn to my head of trading.

"Sarah, can you please finish the presentation for me? I need to go."

She nods, surprise and understanding mingling in her eyes.

I don't wait for anyone else to respond. I'm out the door in seconds, jaw set as I stride down the corridor. My secretary scurries behind me in her heels, struggling to keep pace.

"Call me a car," I instruct her, jabbing the elevator button impatiently.

"I already did, Mr. West. It's waiting for you downstairs."

I nod my appreciation, stepping into the elevator as soon as the doors slide open. The descent seems to take forever, my foot tapping an anxious rhythm on the floor.

I burst through the lobby doors and into the waiting car. "Clinlada, as fast as you can," I urge the driver.

As we weave through the New York traffic, my mind races faster than the passing city lights. Is Rowena okay? Is the baby? It's too soon. Why didn't she call me herself?

I check my phone and find her frantic voicemail. Damn it. I vow to never turn it off ever again, no matter how important the meeting.

The journey feels interminable, each red light a personal affront. When we pull up at the clinic, I'm out of the car before it fully stops, throwing a hasty, "Thanks," over my shoulder.

I dash through the glass doors, nearly colliding with a startled nurse. I beeline for the reception desk, my hands gripping the edge.

"Where is my wife?" I demand, almost shouting.

The receptionist blinks up at me, probably taken aback by my intensity. "Sir, I need a bit more information. What's your wife's full name?"

I run a hand through my hair, ignoring the vise squeezing my throat to say, "Rowena. Rowena Taylor or West."

She types the info into her computer, each click of the keyboard grating on my overtaxed synapses. It's forever before the receptionist looks up with a smile.

"Your wife is in the delivery room. Please follow me, we'll get you scrubbed up and ready to go."

Relief floods through me as I trail her down the sterile hallway. I'm led to a small bathroom where I hastily wash my hands and don the blue protective gown, cap, and shoe covers.

Then a nurse ushers me into the delivery room. The bright fluorescent lights momentarily blind me as the distinct aroma of disinfectant hits my nostrils. I blink rapidly, taking in the ambience, carefully furnished for comfort, yet unmistakably clinical in essence—a lilac yoga ball, a plush recliner tucked in the corner, the walls painted a soothing sage green.

And there, at the center of it all, lies Rowena on the hospital bed. Tendrils of hair cling to her flushed, glistening face. She looks utterly spent, yet somehow she's still the most beautiful woman I've ever laid eyes on. The midwife stands at the foot of the bed, her voice a soothing murmur of encouragement I can't quite make out.

Rowena's weary eyes find mine and instantly brighten, relief visibly washing over her. "You made it," she gasps, a tired but genuine smile gracing her lips.

"Of course I did," I reply, stumbling over the words, the air in my lungs thicker than normal.

I move swiftly to her side and reach for her hand. She grasps it like a lifeline, her grip startlingly strong for someone who's been through the wringer.

I press a kiss to her damp forehead, breathing her in. Until her face contracts in a painful wince and in a panic, I ask the midwife how I can help.

"Rub her shoulders; human touch is healing."

I do everything I'm told as hours blur together in

a haze of contractions and medical jargon. The steady beep of the monitors and the reassuring chatter of the nurses create a strange symphony that fills the room. Through it all, I stay glued to Rowena's side, my hands on her, rubbing, kneading, soothing.

I stroke her hair, whispering words of love and encouragement, my heart feeling like it might burst with a heady cocktail of anticipation and apprehension. "You're doing amazing, Sunshine. Just a little longer."

She nods, her breath coming in short, focused puffs. The determination in her eyes holds me spellbound.

Finally, the moment arrives. The midwife looks up with a smile. "Alright, Rowena, it's time to push. On the next contraction, give it everything you've got."

Rowena bears down, a warrior goddess in a hospital gown, showing a strength I never knew a human could possess.

"Push, two... three... four... five..."

She collapses back against the pillows, breath heaving, only to gather herself and go again. And again. Each time, I'm in awe of her, of the raw power of her body, of her indomitable spirit.

After what feels like a lifetime compressed into mere minutes, a high, thin cry pierces the air. "It's a girl!" the midwife announces, her voice bright with joy.

Tears blur my vision. I blink them away, desperate not to miss a single second. The nurse places a tiny, writhing bundle on Rowena's chest, a shock of dark hair stark against the reddened skin.

Rowena cradles her daughter, wonder and love transforming her exhausted face into something ethereal, something divine. Tears trace silvery paths down her cheeks, but her smile... Fuck, her smile could light the world.

I lean down, pressing my lips to her sweaty forehead. "She's perfect." My voice comes out raw. "You're perfect."

Rowena nods, words beyond her, gaze locked on the little miracle in her arms.

We sit like that, suspended in a bubble of pure happiness for the longest time.

Eventually, Rowena looks up at me, her eyes shining with exhaustion and bliss. "I haven't chosen a name," she murmurs, her voice soft, almost reverent.

I smile, awed by the miracle her daughter is— those impossibly tiny fingers, that button nose, those rosebud lips. "How about Soleil?" I suggest, the name coming to me in a flash of inspiration. "It means sun in French. She's a little sunshine, just like her mom."

Rowena's face lights up, her smile brighter than any star. "Soleil." She repeats the name as if trying it on for size. "It's perfect."

42

ROWENA

Three months later

I wake to the soft whimpers of Soleil from her bassinet beside the bed. My eyelids feel like lead weights as I pry them open, the room still shrouded in darkness. The glowing numbers on the bedside clock read 4.37 p.m. Has it really been only an hour since I fed her last? I thought it was night already. But time has lost all meaning in this endless loop of diaper changes, feedings, and stolen winks of sleep.

Carefully, I scoop Soleil into my arms, her tiny body molding against my chest as I settle into the rocking chair. As she nurses, I find my mind drifting, wondering how something so natural can feel so foreign and overwhelming.

The past three months, since Soleil has been born, have been an endless blur of hours bleeding together, day and night swirling into an indistinguishable haze as I tend to Soleil's constant needs. Sleep, when it comes, arrives in fleeting wisps—one hour here, two hours there—before her plaintive cries pierce through my exhaustion, summoning me back to the present. I feel like a ghost inhabiting the shell of my former self, my body heavy with a deep-set fatigue.

Every night, when Adrian returns home from work, he tenderly takes Soleil from my weary arms, urging me to rest. I stumble to the bedroom in a daze, collapsing onto the rumpled sheets still warm from my last interrupted attempt at slumber. The mattress embraces me as I drift off, only to awaken what seems like moments later, for a night feeding and then again after a few hours. Did I even eat dinner? My eyes squint against the early morning sun slanting through the window. Adrian's side of the bed lies cold—I vaguely recall hearing him getting up at dawn, Soleil nestled against his chest as he gave her a bottle of my milk that I pump whenever I have extra and hummed a lullaby I didn't recognize.

Afterward, he dropped her in her crib and crossed the room to press a light peck on the top of my head. "You can rest; she's burped and will be out for a few more hours."

I nodded gratefully, but a part of me ached for more than this brief interaction, more than the chaste kisses that are all he gives me these days. I know it's too soon for intimacy—I'm still healing from the birth—but I long for the passion, the deep connection we once shared. Does he not desire me anymore now that my body has changed? The thought gnaws at me.

Adrian is being an amazing father, even if Soleil isn't really his daughter. He's present, helps me in any way he can, but I notice a distance expanding between us. There's a shift in Adrian's touch, his kisses growing lighter, briefer. I yearn for the heat of his skin against mine no matter if it's too soon for sex. Even without going all the way, there are a million other things we could do, ways we could be intimate, but he doesn't seem interested. It's like the fire in his eyes for me is gone. And even the smaller intimacies, the long embraces and playful caresses, have faded, leaving an aching void in their wake.

One morning, I catch sight of my reflection in

the bathroom mirror, shadows smudging the puffed skin beneath my eyes, my hair limp and tangled. When was the last time I showered? I can't remember. Does he no longer desire this unfamiliar body, so changed from the one he once couldn't keep his hands off? The thought pierces me, sharp and insidious. I think of the confident businesswoman I had become just before giving birth. That version of myself seems like a distant memory, buried underneath layers of doubt that whisper that I'm failing at everything—as a mother, a wife, a professional.

Sinking onto the cold tile floor, I draw my knees to my chest, hot tears streaming down my cheeks as an overwhelming sense of inadequacy crashes over me. I'm drowning in it, flailing for a foothold, for a glimmer of the woman I thought I could become. But she's lost, subsumed by this new identity I wear like an ill-fitting coat, the weight of it threatening to suffocate me. So I retreat inward, withdrawing even from the person I want the most, fencing in the fragile remnants of my heart behind my solitude as I navigate this unfamiliar terrain alone.

More days blur together in an endless cycle around the baby's schedule. I go through the motions mechanically, my world narrowed to the confines of our home and childcare. Life beyond these walls feels distant, almost unreal. I'm lost in a haze of exhaustion and isolation.

One morning, a ping from my phone jolts me out of my daze. It's my business partner, checking in on the status of the project. Guilt twists in my gut as it occurs to me that I haven't made any progress in weeks. Thank goodness I signed that contract before giving birth, buying myself a bit of grace, but they won't wait forever. Either I start delivering or it'll all fall through.

Noticing my struggle, Adrian suggests hiring a nanny. I refuse the offer as strongly as I secretly want to accept it, feeling like a failure for even considering time away from Soleil, even just a few hours each day. The guilt of wanting that space from my daughter is overwhelming, and I punish myself for it, refusing any help. I only tolerate the cleaning ladies because they were here before we arrived. And honestly, if it weren't for them, we'd be living in a junkyard.

I try to rally, to summon the energy to tackle my overflowing inbox. But every time I sit down at my desk, Soleil's cries pull me away. The constant interruptions shatter my focus, leaving me feeling scattered and ineffective. Each abandoned task feels like another mark of defeat, another shortcoming to add to the growing list.

Adrian has no idea how deep I'm spiraling. I haven't told him I signed a deal. I accepted the offer just before going into labor and in the first few weeks, it slipped my mind. Now, I'm unsure why I never mentioned it to him. Or why I don't seem interested in the project that consumed my life in the months leading to the birth.

In the rare moments when Soleil sleeps peacefully, I stare blankly at the walls, scrolling mindlessly through social media, desperate for a connection to the outside world. But the happy family photos and career achievements of my peers only amplify my sense of failure.

As the days stretch on, the doubts grow louder, more insistent. Am I cut out for this? What if I'm failing my daughter, depriving her of the mother she deserves?

The pressure to be perfect—the ideal mom, the supportive wife, the successful entrepreneur—feels like a weight on my chest, crushing me. I should cherish this time, not be drowning in anxiety and self-doubt.

But the joyful, competent mother I imagined myself being seems like a distant mirage, slipping further out of my reach with each passing day. In her place is a stranger—overwhelmed, uncertain, and utterly lost.

There are a few bright moments that pierce through the darkness. Like one night, I wake with a start, disoriented, to find Adrian cradling Soleil in his arms. He's perched on the edge of our bed, our daughter snuggled up to his chest as he feeds her a bottle.

His low, soothing voice wraps around us in the moonlight as he sings "You Are My Sunshine" to her.

I lie still, not wanting to disturb the tender moment. Adrian's eyes are fixed on Soleil's face, his expression soft with adoration. At times like this, the weight of the world seems to lift from my shoulders.

As the final notes of the song fade away, Adrian presses a loving kiss to Soleil's forehead. "You are my sunshine, little darling," he whispers, "you and your mom."

Tears well in my eyes, but for once, they're not born of despair. My heart swells with love for this man and I think maybe there's still a future for us.

That hope is crushed two days later when a delivery man shows up at my door, shattering the routine of another dull morning. The doorbell startles me from a sleep haze. I'm not expecting anyone. Soleil is finally napping, and I meant to get some work done but fell asleep instead.

I open the door to find a man in a generic pizza delivery uniform. The vision confuses me. I thought it was still early. Who ordered a pizza in the morning? Is it morning or have I lost track of time again?

"Rowena Taylor?"

"Yes?"

"You've been served." The man thrusts a large envelope toward me.

Confused, I take it. "There's been a mistake. We didn't order any pizza—"

But the delivery guy is already walking away, disappearing into the elevator. With a sinking feeling in my gut, I tear open the envelope.

The words "Petition for Divorce" stare back at me, cold and unforgiving. There's an official summon a week from now for Adrian and me to finalize the end of our marriage according to what was pre-arranged in our prenup. The papers slip from my numb fingers, fluttering to the floor.

I pack my and Soleil's stuff in a blur, only the essentials, only what I can carry with me. I consider reaching out to my friends but feel too ashamed to do so. Instead, I use the money from the advance on my toy deal to check me and my daughter into an aparthotel. I go in a taxi, not wanting Sam to know where we are.

Adrian calls me that night. I pick up in a haze of fury, yelling at him that I can't wait to be divorced and move to California and never have to deal with him again. I tell him we'll meet at the lawyer's office to sign the divorce papers next week. I hang up before he can put two words in.

I'm spiraling. My phone rings a second time. I expect it to be Adrian again, but it's Nina instead. She and Hunter insist on coming over. Adrian must've called them. I try to refuse, but then cave in at their insistence. I don't have the force to argue. When they arrive, I must be in an awful state because they don't ask anything, they just offer to take care of Soleil while I shower and rest.

I accept, only to be alone in the bathroom and not have to deal with anyone. After that first day, they come over every night to help with the baby. But whenever they attempt to ask about me, about what's going on with Adrian, I shut it down, claiming I'm tired, that I need to rest or shower or whatever will keep them off my back.

The days blur into a haze of silence and loneliness. Even when Nina and Hunter are here, I feel isolated, like I'm drifting somewhere far away. I plaster on a smile when they're around, doing my best to seem present, but inside, I'm unraveling. I'm grateful for their help with Soleil, but each time they leave, I'm left alone with the thoughts I've been avoiding. Thoughts of Adrian. Thoughts of the future.

My phone buzzes again—a missed call from him. The third one today. He's relentless. Each time my phone rings, my heart jumps in my chest, torn between the desire to hear his voice and the knowledge that I can't afford to fall apart. Not yet. I can't trust myself to talk to him now, not when I'm this fragile. If I hear his voice, I might shatter. And I can't afford to splinter apart. Not when I have Soleil to think about. I need to be strong for her, to get through this week with my head on straight. If I crumble now, I'll never make it to that lawyer's office.

My phone buzzes again—a text this time.

ADRIAN

Please talk to me

Just talk, Rowena. Please. I need to explain

Explain what? Why he changed his mind about us? Why he wants a divorce? Dread sets deep into my gut. I don't want to hear his explanations. I can't. I'm not ready.

I stare at the screen, my thumb hovering over the virtual keyboard. The urge to respond is over-whelming, but I know what will happen if I do. One word from him, and I'll lose the fragile grip I've been holding onto. My mind keeps flashing back to the divorce papers. The stark finality of it all. If I let him back in now, if I allow myself to feel what I'm holding at bay, I'll break apart completely. I need to keep my distance to protect myself, to survive this. For Soleil.

I finally type a reply.

ROWENA

Please stop calling me, Adrian

Not because I don't want to talk to you, I know we need to. But because if I do, I'm afraid I won't be able to keep it together. I need space to figure things out, to be strong enough to face everything that's coming. For Soleil

Please. Just give me some time

I hit send, my heart sinking as I do, then fibrillating as another ping pierces the silence.

ADRIAN

I'll do as you ask

But I'm always here if you change your mind

"It's not me who changed her mind," I say, staring at the screen, his last words blurring as fresh tears roll down my cheeks.

The silence that follows is worse than his calls, but it's the silence I need right now. A silence where I can rebuild the pieces of myself, one fragile sliver at a time.

* * *

Adrian is true to his word, and I don't hear from him again. After a week of this hollow existence, emptier even than the half-life I was leading before, I leave Soleil with Nina and Hunter to go to my appointment with Adrian and the lawyers.

After feeling loved and desired by him, then the opposite—rejected and repulsive. After seeing him being the perfect dad, calling me and Soleil his sunshines, and then receiving divorce papers not two days later. Now I stare into his dark eyes as we sit alone in this cold room, cleared of all the leeches with him asking me why I spilled coffee on our divorce papers, and I've no idea what to say.

43

ROWENA

Now

"Rowena," he says, his voice low and serious. "I need to know. Do you still want to be my wife?"

I open my mouth to speak, but the words stick in my throat, trapped by the warring emotions within me.

At my indecision, his gaze still inscrutable, Adrian speaks again. "How about I go first?"

I shut my gaping mouth and nod.

His eyes bore into mine with a single-mindedness and determination I've never seen before. "I love you." Three simple words that make the ground tremble underneath my feet. "I love our daughter." *Our* daughter; he didn't call Soleil my daughter. "I want us to stay a family."

Am I losing my sanity? Am I still asleep? Is this a dream? Adrian can't be saying those things. He can't mean them. "B-but you served me divorce papers."

He shakes his head, frustrated. "I arranged everything almost a year ago; we were supposed to stay married six months and then divorce. The firm sent the documents following my instructions last June. I didn't think they'd just send you the petition without notifying me first."

"So it was a mistake?" I ask, still incredulous.

"Yes, Rowena. I haven't slept a full night in three months, I'm not on top of everything."

The notion that I'm not the only one struggling is oddly comforting.

"And you want to stay married to me?" I point at my chest. "Because you love me?"

"Yes. And *also*, yes."

The temptation to just believe him is strong. The me who dated Liam would. Heck, the me of a week ago would take his words at face value. But I'm so tired of constantly living in doubt. "I don't believe you."

His eyes widen in shock. "Why?"

"You haven't so much as tried to touch me since

Soleil has been born." My voice cracks. "I know you find me gross."

Adrian is up in a blur of Armani. In a few quick strides, he rounds the table, grabs my spinning chair, and turns it so that now I'm facing him. My husband kneels on the floor before me, his hands gripping the armrests until his knuckles go white. "You are the most beautiful woman I have ever known, and the thought that I could find you anything but breathtaking is absurd."

"Then why haven't you even kissed me in the past three months?"

He glances away guiltily. "I was just trying to be respectful."

"Respectful?"

"I've been keeping my distance because I thought that's what you wanted, what you needed while you healed. Not because I don't want you— because, believe me, Rowena, wanting you has never been the issue. But I've read everywhere that new moms don't want to be pressured about sex by their husbands, that they find the stress of more demands put on them overwhelming and then there's the fact that you've been..." He trails off.

This is it. This is when he tells me he finds me repulsive. "Gross?"

His eyes fleet to mine, disappointed almost by my suggestion. "It's not because of how you look—it never was. But you haven't been yourself." Now his gaze turns considerate. "I kept telling myself that you were okay, that it was just an adjustment period to a big change but then the way you reacted to the papers, not even giving me a chance to explain. Rowena, I'm saying this from a place of deep love and without judging, but I think you might be suffering from postpartum depression."

The words come at me like a needle piercing through a bubble. My ears pop. At once, I know he's right. I can finally put a name to this darkness that's been churning inside me. And suddenly, I can't keep all the fear and anxiety contained anymore. I start crying, full-on bawling. Adrian pulls me up and crushes me into a hug.

Between sobs, I tell him how I've been feeling all these months: alone, helpless, inadequate. He cradles me, caressing my hair and whispering he's sorry for not noticing first, for not offering more help, for not insisting I accept it.

I shake in his arms. "I thought you didn't want me anymore."

He tilts my chin up and looks at me. "I never, for one second, stopped wanting you." And then he kisses me. Nothing platonic about it. He consumes me as if I were the oxygen he needed to breathe. It's fierce and claiming. There's fire and there's need. And there's love.

My doubts scatter like a deck of cards flung into the air, all my insecurities replaced by the warmth of his lips and the strength of his embrace. I grip him back, matching his urgency, tasting the promise in his kiss—the promise that things can still be good between us, maybe even better than before because now we're not tiptoeing around each other anymore.

When we pull apart, the room is spinning, or it could be just me, dizzy with the revelations tumbling through my mind like laundry in a dryer. "Okay," I choke out, clinging to him for dear life. "Okay, what do we do now?"

Adrian's smile is slow and warm, like honey drizzling over pancakes. "First, we get you professional help, both for Soleil and with a therapist. I've already researched the best nannies and psychologists in the city. And once you're on your feet again, we can pack everything and move to California."

I blink, not understanding what he's talking about.

He explains without me needing to ask. "If you're moving to California, I'm coming with you."

I vaguely remember yelling at him that I was moving and couldn't wait to be rid of him in the haze of my rage. "You'd move to California with me?"

"Sure."

"W-what about your job here?" Dominic still hasn't given him the promotion but it should arrive any day now.

"I don't care about it as much as I care about you and Soleil."

I'm floored. "You'd sacrifice everything you've worked for your entire life just for me."

"Yes, gladly." He cups my face. "And there should be no 'just' when you refer to yourself. Because you're everything, and you should never discount how amazing, strong, capable, beautiful, desirable, and irreplaceable you are." He kisses me again then pulls back abruptly. "Did I say sexy as hell?"

I smile. "You did not."

"The sexiest."

We kiss again, and he lifts me up and puts me on the table, pushing between my legs and grinding against me in a way that's not even remotely appropriate for a conference room with glass walls. I couldn't care less.

I catch my breath and pull back slightly, my fingers still tangled in his hair. "So what would you do in California?"

"I'm sure one of those hippie start-ups could use a good CEO."

"And you wouldn't miss New York."

He hesitates just a second too long for his answer to be genuine. "No."

"Pity, because *I* would. All my friends are here."

His grip on my hips tightens. "But you said..."

"I lied. I was mad at you and I wanted to hurt you. But we don't have to move. I turned down the offer from California months ago and signed with MC Toys the same day."

"When?"

I beam up at him. "Oh, about five minutes before going into labor."

His eyes search mine. "Why have you waited all this time to tell me?"

"The tiny human I was trying to push out of a very private place was a bit of a distraction, and after Soleil was born..." Tears fill my eyes again as I try to explain. "I kept it to myself because I was lost. I felt like I was failing at everything and didn't want to burden you with one more thing. I felt invisible, like my achievements didn't matter when I couldn't even handle being a mom."

He hugs me. "I'm sorry I didn't notice earlier what you were going through."

I shake my head in the crook of his shoulder. "It's not your fault. I did everything I could to hide it."

He pulls back slightly, his eyes filled with determination. "We'll take it one day at a time, Rowena. We'll find the right support and get through this. I'm here for you, always."

I lean into his embrace, the weight on my chest easing a bit.

"You're not alone. You have me. Every day."

I nod, feeling a sense of relief wash over me. "I don't want to hide anymore. I want to be honest with you, with myself."

He smiles, a warm, genuine smile that makes my heart ache in a good way. "That's the first step. We'll figure out the rest together. No more secrets, no more hiding."

I blow air through my lips, feeling lighter than I have in months. "Together. That sounds right." I sniffle. "Now can we please leave this awful place as our first mature, functional couple act?"

"Actually." Adrian scratches the back of his head, suddenly nervous. "There is something else I'd like you to sign before we go. It's the whole reason I made you come here in the first place—well, that and because you refused to tell me where you were living."

"You had a diabolical plan not to divorce me?"

He nods.

"I hope it was better than my improvised coffee spill?"

Adrian scratches his neck self-consciously. "I had a grand speech prepared."

Excitement bubbles inside me. "Please tell me you have talking points saved on your phone."

His nostrils flare in fake annoyance. "I remember things better if I summarize them in a list."

"Ooooooh, so it's back to bullet points, you little secret nerd. Show me."

"Never."

Undeterred, I place my hand forward, palm up.

With a groan, Adrian pulls up the file and hands me the phone. The list is titled: *Reasons Rowena should stay married to me*. It makes me grin.

The first bullet point states: *I love you.*

I look up at him. "Strong start."

Number two is: *I love Soleil as my own.*

It follows with a few solid entries like loyal and ready to move anywhere for you. Next, there's a "good in bed" with a question mark afterward that has me cackling.

I look up at him, beaming. "You can remove that question mark, sir."

He brushes off his shoulders like the total secret nerd he is.

I'm smiling so hard as I continue to scan the list —*I get along with your friends, my mom loves you, your parents adore me*—until my eyes snatch on the last point and my heart fractures all over again and comes back together bigger, stronger.

I re-read the bottom line to make sure my mind is not playing tricks on me. But no, the words are there. Black on white.

I want to adopt our daughter.

I take a moment before I lift my eyes to his. And just as well because the way he's staring back at me —vulnerable, hopeful, and most of all, *real*—says more than words or a list of reasons ever could. It's all there, everything I've been waiting, dreaming, and hoping to see.

"Oh, Adrian." I drop my forehead on his shoulder and burrow into him as I sob.

His strong arms engulf me as he smooths my

hair down, his fingers trailing through the locks. "Please tell me these are happy tears."

"They are. Your diabolical plan worked." I pull back and grab a tissue from my bag and blow my nose. It's not sexy but it's necessary, and I'm not afraid to be my true, flawed, unguarded self in front of him anymore. "Is that what you want me to sign today?"

"Yes." Hands in his pockets, he tilts his head. "The adoption papers are drawn, will you... sign them?"

I smile brighter than I have in my entire life. "Bring all those lawyers back in here and tell them to leave the coffee out this time because I'm not spilling on those."

44

ADRIAN

At the office, I scratch out my signature on a document and flip the folder shut. Rowena's face drifts through my mind, her eyes sparkling, lips curved into that irresistible smile that makes my heart thump double-time. After patching things up with her yesterday, my life feels like it's finally fallen into place. We're together now, for real, a family, no more doubts about where any of us stands.

It's barely 11 a.m. and I already can't wait to go home to her, to both my girls. I wonder what new trick Soleil will have learned today, even if I'm sure nothing could ever top the first time she smiled at me.

The intercom on my desk buzzes, interrupting

my reverie. "Mr. West?" My secretary's voice crackles through the speaker. "Mr. Fulton wants to see you in his office. Right away."

I frown and press the reply button. "Did he say what it's about, Wendy?"

"No, just that he needs to speak with you." Her tone carries an undercurrent of curiosity.

Unease slithers down my spine as I push back from my desk. It has to be about the promotion— Dominic must have made his decision about who will replace him when he retires. He was supposed to already have retired by the end of the year, but he postponed. I suspect he wanted to see how the deal with the police fund would go, leaving Preston and me in a sort of limbo.

And after this eternal wait, it seems fitting that the decision would arrive today, the final tassel missing in the perfect puzzle of my life.

Truth is, last summer, this would've been the single defining moment of my existence. But now I know that even if I don't get the job, I'll survive.

I still want it. I've worked my ass off for it—but if Preston gets it, it won't be the end of the world. I already dodged that bullet yesterday when I thought Rowena was leaving me, taking Soleil with her. So, today, I can be at peace with whatever decision Dominic makes.

Rolling my shoulders back, I stand, buttoning my suit jacket, and stride toward the elevators, determination quickening my steps. I jab the up button and watch the numbers slowly ascend as the stress of the last few months uncoils from around my spine. The doors slide open with a soft ding, and I step inside, steeling myself for whatever news awaits me in Dominic's office, good or bad.

As the elevator lurches upward, I check myself in the mirror, smoothing my tie for the dozenth time.

When the doors slide open, Dominic's assistant waves me straight into the corner office. I settle into the leather chair opposite my boss's expansive desk, willing my face into its usual unreadable mask.

"Adrian," Dominic greets me, sharp eyes flicking up from a stack of papers. "I'll cut right to it. I've made my choice about the CEO position."

My mouth goes cotton dry. This is it—the moment I've been gunning for my entire career.

"But first, let's discuss your performance these last few months." He stacks the papers and pushes them aside. "Since I announced my retirement, you've taken more days of leave than in your previous ten years combined."

"I had to accompany Rowena to medical appointments," I interject, scrambling for an explanation that doesn't make me sound like a total flake. "She—"

Dominic holds up a hand, silencing me. "You've been delegating more than usual to Sarah. Logging fewer hours than ever. Frankly, you look exhausted most days."

Heat crawls up my neck. I want to protest that Soleil has yet to sleep through the night, but Dominic forges on.

"I'm aware you have an infant at home."

Frustration surges through me, hot and stinging. The long nights walking the halls with a wailing newborn, the endless diaper changes and leaky bottles, all piled on top of my brutal work schedule— does he think any of that is easy? I bite the inside of my cheek hard, choking back the snide retort burning on my tongue.

Even if putting my family first has torpedoed my shot at being crowned king, I don't regret a single minute spent by Rowena's side. She and Soleil are my entire world. They're what matters most, promotion be damned.

Dominic leans forward, elbows propped on his massive desk. "And let's not forget the police pension fund deal. You busted your ass to land our biggest whale to date, only to walk out mid-meeting."

"We still got the funds," I grit out, my agitation rising by the second. Rowena was in labor, what was I supposed to do?

"I know." Dominic's steely gaze pins me in place. "That's not the point."

Adrenaline floods my system, anger simmering just beneath my skin. Does he seriously not grasp the magnitude of what I've sacrificed? The parts of myself I've carved out and laid at the altar of this firm?

"Moving forward, all fund profits will be directed into a charitable foundation." Dominic knocks once on the desk. "I've asked Ella Harris to become president of the foundation, given her extensive non-profit experience."

Ice water replaces the blood in my veins. If Preston's wife is landing the foundation gig, does that mean Pretty Boy Preston is a shoo-in for my job?

A trickle of sweat slithers down my temple as a sickening sense of revulsion curdles in my gut. I don't know if I'll want to stay on if I have to report to

Preston. California or not, it looks like I'll be in the job market soon, anyway.

Dominic leans back in his leather chair, steepling his fingers. "Which brings us to the role of CEO." He pauses, letting the suspense build until I'm ready to vibrate out of my skin. "If you want it, it's yours."

I blink once. Twice. The words hover in the space between us, too far-fetched to feel real. If I weren't already sitting, I'm pretty sure I'd crumple to the floor.

"I... I don't understand." I rub my brow. "You just spent the last ten minutes describing what a shit employee I've been. Why on earth would you give me the job?"

My brain scrambles to process this dizzying turn of events. Is it a prank? A test? A trap?

Dominic regards me steadily. "Because now you get it, Adrian. There's more to life than putting in face time at the office. I need someone in the big chair who sees my people as human beings, not cogs in the money-making machine. People with families, with personal lives and challenges that can't always be put on hold for the sake of the almighty dollar."

He leans in, his expression deadly serious. "Seventy per cent of our fund's profits will seed the foundation. The other thirty? Half will go toward employee benefits—better health insurance, paid family leave, the works. And half will be redistributed as year-end bonuses, rewarding everyone's hard work. I want to make money for charity, yes, but not at the cost of bleeding my people dry." Dominic's eyes are alight with the new vision. "I want to build a different company, Adrian. One where employees love coming to the office every day, without having to sell their souls like all the other corporate drones on Wall Street. And you"—he points a weathered finger at me—"are the man to make it happen."

"Me?" I gape, still reeling. Then, as if realizing I should project more confidence, I repeat, "Me." No question mark.

"Yes, you. You've always had killer instincts, Adrian. You're a damn right sicario. But now"—a slow grin spreads across his face—"you've got a heart to match. Courtesy of that firecracker wife of yours."

At the mention of Rowena, a matching smile blooms on my face. "She's... everything."

Dominic nods sagely. "Hold on to that, you hear

me? That woman is one in a million. Don't you dare screw it up."

"Never," I vow fervently. "They're my whole life."

"Good man." Dominic pushes to his feet, extending a hand across the desk. "So what do you say, West? You ready to usher Fulton Capital into its bright new future?"

I stand so quickly my chair nearly topples over. My palm meets his in a firm shake, sealing the deal. The grin on my face threatens to crack it clean in two.

"I was born ready."

EPILOGUE
ROWENA

Five months later

Soleil giggles in my arms as she gnaws on the puffy ear of her stuffed bunny, blissfully unaware of the tense anticipation filling the sunlit courtroom. Adrian and I sit rigidly on the polished wooden bench, hands clasped tightly as if our interlocked fingers could somehow influence the outcome we've been praying for these past months. Our lawyer, a reassuring presence in her tailored suit, flips through a folder of documents beside us.

The courtroom door opens and the chatter of waiting families hushes. My heart hammers against my ribcage as the judge strides in, her black robes billowing. She takes her seat at the bench, appraising the room with kind but attentive eyes. Adrian brushes his thumb over my knuckles, capturing my hand with his. I glance up at him, recognizing my anxiety and hope mirrored in his handsome face.

There are a couple of proceedings before ours, and then the judge reaches our case.

"We are here today to finalize the petition of adoption for Soleil Amelia Taylor by Adrian James West," she begins, her voice echoing in the reverent silence.

I pull Soleil closer, breathing in her sweet baby scent, as the judge reviews the files. Each second seems to stretch into an eternity. Then, the words we've been longing to hear:

"Upon review of the petition for adoption and the supporting evidence, it has been determined that the biological father has failed to acknowledge paternity or respond to the court's summons. Given his lack of involvement and the best interests of the minor, the court hereby grants the adoption request, terminating the parental rights of the biological father and establishing the petitioner as the child's legal parent. Congratulations."

My throat is full and heat rushes up the back of

my nose as a tsunami of relief and joy crashes over me. Adrian turns to me, his eyes shining with relief and adoration. Soleil coos between us, reaching out a chubby hand to pat her daddy's stubbly cheek.

"We did it." Adrian's voice wavers with emotion. "We're officially a family."

He leans in, capturing my lips in a tender kiss as Soleil smooshes herself between our faces, demanding to be part of this celebration. Adrian and I laugh, peppering her rosy cheeks with kisses until she shrieks with delight. In this perfect, golden moment, everything we've been through—the heartache, the hurdles, the sleepless nights—it all feels worth it.

We emerge from the courthouse into a bright sunny afternoon, a gentle fall breeze tangling in my hair. Soleil is nestled against my chest, tuckered out from all the excitement. Adrian wraps an arm around my shoulders, and we pause at the top of the steps, just breathing.

It feels surreal, standing here with my husband and daughter, when only months ago I'd been drowning in the depths of postpartum depression, convinced I was signing divorce papers instead of adoption forms. But with a lot of therapy, love, and support, I've come out on the other side. I'm not "cured" by any means, I still struggle every day, but now I have the tools to manage my mental health without spiraling into depression. And having a partner like Adrian, who's been my rock through it all, makes everything feel possible.

"Penny for your thoughts?" Adrian leans in, tucking a windswept lock of hair behind my ear.

"Just feeling grateful," I reply, leaning into his solid warmth. "For you, for Soleil, for our family. And excited for whatever comes next."

"Me too. I love you, Sunshine."

"I love you, too, Bunny."

I smile up at him, marveling at the journey that brought us here. This blended family we've created, with all its beautiful imperfections and boundless love.

* * *

Back home, as we step into the penthouse, a chorus of cheers and applause erupts from the living room. "Surprise!" Our friends jump out from behind furniture, their faces alight with joy. Soleil startles in my arms at the sudden noise, but then breaks into a gummy grin, waving her chubby hands excitedly.

A colorful banner dangles from the ceiling with

the writing "Welcome home, Soleil Taylor West!" hand-painted with exquisite detail that could only be Nina's handiwork. Streamers and balloons in soft pastel tones adorn every surface, transforming our usually sleek space into a whimsical wonderland.

The delicious aroma of homemade dishes wafts from the kitchen, mingling with the laughter and chatter of our loved ones. Adrian squeezes my hand, his eyes suspiciously misty. "I know you didn't want to jinx the hearing by organizing a party before we had the final decision, but I couldn't help myself. They were all so excited to celebrate with us."

Emotion swells in my chest as I take in the smiling faces of our friends.

Nina beams with pride. "Congrats, mama bear! And papa bear, of course." She winks at Adrian, who chuckles.

Hunter, radiant like I've never seen her before, pulls me into a warm hug, mindful of Soleil between us. "I'm so happy for you, Winnie."

Dylan, his arm slung around Hunter's waist, grins broadly. "Couldn't have happened to a better couple. Soleil's one lucky kid."

I move past them only to be pulled into another hug by Reese. "Congratulations, we're so happy for you."

She and Thomas wear matching grins.

Our work relationship has progressed into more of a friendship, and with the official launch of my console scheduled for next week—to catch the holiday season shopping frenzy—I couldn't be happier to have them here.

As if on cue, K-2P scurries in from the kitchen, carrying a tray of hard-boiled tiny eggs.

He lifts it up to me. "Quail eggs?"

"No, thanks," I refuse with a smile.

The droid beeps in approval. "You're right. I wouldn't want to eat something that came out of a bird's ass either."

Thomas, Reese, and I all burst into laughter, and K-2P scurries on to delight his next victim. I follow him, wanting to greet everyone.

As I make my way through the room, accepting hugs and well-wishes, a profound sense of peace settles over me. These people, who've been by my side through the highest highs and lowest lows, are more than friends—they're the family I chose. The family that chose me. Like Adrian chose me and Soleil.

I watch my husband move effortlessly through the crowd, Soleil perched on his hip as if she was always meant to be there. The easy rapport he's developed with my friends—*our* friends now—fills me with warmth. Two worlds, colliding and inter-twining into something beautiful.

"Better get used to being outnumbered, Adrian!" Hunter calls out, eyes twinkling. "You're officially a minority. Girl power woo-hoo!"

Adrian laughs, bouncing Soleil playfully. "I think I can handle it."

The room dissolves into good-natured ribbing and shared laughter, the camaraderie palpable. As the celebration continues, stories and memories flow freely, painting a picture of the winding road that led us here.

"Remember when Winnie called in a panic, con-vinced she was in labor at thirty weeks?" Nina gig-gles, sipping her champagne. "Turns out, it was just gas."

"Hey, in my defense, it felt very convincing at the time!" I protest, chuckling.

The tales continue, each one a thread in the ta-pestry of our shared history. The late-night cravings runs, the nursery decorating debacles, the moments of sheer terror and overwhelming love. And through it all, the unwavering loyalty of the people in this room.

As I lean against Adrian, Soleil back in my arms

and dozing contentedly, I'm struck by the incredible journey that brought us to this moment. The path wasn't always smooth or straightforward, but every twist and turn, every challenge and triumph, led us right where we were meant to be.

Here, surrounded by the love and laughter of our chosen family, I've never felt more at peace. More at home.

* * *

Later that evening, after our friends are gone and the apartment is quiet again, Adrian and I put Soleil to bed together. The nursery is awash in a soft, golden glow from the crescent moon night-light, casting playful shadows on the pastel-colored walls.

"Once upon a time, in a land far, far away," Adrian narrates Soleil's favorite bedtime story. He takes on the role of the brave knight, his voice deep and heroic, while I play the part of the wise and kind fairy godmother.

Our daughter's eyes sparkle with delight as Adrian brings the story to life, her tiny hands reaching out to touch the colorful illustrations. When he gets to the part where the knight faces off against the wicked ogre, Adrian's voice drops to a comical growl, sending Soleil into a fit of giggles.

I watch them, my heart so full it feels like it might burst. The love between them is palpable, a bond that has grown stronger with each passing day —beyond biology and genetics. And now, with the adoption finalized, we're even more united than before.

As Soleil's eyelids droop, we tuck her in, placing gentle kisses on her forehead. "Sweet dreams, my little love," I whisper, marveling at the perfect miracle that is our daughter.

Hand in hand, Adrian and I move to our bedroom, the events of the day still swirling in my mind. The moment the door closes behind us, he pulls me into his arms, his lips finding mine in a kiss that is both tender and passionate. Restless and content.

We make love slowly, savoring each touch, each sigh. In the afterglow, Adrian holds me close, his fingers tracing lazy patterns on my skin. "I love you, Sunshine." The words are thick with emotion. "I promise to always be there for you and Soleil, to love and support you both, no matter what."

Unshed tears sting my eyes as I gaze up at him. "I know you will," I whisper back. "You've already proven that, time and time again."

We talk about the future, about family vacations and holiday traditions, about the adventures we'll have and the memories we'll make. We discuss our hopes and dreams for Soleil, imagining her first steps, her first words, her first day of school.

And as we drift off to sleep, our fingers intertwined, a sense of peace and contentment washes over me. Gone are the doubts and fears that once plagued me, replaced by an unshakable faith in the strength of our love and the promise of our future together.

This is where I'm meant to be, with my husband and our daughter. And I know, with absolute certainty, that no matter what challenges may come our way, we'll face them together, hand in hand, heart to heart.

Always.

AFTERWORD

Dear reader,

Thank you for spending time with Adrian and Rowena. I hope you enjoyed yourself. Sad it's over? Not so fast... I've hidden an extra spicy morsel at the end—consider it the book equivalent of finding that last French fry at the bottom of the bag.

I wrote an extended sexy scene of Rowena and Adrian's first time together on their honeymoon that'll steam up your reading glasses.

You can find it in my newsletter here: https://bit. ly/CamillaIsleyNews

Proceed at your own delicious risk... Don't say I didn't warn you!

Happy reading,

Camilla

PS. If you enjoyed this story, please consider leaving a review on your favorite retailer's website, on Goodreads, Bookbub, or in a BookTok or Bookstagram post. Reviews help my work be known and encourage me to bring you even more romantic stories...

PPS. If you loved Reese and Thomas, and especially K-2P, you'll be happy to know they have their own book, *The Love Algorithm*.

ACKNOWLEDGMENTS

Well, here we are again, at the part where I get to thank all the people who made this adventure possible. There's something surreal about finishing a book and knowing you'll soon share it with the world. If this one is now in your hands, that means it's out there, and I'm equal parts thrilled and terrified. But hey, that's part of the fun, right?

To my editor, Megan Haslam, thank you for understanding the depths of my scattered notes and helping turn them into something coherent and, dare I say, entertaining. To my copy editor, Candida Bradford, and proofreader, Susan Sugden—you deserve medals for braving my creative punctuation and surviving.

To my publisher, Boldwood Books. To the production team, for wrapping my stories in such pretty packages. To the marketing and sales teams, thanks for dealing with my anxieties and constant questions.

A huge shoutout to my partner, who, without fail, always knows when to intervene with snacks or make strategic exits during my writing marathons. To my family, for pretending to be fascinated by every plot twist I rambled about. Your Oscar-worthy performances have not gone unnoticed.

To the readers who keep this journey alive, whether you've been with me since day one or this is the first of my books you've picked up—thank you. Your support fuels the creative madness, and I wouldn't have it any other way. If you leave a review for this book wherever on the world wide web, you're even more of a star.

To all BookTokers and Bookstagrammers out there, I love your posts. Thanks for sharing your love of stories with the world and for all the great reading recommendations you give.

ABOUT THE AUTHOR

Camilla Isley is an engineer who left science behind to write bestselling contemporary rom-coms set all around the world. She lives in Italy.

Would you like to read a bonus epilogue? Then sign up to Camilla Isley's newsletter and you'll get it in your inbox!

Visit Camilla's website: https://camillaisley.com/

Follow Camilla on social media here:

f facebook.com/camillaisley

X x.com/camillaisley

O instagram.com/camillaisley

BB bookbub.com/authors/camilla-isley

ALSO BY CAMILLA ISLEY

ALSO BY CAMILLA ISLEY

The Love Theorem

Love Quest

The Love Proposal

I Love to Hate You

Not in A Billion Years

Baby One More Time

It's Complicated

The Love Algorithm

Stoned With A Book

The Is Not a Holiday Romance

A the King Pin

WHERE ALL YOUR ROMANCE
DREAMS COME TRUE!

THE HOME OF BESTSELLING
ROMANCE AND WOMEN'S
FICTION

 WARNING:
MAY CONTAIN SPICE

SIGN UP TO OUR
NEWSLETTER

https://bit.ly/Lovenotesnews

Boldwood

Boldwood Books is an award-winning fiction publishing company seeking out the best stories from around the world.

Find out more at www.boldwoodbooks.com

Join our reader community for brilliant books, competitions and offers!

Follow us
@BoldwoodBooks
@TheBoldBookClub

Sign up to our weekly deals newsletter

https://bit.ly/BoldwoodBNewsletter

www.ingramcontent.com/pod-product-compliance
Lightning Source LLC
Chambersburg PA
CBHW010656100726
47900CB00010B/2686